CANDLELIGHT

Ecstasy Supreme

"I FELL FOR THAT PURE AND NOBLE ROUTINE OF YOURS ONCE, RUTH. BUT I'M SAVVY TO IT NOW."

"What do you mean, Jacob? Why are you so angry at me? I don't understand."

"Well, see if you can understand this: I'm tired of being used. I'm sick of being your patsy. You're just like all the other city women I've known. They're only interested in what they want and they don't care what they have to do to get it. Was I supposed to be satisfied with all the sex I could handle for a year while I helped you with your research? Is that how you reward all your assistants?"

She stared at Jacob in shock. "What I felt for you was genuine. I'd never barter my body—not even for you! Why don't you believe that?"

"I don't believe that because I'm sick to death of your lies," he told her, and strode angrily away.

CANDLELIGHT ECSTASY SUPREMES

WITH OPEN ARMS

Kathy Alerding

A CANDLELIGHT ECSTASY SUPREME

Published by
Dell Publishing Co., Inc.
1 Dag Hammarskjold Plaza
New York, New York 10017

*This book is dedicated to the people of Elkhart
County, Indiana, who have always welcomed us
with open arms.*

Dell ® TM 681510, Dell Publishing Co., Inc.

Candlelight Ecstasy Supreme is a trademark
of Dell Publishing Co., Inc.

Candlelight Ecstasy Romance®, 1,203,540, is a registered
trademark of Dell Publishing Co., Inc.

ISBN: 0-440-19620-5

Printed in the United States of America

First printing—February 1986

To Our Readers:

We are pleased and excited by your overwhelmingly positive response to our Candlelight Ecstasy Supremes. Unlike all the other series, the Supremes are filled with more passion, adventure, and intrigue, and are obviously the stories you like best.

In months to come we will continue to publish books by many of your favorite authors as well as the very finest work from new authors of romantic fiction. As always, we are striving to present unique, absorbing love stories—the very best love has to offer.

Breathtaking and unforgettable, Ecstasy Supremes follow in the great romantic tradition you've come to expect *only* from Candlelight Ecstasy.

Your suggestions and comments are always welcome. Please let us hear from you.

Sincerely,

The Editors
Candlelight Romances
1 Dag Hammarskjold Plaza
New York, New York 10017

PROLOGUE

Listening to her own footsteps echo down the long corridor, Ruth Mueller walked at a steady pace.

With classes over, only the muffled voices of a few departing students broke the silence of the late afternoon, as pale-spring sunshine tossed slender shadows across the polished wood of the hallway floor.

This was Ruth's favorite time of day—when the old, ivy-covered buildings of the university seemed to breathe a sigh of relief. The clamor of impatient students faded from the classrooms, and the campus began its twilight transformation into a peaceful island of silent study and thought.

Ruth had made this same pilgrimage down this corridor hundreds of times over the past six years, often at this very time of day. But on this particular afternoon, her footsteps suddenly faltered from their normal pace. The echo that announced her approach stopped abruptly; Ruth hesitated before the closed door of Dr. Phillip Lane's office.

This was no ordinary meeting. She felt it distinctly. Something undefinable told her to prepare for a shock.

Ruth straightened to her full height, feeling a terrible sensation of foreboding.

Leaning against the smooth wood of the door frame, she took a deep breath. Ruth was only twenty-eight, yet it seemed as though she'd lived a lifetime in the six years she'd been with Phillip Lane. An entire lifetime that revolved on only one central theme: her devotion to a man who'd never acknowledge her.

She heard a muted "Come in!" from inside the office. Ruth pushed open the massive mahogany door and stepped over the threshold.

"Sit down, Miss Mueller," Lane said flatly, without looking at her. He appeared engrossed in a book spread open on the imposing oak desk that dominated his luxurious office.

Taking her usual seat in one of the two highbacked leather chairs that faced Lane's desk, Ruth silently appraised the tall, handsome man before her.

He was approaching his fifties but looked much younger. Phillip Lane was always immaculately dressed, the very image of diplomacy and scientific purity. The world press revered him, the university treasured him, and students nearly worshipped him as one of the world's leading anthropologists. But Ruth Mueller alone had patiently devoted herself to him.

Lane continued to ignore Ruth's presence—turning the pages of his book carefully as he slowly read on.

As she watched Ruth remembered how she had originally come under this magnetic man's spell.

As an undergraduate student majoring in anthropology, she had sat enthralled during his lectures. His glowing oratory transported her imagination from the jungles of New Guinea to the bitter snows of Greenland. His lectures had been the most important factor in her decision to apply to graduate school and then to go on to a teaching position in social anthropology.

Her admiration for Lane had become a fixation, and before Ruth realized it, her total ambition turned to working with him. Eventually he had noticed her, and he had offered Ruth a prestigious position as his research assistant.

That was six years ago now—and thousands of torturous hours of work. In that space of time, Dr. Lane's academic sheen had dulled for her. Sometime during those years Ruth Mueller had been forced to see him as he really was: not a scientific demigod, but a very human man with very human weaknesses. The reality of the discovery tarnished her idealism but did little to discourage her devotion to him.

Ruth had begun to deceive herself into believing that her care and dedication could infiltrate his sullen heart one day. It was the reckless, unfounded dream of a young woman in love with love.

By now the early hope of Lane returning her love had dimmed; Ruth had accepted the fact that her feelings for him could find expression only through their work. And for years, being a part of his academic achievement had sustained her.

Still, even as she sat there, waiting to be recognized, Ruth wanted to believe in Phillip. Pompous as he was, cold and aloof as he had frequently been to her, he had always had her respect. Though their six years together had generated little more than professional courtesy, she still believed in Phillip Lane's dedication to their science. Ruth never allowed herself—or anyone else—to criticize his integrity.

And until recently Ruth had refused to listen to the rumors and accusations that so many of the instructors insisted on circulating about his relentless competition for the university presidency.

Lane closed his book with great ceremony and rose to place it back in its proper place on a shelf.

Once more, watching him cross the room, Ruth tensed, waiting for the cause of her uneasiness to materialize.

"Have you completed cataloging the research notes from the Guatemalan expedition?" Lane finally began with blunt precision and, as usual, without any greeting.

"Yes," Ruth replied evenly. "Everything from last summer's research was completed this week."

Lane still hadn't looked at her, but that wasn't unusual. He normally addressed people as if they were no more real than thin air. "Are the plans for this summer's expedition finalized yet?" he went on while organizing bundles of papers across the desktop.

"Everything's in order," Ruth replied. "Your visa and research permits should arrive this week." Ruth pulled herself forward in her chair and pointed to a large file folder on Lane's desk. "All the travel schedules, tickets, equipment lists, and so forth are—"

"I've seen them," he interrupted her, and for the first time since she entered his office, Lane looked at her. "How many classes are you teaching this term, Ruth?"

As chairman of the university's School of Social Science, Lane knew precisely how many classes and the exact number of students Ruth was responsible for in addition to her nonstop, unsalaried position as his assistant. His question annoyed her, but patiently she replied, "Four undergraduate courses and one graduate seminar." She reminded herself that it was a remarkable teaching load to maintain while working no less than forty hours a week on Lane's projects.

With his hands clasped behind his back, Lane began to pace slowly behind the desk. "Your work is usually satisfactory, Ruth," he said without expression. His back to her, Lane peered nonchalantly out the office window.

Usually satisfactory was even less than Lane's normal description of Ruth's competency. She had grown used to his pasty *satisfactory* appraisals; the word *usually,* however, made her nervous.

10

"I'm afraid, however," he went on, still gazing out at the campus, "this past year has seen an appreciable drop in your overall performance."

Half rising, Ruth gripped the arms of her chair. "Are you referring to my teaching?" she asked, trying not to sound flustered.

She'd been assigned two additional classes to teach at midterm—at the same time Lane had decided to prepare an extensive series of articles for a national magazine. Preparing for additional courses *and* having to translate his sketchy outlines into viable reading material—while setting up their annual summer expedition plans—had almost surpassed even Ruth's extraordinary organizational capacities. What did he expect of her? That was a moot question; he always expected superhuman performance.

Then what was he driving at? That was the primary question.

"Actually," Lane replied, turning to take his seat at the desk once more, "your teaching appears satisfactory. It's your attention to my research requirements that seems to have diminished substantially."

As Lane delineated a list of trivial—nearly nonsensical—transgressions, Ruth forced herself back into the chair. Initially his statement sent her mind into shock. She was astounded that he would find fault with her research efforts on his behalf; after all, Lane had always demanded that *his* work come before anything else—even classroom preparation—and she had always complied.

Suddenly she realized what was happening. She had heard that Lane was considering another young woman as his research assistant—a young woman whose father was the chairman of a substantial private endowment foundation. Rumors were always abundant, and she'd never given the grapevine any cre-

11

dence, but perhaps, she thought, she should have paid more attention.

All the pieces suddenly fused into a complete picture in her mind, and Ruth was shaken to the core at the thought of what might happen to her.

Lane was replacing her with another idealistic graduate student simply because that student's father could provide more funding for Lane's pet projects! That had to be it, Ruth realized, feeling suddenly very ill.

Ruth had done nothing wrong—she just wasn't useful to Lane's ambitions anymore. He was only making excuses—degrading her work—to justify her dismissal. Ruth's energy and intellect were nominal assets compared to those of an assistant with unlimited financial resources.

Where was the man she'd worked for and devoted herself to for six years? The man Ruth had given every ounce of time, intellect, and emotional energy to? Was there nothing of substance to Phillip Lane? Was he nothing more than hollow ego?

The truth came unexpectedly, sweeping over her in a wave of physical pain.

Lane droned on, but Ruth wasn't listening anymore. All her strength was centered on maintaining self-control. She had to get a grip on herself.

As painful as it was for Ruth to face dismissal on such grounds, it was his ultimate emotional rejection that stunned her. Lane had just been using her—nothing more, nothing less.

Used. Her honest affection and dedication reduced to manual labor in Phillip Lane's self-exaltation campaign.

Cold anger replaced Ruth's pain. Cold anger cleared her mind and gave her the strength to seize her full composure in the midst of emotional crisis.

There was more at stake than emotional rejection or the loss of her research position. If she reacted angrily to his disgusting decision, she might give him further justification to void her teaching position and Ph.D. work as well. Above anything else, Ruth had to secure her university teaching position, to salvage the foundation of her career and complete her Ph.D. requirements.

Masking her anger and a mounting trepidation, Ruth tried to appear attentive to Lane's continuing soliloquy.

". . . In summation," he went on, "I believe that if you are ever going to mature into a reputable social scientist, you must learn to function independently. After all, Ruth, you'll never develop intellectual self-sufficiency if I continue as your mental support system."

Ruth smiled at Lane as pleasantly as her tight jaw muscles would allow. "I couldn't agree more," she managed to say.

By the look on his face, Ruth could tell she'd gained Lane's full attention for the first time in their six years together.

Suddenly silent, his eyes narrowed slightly, and he brushed his chin with one well-manicured hand. "I'm glad we've come to a meeting of the minds," he said slowly.

"As a matter of fact," Ruth went on undaunted, taking full advantage of Lane's surprise, "I would like to take this opportunity to ask your opinion of a plan I've been considering for some time."

"I'm very pleased at your acceptance of my decision, Ruth," Lane pushed back at her. "It shows a marked improvement in your maturity. Now, tell me. Just what ideas have you been toying with?"

Ruth smiled again. She was determined to get something of value in return for her misplaced admiration and dedication to Phillip Lane.

"I believe," she began with feigned humility, "that I have been taking the easy road, so to speak. It's been far too simple for me to follow in your footsteps. I need to proceed on my own—as you propose." Though the words nearly stuck in her throat, Ruth was glad she'd forced them out. Lane's ego had been smoothed by her humble supplication. "I would like to take this coming year as sabbatical and work on my doctoral dissertation. That is," she added, "if you could approve my leaving on such short notice."

Ruth knew full well that Lane would be all too happy to have her off campus the next year. The reason for her absence would eliminate any unnecessary gossip over his replacing her.

She also knew that as chairman of the school, Lane had the power to circumvent the red tape normally associated with the approvals of both sabbatical leaves and Ph.D. dissertation topics.

Her calculated gamble worked, and Lane did not hide his obvious eagerness. "That's a splendid idea, Ruth. Splendid, indeed. It's time we see what stuff you're really made of. A year of research on your own should prove invaluable to your teaching performance too, I daresay."

Ruth found it easier to smile now. Lane's unusual interest and animation almost made her laugh, because she knew it was based on his pleasure at having his own way so easily.

"Then I can expect to have my teaching position held open for the next year?" Ruth had to be certain that Lane agreed with every aspect of her proposal.

"But, *of course,* Ruth," replied Lane, standing to indicate their meeting was over. "I'll have all the paperwork initiated tomorrow."

Walking around the desk, he actually escorted her to the door—an unprecedented move that assured Ruth her plan had worked.

"Now, tell me," he asked with pretense of interest, "what subject have you decided on for your dissertation?"

"The Amish," she replied without hesitation. "I want to research changes in contemporary Amish society. I'll have my proposal to you tomorrow," she continued with conviction.

Ruth had prepared the proposal years before, actually. Only time—time spent in Lane's service—had kept her from starting work on the Amish research. And now there was no doubt in her mind that Lane would accept her topic of choice.

"Fine, fine," he agreed as they reached the door. "And you'll be free to leave on your sabbatical at the end of the month—right after final exams."

Ruth turned to face Lane one last time. "I want to thank you for the past six years, Dr. Lane," she said honestly. "I've learned more by being associated with a man like you than I ever imagined possible."

Phillip Lane misread the intensity in Ruth's words, and responded as if he'd been given a sincere compliment.

CHAPTER ONE

Elkhart County hadn't changed in all the years Ruth had been away. Flat, broad farmland still reached in every direction, carefully defined, for as far as the eye could see, by miles of brambled fence rows and stately hardwood windbreaks.

There, in the far northern corner of Indiana, where winter refused spring its full term, the earth was budding quickly in the first heat of summer.

Furrows, like bright-green ribbons, streaked through the fields in neat, even rows. In a race between winters, farmers had planted early; every square inch of land appeared to be sprouting at once.

Here and there a cluster of farm buildings appeared on the horizon—standing out from the clear, June sky like picture-book cutouts. And trees, in full leaf, dotted the roadside, sheltering stubborn wild berry patches that grew abundantly, unattended.

The delight of discovering her childhood world much as she had left it years before was made complete when Ruth Mueller arrived to find Aunt Mamie's farm seemingly as unchanged as the surrounding landscape.

When she turned off the remote county road onto the farm's gravel lane, Ruth stopped the car and sat quietly taking in every detail of the peaceful scene before her. She sighed and smiled, relieved that her destination seemed all she'd remembered it to be.

The Detweiler farm centered on a cozy hub of great whitewashed buildings with grass-green roofs that nestled majestically at the end of a quarter-mile lane. And though the air was full of the clean scent of new-plowed earth, Ruth clearly distinguished the pungent aroma of her aunt's greenhouse.

The greenhouse, where Mamie Detweiler had cultivated herbs and spices for over forty years, still stood joined to the tall frame farmhouse at the far end of the lane. Ringed by wide beds of bright flowers, the house and its multipaned glass attachment seemed to float in a floral sea.

Changeless and enduring, Aunt Mamie's farm held the wealth of Ruth's childhood memories and her early dreams. Here the past was still alive and life's promise was fresh.

Here Ruth could take refuge from her shattered hopes and rebuild her future, in reunion with her past.

Home—she was *home* at last.

Ruth put her head back on the seat and drank in the peaceful feeling as she tried to put aside the recent upheavals in her life. She wanted none of the anger, bitterness, or confusion to mar her homecoming.

With every mile that separated her from the university, Ruth sensed a freedom emerging from within. As the distance melted away, the pain of Phillip Lane's spiteful rejection receded from her conscious thoughts. Disillusionment was offset by the joy of returning to Elkhart County.

After two days of steady travel, she finally exited the sceneless monotony of the toll road and began the last leg of her journey along a straight, narrow state highway. As the territory grew increasingly familiar, so her anticipation increased, and she hummed along with the blurred static of the car radio. A road sign appeared, and she read the town names out loud: Shipshewana—Middlebury—Goshen.

She repeated each name, savoring their sounds, and recited other nearby villages from memory: Wakarusa, Nappanee, Ligonier, and Honeyville.

The words felt good in her mouth; the exotic names pulled long-lost memories into her mind—memories of a childhood spent in these tiny towns where time and the outside world had little relevance.

And now, at last, she sat at the end of Aunt Mamie's lane, her destination just a quarter mile away.

Through captivated eyes, Ruth noticed something moving down the lane toward her. Expectantly, she watched as it approached, then came into sharp focus.

A dark, horse-drawn buggy finally rumbled past the car, throwing fine gray dust into the still afternoon air.

Ruth smiled at the black-bonneted woman driver and received an almost imperceptible nod in return. Turning in the seat, she watched until the buggy clattered onto the paved county road and rolled out of sight.

"Ruthie! Ruthie!" Mamie shouted, holding out her arms. She grabbed Ruth in a tight hug the moment she stepped on to the wooden porch. "Oh, I'm so glad to see you, Ruthie. Just let me look at you."

Though she was in her late seventies, Mamie's grasp had not lost its strength; she held Ruth in place for inspection.

"My word, girl. I believe you've grown another inch or two since I saw you last."

Ruth frowned playfully. "I hope not." She chuckled, giving her aunt a hard squeeze in return. "I've been five foot eight since I was eighteen, Aunt Mamie. And that's tall enough."

"Well, you carry your height much better than you did as a teenager," bubbled her aunt. "Oh, Ruthie, I've missed you," she added quietly, her eyes quickly sobering. "It's been three years since you've been home, and look at you." The old woman wrapped one arm around Ruth's waist, ushering her toward the kitchen door. "Why, you're so grown up now."

Ruth felt remorseful. Her relationship with Lane had proven unworthy of the sacrifice. Precious time, which could have been spent with her family, had been wasted instead. A tinge of anger rippled through her. Lane had cheated her of more than just his respect.

"Well, we'll have plenty of time to catch up now," Mamie continued. "I can't tell you how tickled I was to get your letter last week."

"I'm sorry about giving you such short notice," Ruth apologized as the screen door banged shut behind them. "I hope it didn't inconvenience you."

"Inconvenience? My word, Ruth Mueller. Don't talk nonsense." She pulled out a chair from the table and motioned for Ruth to sit. "Since when is having you around an *inconvenience?* Hmmm? Matter of fact, I've been lookin' forward to the day you'd come back for a good long visit. And when I got your letter—well, I tell you, Ruth, it was more than I'd hoped for."

Walking to the cabinet, she withdrew a cup and saucer before turning to the stove. "I've brewed up some of my special chamomile tea for you. It'll help you relax after your long trip."

Relax? thought Ruth. Just stepping into Aunt Mamie's kitchen was enough to relax anyone.

For as long as Ruth could remember, Aunt Mamie's kitchen had been yellow. The high walls were bright lemon, the woodwork and ceiling always painted a shining white enamel. That was Mamie's kitchen—the

20

place where every guest entered and usually remained for quite a while. In this vast yet cozy space, anyone and everyone was welcomed to visit, to laugh—even to discuss the world's current plight—and, always, to eat.

Mamie and her magic kitchen cured hunger and personal dilemmas with equal speed. And Ruth had spent many an hour there herself, at her aunt's knee.

"I saw a buggy leaving," Ruth said, stretching her long legs under the table. "The herb business must be booming."

"I have my regular customers," replied her aunt. "But business always picks up considerably when the tourists start arrivin'." She shook her neatly waved white head at the tea kettle. "I might just take down that herb shop sign at the end of the lane this summer."

She removed a lid from one of the several pots that bubbled on the stove and stirred its fragrant contents. "All summer long—every weekend the sun shines—there's a never-endin' parade of cars in and out of that lane, up and down the road. It's such a nuisance."

Ruth chuckled at her aunt's grumbling. "You've been threatening to take that sign down for as long as I can remember."

Mamie's herbal blends had quite a local reputation. But the tourists who flocked to the county each summer bought her dried herbal seasonings by the pound. And though she'd never admit it, Mamie Detweiler looked forward to summer selling season and the hordes of buyers; it gave her a chance to talk with outsiders and was a welcomed break from her rural isolation.

Yet her aunt's conscience never let her quite enjoy the attention to its fullest. She constantly reminded herself that her herb business drew too much attention to the immediate area. So many tourists—so many cars and cameras—often disrupted her Amish neighbors' lives, and Mamie somehow felt responsible to her Plain neighbors who patiently endured it all.

"Well, I just might take that sign down yet," Mamie went on, shaking her wooden spoon at Ruth.

But Ruth had lost interest in the sign controversy.

Gentle, fragrant air blew the stiff, starched curtains in and then back against the screens. Her attention was captured by the drying herbs, tied and hanging in bunches about the room. Memories of childhood days spent gathering, tying, and hanging tiny bundles just like these came racing back to her.

"Everything's just as it was when I was here last," mused Ruth as her aunt puttered at the stove. "The room's even the same color. And aren't those the curtains we picked out together in Shipshewana?" Ruth sighed. "And you still have my old highchair in the corner. Aren't you ever going to move it to the attic?"

"That highchair comes in handy when I have very small guests," Mamie replied, walking across the wide room to hand Ruth a cup of tea. "But once you get a closer look at the place, Miss Ruth, you'll see there've been quite a few changes around here since you left." Mamie settled in her chair at the table. "But let's not talk about that now; I want to hear all about *you* and this project you wrote about."

"Okay, what would you like to know?" answered Ruth with a grin. She took a sip of tea, knowing her aunt's curiosity could not withstand much more mystery. Her hasty letter had contained only the bare essentials—just enough to tempt Mamie's curiosity.

"Well, tell me about this sabbatical."

Ruth put down her cup and suppressed a smile as her aunt folded her hands, trying to look nonchalant.

22

"A sabbatical," Ruth began her dictionary definition, "is a period—usually a year in length—that a graduate student is granted to work on his or her doctoral dissertation. A doctoral dissertation," she went on blandly, "is a very long research paper."

Mamie's impatience got the better of her and she drummed her fingers on the tabletop. "That's very interesting, Miss Ruth, but I know all *that.*"

"Do you know what the university is going to give me if I do a really good job on my dissertation?" Ruth went on baiting her.

Mamie waved one thin finger at Ruth. "Do you know what I'm gonna give you if I don't hear some pertinent facts real quick?" Her loving voice belied the threatening gesture.

Ruth quickly hopped up from her chair, circled the table, and grabbed her old aunt in a bear hug. "Do you think you can still paddle me? Huh?" Ruth laughed, as she held her aunt and playfully kissed a powdered cheek.

"I might have to trip you with a broom to get you down to my level, Ruth Marie," Mamie warned in response, "but I can still handle the chore."

With a moan, Ruth released her aunt and plopped back down in her own chair, laughing. "I'll bet you could do it too."

"I *know* she could!" came a deep baritone reply.

Mamie, flushed with laughter and excitement, stood up and began smoothing her green-checked gingham house dress. "Why, Jacob," she said, "is it dinnertime already? Come in, come in. Ruth just got here."

Her aunt started for the door, and Ruth stood to greet the voice behind her.

"Ruth, this is Jacob Yoder."

Turning, Ruth saw only the shape of the man her

aunt addressed. With the sun at his back, she was blinded to all but his size.

Jacob Yoder was a square silhouette whose massive form barely fit within the dimensions of the oak door frame, towering above her and eclipsing the rays of the setting sun.

"I wrote you all about Jacob. Remember?" Mamie added as Ruth struggled to find her voice.

"Oh, yes. Of course," Ruth replied, unable to hide her amazement. "My aunt mentions you so often in her letters."

As Jacob stepped away from the door and approached her, his face became visible at last. And in the light of the kitchen, Ruth was confronted by a striking man not much older than herself. His lightly browned face was smooth and full; the broad cheekbones and fine nose were well defined beneath heavy waves of thick, brown hair. And his eyes—crystal blue, like a cloudless summer sky—left her spellbound.

"I-I-I've heard so much about you." But she never expected *this*—a magnificent giant in crisp denim who overpowered her with disarming eyes.

"By your expression I'd guess you didn't like what you heard," Jacob replied with a wide smile as he accepted her outstretched hand.

His touch was warm and his calloused hand—nearly twice the size of Ruth's own—made her feel strangely uncomfortable as it folded around her palm like a fine leather glove.

Ruth steadied herself. "Oh, no. Not at all. Aunt Mamie has always spoken highly of you, Jacob," she said with forced composure. "It's just . . . well . . ." She smiled and shook his hand. "I was expecting someone who was"—she hesitated—"old. I mean, *older*."

24

Jacob Yoder grinned. "How old?"

"Oh, *at least* as old as Aunt Mamie," replied Ruth, trying to take refuge in humor.

"Nobody's *that* old," retorted Mamie with mock indignation. "And why would I want some old farmer runnin' the place? I never said he was old!"

"No," added Ruth. "You wrote that Jacob was experienced in farming, that he wasn't rowdy, that he kept a tidy barn, and that he liked to putter around the place, fixing things. Now, doesn't that sound like a good description of an *old* farmer to you?"

Jacob pursed his lips and agreed. "Yep. Sounds *real* old to me. Didn't she mention anything in all those letters that sounded young and exciting?"

In reality, her aunt's letters had given astonishing little detail about Jacob. And it wasn't like Mamie to stop short of full disclosure on any subject.

Ruth laughed nervously, avoiding Jacob's steady gaze, a gaze that seemed to hold some undefined challenge.

"To tell you the truth," Ruth went on, covering her lack of knowledge about Jacob with pretense, "Aunt Mamie's been careful not to say much at all about you. I was beginning to think she'd made up that story about working with another farmer."

"Oh?" Jacob responded with a wicked grin. "Did you think that maybe she'd taken up living with some man and didn't want you to know about it?"

"Oh, you two. What nonsense. What pure nonsense!" Mamie protested loudly, obviously enjoying the attention.

She started back to the stove, but Jacob caught her deftly about the waist and pulled her in under his arm.

"We'd make a fine couple, Mamie Detweiler," he teased as she struggled against his hold. "A *proper match*, wouldn't you say?"

"I say *nonsense*, Jacob Yoder. Now you let me go this instant. I have to tend to dinner."

Ruth's laughter caught in her throat as Jacob followed Aunt Mamie back to the stove and continued to tease her. He seemed completely at home with the old woman, and somehow that made Ruth feel jealous. Aunt Mamie seldom acted this happy with anyone, even with her.

"Ah, Mamie, I never told you before," he said, "but it was your fine Dutch cooking that turned my head."

"Out of that pot, Jacob!" warned Mamie, waving a spoon at him. "We'll eat soon enough."

"You found the way to my heart," Jacob added, dodging the flailing spoon.

"I know. I know," Mamie repeated. "It was right there next to your stomach," she added, swatting at him. "Now, go sit down and pester Ruth for a while."

Jacob obeyed, but not before he'd pulled her apron strings and freed the bow.

"Oh, go on," Mamie reprimanded, laughing. "Ruth, see if you can do something with this hungry farmer."

Jacob gave Mamie a peck on the cheek and turned to get a cup from the cabinet. Pouring himself some coffee, he opened several cabinet doors.

"Are we out of sugar?" he asked.

"Oh. Yes. I forgot" came her reply.

Jacob took his coffee with him to the bulletin board next to the kitchen door, and Ruth watched him write something on the household grocery list.

"We'll have to get some more honey this week too," he called back over his shoulder.

"Make sure it's clover honey, not alfalfa," Mamie qualified, still working at the stove. "You don't like alfalfa honey, Jacob. Remember?"

"And *you* don't like alfalfa honey either," he said to

Ruth as he sat down at the table. "Mamie tells me you could always tell the difference too."

"Alfalfa's too strong," Ruth replied. His quick familiarity surprised her, but his great size and striking appearance had thrown her off balance. Jacob Yoder was a mass of tight, toned muscle that moved with inexplicable grace and ease. Nothing about him was awkward—not his actions and certainly not his speech.

But even as his body fascinated her, his comfortable, at-home manner somehow disturbed her more.

"But honey's not your only sweet-tooth specialty." Jacob chuckled. "You can't be trusted to pick strawberries by yourself, because you always eat most of what you pick before you get back to the house."

Ruth swallowed, feeling very odd. "Someone always had to go berry picking with me," she confirmed hesitantly, trying to maintain her smile.

"And . . . let's see . . . ," he blew into his hot coffee. "You were valedictorian of your high-school graduating class, and your favorite colors are yellow and blue. How am I doing?" He smiled broadly.

"A hundred percent so far."

Jacob leaned back and balanced his chair on two legs.

"*And* you and I have something in common."

"Oh? What?"

"We both like your aunt's cooking!" Jacob laughed. "I understand you used to sneak her jelly out of the house and sell it at school."

Ruth's smile had frozen, "Sixth grade," she managed to say.

"Did you really sell three dozen jars before Mamie caught you?"

"Forty-two jars," injected her aunt, shaking her silver head and chuckling. "Did she ever get a spanking for that. Whole season of berry jelly—sold for a quarter a jar!"

Jacob's chair tipped forward. "Maybe if you'd sold them for fifty cents, she wouldn't have punished you." He chuckled again.

Ruth tried to smile, but every nerve in her body was tight. This man apparently knew every detail of her childhood, and she knew absolutely nothing about him. Why hadn't Aunt Mamie provided her with details of him? And why was she feeling like an orphan in her own home—being talked *about*, but not having enough information to participate in the conversation? She felt inexplicably angry at this attractive but somewhat overbearing man. She had returned to Elkhart County to put the pieces of her life back in order and here was a handsome stranger in her home, acting as if he owned it and making her feel like an outsider.

"I guess I'd have been tempted to let everybody know about Mamie's cooking too," Jacob continued warmly. "She's one of the best cooks I've ever known, but I'm trying to discourage her from working so hard at it. She'd stand over that stove twelve hours a day, if I let her," he said with sudden seriousness. "Your aunt's not getting any younger, and I think she ought to slow down some."

"You'd better let her be the judge of that," Ruth replied sourly. Even though she agreed, there was something in Jacob's attitude that smacked of genuine intimacy with her aunt and Ruth hated it instantly.

Ruth had never had to compete for her aunt's affection, and she didn't intend to now. Especially now—when she needed every ounce of security Aunt Mamie's love could provide.

"I can talk Mamie into just about anything," he stated confidently, his words sounding cocky and smug. "I did get her to move downstairs to the guest room this last winter," Jacob continued in a whisper, glancing over to see if the older woman was listening. Satisfied that she was absorbed with her cooking, he went on. "Her arthritis kicked up and those stairs were hell to climb. I'm glad you're back, Ruth. Mamie can use both of us helping around here."

The powerful attraction she'd felt for him initially was now displaced by equally powerful distaste. *Who is this man?* thought Ruth vehemently. *Who does he think he is,* strutting around the place as if he owns it and talking about Aunt Mamie as if she were *his* responsibility?

But most disturbing was the fact that her aunt seemed to enjoy his possessiveness.

Ruth definitely did *not*.

"So how was your trip from Boston?" he asked.

"Very long and very boring," she replied a little coldly. Her body felt brittle and sore, but her voice was even.

"You know," Jacob went on lightly, not noticing the dramatic change in her, *"you* weren't exactly what *I* expected either." His large blue eyes were warm and friendly, but Ruth refused to see it.

At that moment, it was impossible for her to understand the intense, meaningless jealousy that flooded over her. Normally, she would have dismissed such ridiculous feelings. But weeks of emotional turmoil and days of sleepless travel had drained away her objectivity.

"And just *what* did you expect?" she replied through the faded smile.

"Well, it's hard to put into words." Jacob mimicked her original response. "I guess I was expecting someone . . ."

"Shorter?" she interrupted sharply.

"No, *older.*" He chuckled, stretching his long arms

over his head lazily. "Every time I read one of your letters or saw an article about the work you and this Dr. Lane are involved in . . . well, I just couldn't believe a woman of your tender years would have the knowledge—let alone the courage—to do all that."

"*You* read *my* letters?" Ruth came back at him, outraged.

"Your aunt shares them with me," Jacob answered, ignoring the icy change in her voice.

"We read every single one of them. Two and three times," Mamie added proudly from across the room. "Her letters are even better than her articles for *National Geographic,* aren't they, Jacob?"

"That expedition to New Guinea two years ago was especially interesting," Jacob went on quickly. "When will your article on last summer's expedition be published? The one to Lapland?"

"In November," Ruth answered in a short, clipped tone. One part of her mind told her to be thankful Aunt Mamie had a confidant like Jacob—someone to share her time and thoughts with. But another, darker part of her mind refused to be rational; it told Ruth that her aunt's love and affection had been usurped, that her place in Aunt Mamie's heart had been taken by a stranger.

"Dinner's ready!" Mamie announced cheerily. "You two set the table so we can eat."

The distraction of placing Mamie's flowered china on the red-and-white checked tablecloth was enough to temper Ruth's growing resentment. Silently she concentrated on the simple task, telling herself she'd feel better after a good meal. Nothing was going to spoil her homecoming, she told herself forcefully.

Her inner dialogue seemed to help, and by the time they all sat down to dinner, Ruth really believed she'd conquered her anger.

"I made chicken and dumplings for you, Ruth." Thankfully, her aunt had kept up a steady stream of instructions and chatter that displaced Ruth's silence. "I know how you love them. And there's shoofly pie for dessert. That's a favorite of Jacob's."

"I promise you won't get any competition over dessert, Jacob," Ruth said evenly. "All that molasses and cream are just too rich for me."

"Staples of a good Dutchman's diet," he told her. Aware that he had unintentionally offended her, Jacob spoke carefully, seeking the right combination of words and emphasis to kindle some kind of friendly flow between them. He'd liked that feeling when they'd first met—and, puzzled by his own reaction, Jacob wanted more—even as he recognized something had gone wrong, somehow.

"Now, we want to hear all about this new project of yours," Mamie went on, ignoring her own dinner. "Ruth's decided to finish her Ph.D., Jacob."

"So you're retiring to the country to write," he murmured. "Well, you'll complete that paper in record time. Not much to distract you from work out here."

Ruth bit into another dumpling and nodded an affirmative.

"I hate to admit my memory's failing, but I'm confused by all this." Mamie frowned. "I thought you were planning to be in Central America with Dr. Lane this summer."

Her stomach tightened. "I was," answered Ruth. Even though she'd known all along that she'd have to explain it all, Ruth hadn't expected to recount the details to anyone but her aunt. Jacob's presence inhibited her; she felt self-conscious and defensive.

"Well, what will Dr. Lane do now?" her aunt probed, unsuspecting.

"He'll have to work with a new assistant, that's all.

31

Would you pass the butter, please?" Ruth answered, stalling and hoping to break Mamie's train of thought.

Her aunt handed her the butter dish. "A qualified assistant won't be so easy to find. I mean, someone with your experience doesn't grow on trees, Ruth. This is so sudden." Her voice rose. "You didn't have a disagreement with Dr. Lane, did you?"

"No. Nothing quite so dramatic. May I have another cup of tea?" Her evasive maneuver didn't work. Mamie quickly went to the stove, but held tight to her line of questioning as she brewed more tea.

"Well, I'll bet he was awful unhappy to hear you wanted to work on your dissertation instead of working with him."

Ruth accepted her teacup back. "Actually, he thought it was a good idea. Dr. Lane thinks it's time I completed my Ph.D."

"But wasn't he upset? After all, you two have been together for years." Mamie paused to breathe. "And how can he possibly find a good replacement on such short notice?"

Her aunt's knack for getting down to all the sordid details of a situation was beginning to grate on Ruth. She didn't want to hide the truth from Mamie, but she didn't want to share it with Jacob either. So Ruth just took another bite of her dinner and tried to suppress her anxiety.

Jacob sensed that Ruth was being forced into a corner and detected her discomfort under Mamie's cross-examination.

"Dr. Lane shouldn't have too much trouble finding a replacement for Ruth," he spoke up before Mamie could launch another barrage of questions. "Research assistants come and go pretty regularly, I'll bet. Although," he quickly clarified, "I'm sure he won't find any one as capable as Ruth."

"And I suppose you're an expert on scientific protocol," Ruth retorted. Where her aunt's innocent questioning was understandable, Jacob's interference seemed intolerable. Her anger boiled to the surface in one great bubble.

"Not really," admitted Jacob, amazed she'd taken offense. "It seemed logical."

Ruth ruffled. "To a farmer, I suppose that kind of superficial logic could explain most anything."

Jacob looked into Ruth's blazing eyes and read more vehemence into her icy rebuke than even she had meant. His face hardened.

"Then Dr. Lane approved of your sabbatical?" Aunt Mamie said, determined to keep the conversation civil.

"Yes, Dr. Lane approved," Ruth answered. She pulled away from Jacob's stony glare.

"Ruthie, are you sure this won't hurt your chances for a permanent teaching position with the university?" Her old aunt's voice rose with concern.

"No," Ruth assured her patiently. "You see, Aunt Mamie, it was time I took store of my position with Dr. Lane. And when I looked carefully at the situation, it was evident that being his research assistant was conflicting with my own career progress."

"Even to a stupid farmer *that's* real logical," Jacob muttered so only Ruth could hear.

Ruth ignored his words. "Because," she continued with increasing assurance, "my time has always been divided between my teaching responsibilities and Dr. Lane's research requirements. That leaves no time to pursue my own research objectives." She glanced at Jacob. "I have scientific ambitions of my own."

"I'll bet you do," Jacob responded quietly. "And all this globe-trotting with the eminent Dr. Lane has probably put a crimp in your plans."

Not hearing the contempt in Jacob's statement, Aunt Mamie agreed. "I can see how the demands of this research position could keep you from getting on with your degree work and into meaningful research on your own. But . . ." She shook her head. "You'll have to forgive me, Ruth, but I'm just an old farm woman and I don't understand all this *logic*, like you younger folk."

"It's okay, Aunt Mamie," Ruth comforted her by patting her hands. "What do you want to know?"

"Well." She hesitated. "How can working with a very famous and respected man like Dr. Lane be bad for your career? After all, you two are working *together* in all this research. You said *that* yourself; I'm sure everyone who's anyone in anthropology knows that you're contributing to the work as much as Dr. Lane. How can that be bad for your career?"

Ruth refused to lie to her aunt. The old woman's observation was absolutely on target. Her research job had been an ideal position for an aspiring scientist. What her aunt didn't know was that Ruth's contribution would never come to light—Dr. Lane would make sure of that. The seething anger she'd held for weeks began to bubble to the surface of her thoughts again.

"You see, Aunt Mamie," she began tensely, "that's just the point I'm trying to make. I've outgrown this research assistantship. I have a lot of ability, and I'm ready to start building my own personal reputation based on research projects of my own design. Why invest all my energy and talent with Dr. Lane and let him claim all the glory?"

"No guts, no glory." Jacob ground out the words between his teeth. Ruth looked at him sharply.

"I certainly agree you have the talent," Aunt Mamie assured her. "But what about your teaching position?"

"My teaching position can only be *improved,*" Ruth explained honestly. "Once I have my Ph.D. I'll be eligible for a professorship; right now I'm only an instructor."

"Always a bridesmaid . . ." Jacob murmured acridly.

Ruth flashed him a warning look.

"So this all fits together," mused Mamie, beginning to understand. "You'll take this next year to write your dissertation. Then you'll receive your Ph.D., which means you'll have a permanent teaching job with the university and can work on your own research projects independently."

"That's right," Ruth answered firmly.

"Good." Mamie thumped the table for emphasis. "Now that I have all that understood, tell us about your dissertation. Are you going to write about one of the expeditions with Dr. Lane?" she asked with new enthusiasm. "I hope it's about the natives on that tiny island in the Pacific. That was so interesting. You remember that expedition, don't you Jacob?"

"Yes, I remember. That was the summer you studied the cannibals of Papua," Jacob replied, looking Ruth squarely in the eye. "And to think"—he grinned—"*we* were worried about *your* safety."

"They were *headhunters,*" she corrected him sharply. "And I assure you that I never felt endangered."

"I wonder how the headhunters felt?"

"Oh, Jacob." Mamie chuckled. "Be serious now. Go on, Ruth. What's your dissertation subject?"

Ruth looked directly at Jacob, and their wills locked in silent—yet mutually acknowledged—conflict. "I've decided to produce my dissertation from new re-

35

search," she informed her aunt, breaking away from Jacob's blazing gaze. "And that's why I'm here."

"Go on, go on," bubbled Mamie, on the edge of her seat. "The suspense is killing me."

Ruth smiled, because it was clear she had succeeded in recapturing her aunt's full attention. "I'm going to research Amish culture and write about changes in their life-styles over the last decade."

"That shouldn't take long," Jacob responded in a clear, steady voice.

Mamie stiffened in her chair.

"Oh? Are you sure of that?" Ruth charged back.

"Quite sure," he said without hesitation. "There haven't been any significant changes with the Amish in a hundred years."

"Well, it might appear that way to a casual observer like yourself, Jacob." Certain of her ground, Ruth held firm. "People like you and Aunt Mamie have lived around the Amish for so long that you've stopped seeing them. They're in the background of your daily life, so to speak. You're used to them. Just because they may *appear* unchanged doesn't mean that they aren't undergoing important cultural changes. That's a determination that can only be made by a skilled observer."

"A skilled observer like you, huh?" Jacob shot back, undaunted.

"Yes, an anthropologist like myself," she asserted with brash superiority.

"I think what Jacob is saying—" her aunt tried to clarify, but Ruth cut her off.

"I think Jacob's position is representative of that of the vast majority of people," Ruth declared. "They don't understand that groups like the Amish will eventually disappear and be absorbed by the predominant culture. It's important to understand how and why subcultures are assimilated." Her voice was tight, her words cold and sterile—products of some angry, disheartened creature masquerading as Ruth Mueller.

"I wouldn't hold my breath, waiting for the great disappearance if I were you," Jacob said forcefully. "And I wouldn't waste my time concocting a lot of scientific mumbo-jumbo to prove your theory either."

"I won't have to concoct anything," she assured him, glaring. "The Amish of Elkhart County are going to provide the information themselves."

"Don't bank on it," he snapped, getting up from the table and stalking to the door. "You'll be lucky if they give you time of day."

"Come now, Mr. Yoder. That's not exactly a rational position to take." Ruth smiled at his retreating form victoriously.

"No, it's not rational," he answered, opening the screen door. "But it's factual."

"What makes you think you can accurately predict their response to my research?"

Jacob walked across the threshold, stopped, and turned to face her. "Because I know how they are, how they think," he said slowly. "I ought to; I was born and raised Amish."

CHAPTER TWO

"Maybe I should have told you more about Jacob, Ruthie." Mamie's weary voice cut the terrible silence left in the wake of Jacob's abrupt departure. "But I didn't think it was my place to gossip about his personal life."

She stood slowly and began clearing the dishes from the table.

Ruth, stunned and silent, sat staring at the kitchen door. The unquestionable fury in the big man's quiet words had shaken her. *Born and raised Amish?* But how could she have known? His dress—his open, playful manner—where had the key been?

Perhaps she should have read more into the clues his body gave. Only a life devoid of modern luxuries and centered on intense physical labor could have produced that sinewy, seasoned structure.

"He left the order years ago." Mamie put the dishes on the counter and stared out the kitchen window. "He never talks about it much, and I didn't want to . . ." She shook her head, distressed by what had happened. "It's been an awfully hard decision for him to live with. I've always thought it best not to speculate about his past in my letters. We have enough idle talk about him around here as it is," she added softly and sighed. "I didn't think Jacob would want me doin' any extra advertising about it."

She glanced at her niece, expecting a response. Instead, Ruth sat immobile and mute.

Mamie crossed the room again. "I swear I've never seen him like this before, Ruth. But I'm sure he'll come around after he's thought it over. He knows all about the work you do, and he's told me more than once how much he respects your research," she rambled on, gathering more dishes. "It's not like you were going to study him personally."

With her hands full of dinner plates, Mamie turned back to the sink, wondering what had happened to the two people she loved most in the world. Not only was Jacob's flash of temper surprising, but Ruth wasn't acting like herself either.

"I'm very fond of Jacob. I only wish you two had met under different circumstances." Mamie continued worrying out loud, more to soothe her own mind than to explain what had happened. "Maybe it was just too much for him—after a hard work day and all. And you're tired from traveling." She shook her head again. She couldn't understand what had caused such a confrontation. And here was her own Ruthie, not even talking to her. "Another cup of tea?" she wheedled, trying to entice Ruth to speak.

"Yes" was all Ruth said as she pulled her attention away from the door and began massaging both temples with her fingers.

In a disturbing, heavy silence, the old woman brewed another pot of tea, picked up the last of the dishes from the table, and eventually settled back down in her chair next to Ruth.

"Jacob is *really* a very nice person, Ruth," Mamie began hesitantly. The silence between them was painful—unnatural. "He's usually so . . ."

"You don't have to apologize for him," Ruth finally

39

said, her eyes closed to the room's light. She tried unsuccessfully to rub the pain from her head.

"Oh, but he's never . . ."

"You have nothing to apologize for," she repeated. Opening her eyes, Ruth could see the hurt in her old aunt's face. "And Jacob doesn't have anything to apologize for either. I think his behavior was a perfect reaction to my misbehavior." She gave Mamie a rueful smile.

Thinking how tactless and unfeeling she'd been in approaching the subject as she did, Ruth feared she'd lost her sense of proportion and an equal measure of humility. But what struck her the hardest was that she had sounded exactly like Dr. Phillip Lane. Her tone of voice, the condescending attitude, that ring of intellectual superiority—just the thought of it made her sick at heart.

"Drink some of this. It will relax you, honey," her aunt said, pushing a brimming teacup closer to her hand.

"I'll need something stronger than chamomile to relax," Ruth said with a chuckle. Her eyes felt strained, her neck was tight, and her head throbbed. But it was wonderfully comforting to have her aunt still trying to mend her troubles with herbal tea, just as she'd been doing since Ruth was small.

"It's all the stress of driving so far," Mamie announced. "You'll feel much better in the morning, after a good night's sleep."

"I don't think so, Aunt Mamie. Better, maybe. But I won't be able to *cure* this problem with sleep."

Mamie reached over to hold her trembling hand. "Do you want to tell me what's troubling you, Ruth? You know, we've always been able to confide in one another."

She squeezed Ruth's hand and a new flood of memories came into the younger woman's mind. She envisioned the times she'd talked for hours with her aunt, here in this very same room. There wasn't a thing she couldn't tell her about. Though they frequently disagreed, as the generations often do, she and Aunt Mamie had always understood each other.

"You always know when I'm having a problem, don't you?" Ruth asked.

"Well, I certainly hope I do. After all, Ruth Marie, we think an awful lot alike, you and me. Why, in many ways you're just like I was when I was your age!"

Ruth had to laugh; she'd heard those very words so many times before—and they always reassured her. It was as if Aunt Mamie were her older sister rather than an elderly aunt. Their wide age difference meant little to Ruth. Aunt Mamie had always been young at heart, open and unjudging in her mind.

"I knew something was real wrong the minute I set eyes on you," Mamie added. "You look so tired, Ruth. Is it your job at the university?"

Ruth took a sip of her tea and nodded slowly.

"It isn't like you told Jacob and me, is it?"

"Yes. And no" came Ruth's answer. In the still kitchen, with only Aunt Mamie to listen, she now felt like talking. Even so, the words didn't fit together well. Perhaps it was because her thoughts on the matter hadn't come into focus yet. She hadn't been able to shake her anger, and until she could, the real problem would be muddled.

"I didn't just decide to leave Dr. Lane and work on my dissertation," she said slowly. "Dr. Lane replaced me. He's hired another assistant."

Her aunt's face reflected her disbelief. "Why—why—" she stuttered, "whatever for? You've done a wonderful job for him. You've worked so hard, Ruth."

Ruth smiled and tried to relax in her chair. "Jacob guessed why," she said, making her voice lighter. "It's not all that unusual for research assistants to be replaced. Actually"—Ruth leaned toward her shocked aunt and winked—"I hold a record of sorts. After all, I've been with Dr. Lane six years."

"So, to show his gratitude, he fires you!" Mamie retorted with loving indignation. "I'll be blessed if I ever understand how some people's minds work. Or how any blasted system works—universities, governments . . ."

"You and me both!" answered Ruth. Mamie's fiery words had already made her feel better, less burdened by her own inability to comprehend the *why* of it all. "Now, do you want to hear his reason for letting me go? Or do you want to hear what he said to me?"

"I'll put the tea kettle back on a boil. I can see we're going to need a couple of stiff cups to get through this one."

By the time the kettle whistled, Ruth had finished a word-for-word replay of the last meeting with Phillip Lane.

"Now, that's what he *said,*" she finished.

Mamie, on the edge of her chair, frowned. "I've got that. Now what did he *mean?*"

"It's politics, don't you see?" Ruth rushed on, explaining that her replacement might provide Lane with more financial backing for his projects.

"But isn't that *good?*" her aunt countered. "I thought you always said that funding was critical to good science programs at any university."

Ruth could tell she hadn't made her point. Baffled, she struggled to find the right logic. She shrugged and tried to think.

"I don't mean that it was *right* for you to be re-

42

placed for a silly reason like that," Mamie added quickly, thinking she had offended Ruth.

"I know, it's okay. It just makes me so angry."

"Well, you have every right to be *very* angry, I would say," agreed her aunt.

"It's not the job, Aunt Mamie. I'm angry about the system. The politics." Ruth slapped the table. She was beginning to see the reasons for her own anger. And they weren't what she had first suspected. "You know, when this happened," she explained to her aunt as well as to herself, "I was hurt because I'd dedicated my time and energies to a man who never appreciated my efforts. Never appreciated *me*. A man who was more interested in university politics than real science. But now I see it better." Her anger had faded and turned into resignation.

Ruth's face grew solemn. "You know, all I've ever wanted to do was work. I've always wanted to study people and to teach about people. Sounds pretty silly, doesn't it? That's such a little goal to have in life."

"It's *not* silly. It's a very noble goal—to want to help people understand other people," responded Mamie.

"But that's not what the system is after," Ruth said with a sigh. "It's a game, and whoever gets the most research money wins. It shouldn't be that way. Teaching and science should be immune to politics. Shouldn't they?"

"They are," answered her aunt warmly. "You have to look at the individuals, not the institutions. In spite of all the politics, a lot of people like you are doing good things in science."

"Maybe," Ruth replied, and laughed. "Doesn't this sound ridiculous?" Mamie frowned back. "Here I am," Ruth explained, "a twenty-eight-year-old Pollyanna—all hurt and weepy because the world isn't like I think it should be."

She had to laugh again as she began to look at herself objectively. "I must be a very slow learner, Aunt Mamie. It's taken me forever to see beyond my ivory tower." Holding up her teacup, she offered her aunt a toast. "Here's to my entrance into the real world." She clinked her cup to Mamie's. "Now I understand."

"Don't be so sure of that," warned her aunt, though she was glad to see Ruth returning to normal. "I'm a lot older than you, and just when I think I've got a handle on the way the world turns, somebody comes up with a new-fangled notion that turns it all upside-down again." With satisfaction, she tapped Ruth's cup. "Let's say you understand it today. Tomorrow it'll be all topsy-turvy again. You'll just have to work around it."

Ruth suddenly remembered Jacob and their ugly, senseless scene. "Well, today didn't go very well on the understanding side," she admitted. "I wonder if Jacob will ever speak to me again. I didn't show him much of my understanding and concern, did I?"

Aunt Mamie took a deep breath and smiled. "Don't worry about Jacob. Once he gets to know you, he'll come around. He'll see that you were having a bad day, not attacking him."

"But I *was* attacking him, Aunt Mamie. I *was* trying to put him down."

Mamie was startled at Ruth's admission and her eyes grew large. "Why, Ruth? Was it something he said that I didn't hear? Something he did?"

"Nothing he meant to do or say, I'm sure, Aunt Mamie. I'm the one who wronged Jacob—not the other way around. As juvenile as this must sound, I guess I was jealous of him—from the minute he came in."

Mamie's wise eyes glittered knowingly. "You wanted everything to be just as you had left it," she said, as if reading Ruth's thoughts. "And when Jacob came in—teased me and hugged me—you didn't like it."

"It was as if he'd replaced *me*. Does that make any sense?" Ruth was bewildered by her own emotional reaction to Jacob. It had been uncontrollable—and that disturbed her.

"It makes all the sense in the world, Ruth." Her old aunt smiled and patted her hand. "It's always been you and me, hasn't it? When you were a very little girl, living with your dad over at Honeyville, I'd drive our old truck over every other day to pick you up and bring you out here. When you got older, you'd ride your bike over all the time." She smiled lovingly at Ruth, whose mother had died when she was an infant. "We were a team from the very beginning. And here you come back home and find someone else is on the team. I can understand why you'd be jealous."

Standing, she came over to where Ruth sat quietly and put her arm around her niece's shoulder. "When you left to go to graduate school, Ruth, I was so lonely I thought I'd die. Your dad had sold his farm and retired to Florida. I'd lost your Uncle Clarence. I'd just never been so all alone."

Ruth looked up to see tears in her old aunt's eyes. "I should have stayed, Aunt Mamie," she exclaimed, feeling suddenly guilty.

"Nonsense," Mamie said. "You had a life to live. And I'd lived most of mine. Clarence and I were married for fifty-one years. Never could have children of our own, but *you* filled that spot just fine. We had lots of love between the three of us, Ruth. But then you went off to Boston. Clarence died . . ."

Mamie leaned against the table and took Ruth's

chin in her hands. "And then Jacob came along. He offered to live here and work the land for me. And, Ruthie, I haven't been lonely a day since."

"I'm happy for you, Aunt Mamie, really," Ruth insisted.

"I know you are. But what I'm trying to tell you, Ruth, is that there's room in my heart for both of you. I love you in different ways. You're like a daughter to me; you've made my life worth living. But, Jacob, he's a special addition—a ray of sunshine in my life. Just when everything looked gloomy, Jacob came along and brightened it up for me. Can you understand that?"

Ruth hugged her aunt. "Sure." She tried to smile. "But now you see I'm not as mature and worldly as you thought. The big-time social anthropologist is really a mean little kid at heart."

Mamie's laughter rang cheerily through the cool night air that had filled the kitchen. "I won't tell anybody, if you don't, Ruth," she assured her merrily, and sat back down.

All Ruth's problems seemed to evaporate in the face of Mamie's laughter and reassurance. "I suppose I'm just human," she admitted, chagrined. "What a disgusting thought!"

"You're *very* human, Ruthie. And I don't think that's bad at all. But remember, Jacob's human too," she added tenderly.

"Tell me about him. I'd really like to know more," Ruth said honestly.

"I suppose it's all right," mused Mamie. "I don't really know very much, actually—not about his life before he came to work here. Let's see . . . more tea?"

"I can't; I'm floating already."

"Oh, all right. About Jacob." She sat up straighter

and put both elbows on the table. "As you know, for two years after your uncle died, I rented out all of our acreage to a fella who lives a few miles down the road. And I received a very tidy rent check each fall, after harvest. Well, that was fine, except he was one of those modern farmers and used a lot of high-tech fertilizers, insecticides, pesticides, and twelve other chemicals I couldn't even pronounce. You know how Uncle Clarence never went for all those chemicals. He believed in a lot of the old-fashioned ways." Mamie chuckled. "Everybody used to think we were Amish, 'cause Clarence didn't even buy a tractor till the war years, and he only did it then so we could produce more for the war effort. Had to do our part, you know." She sighed heavily. "My, my, how that man loved to farm."

Ruth listened patiently. She'd asked and now she was going to get every detail, even parts of the story she already knew by heart.

"Well, I didn't like this fella's chemical farming. That stuff smelled somethin' terrible. Still, I didn't think too much about it; the rent checks helped out, and I told myself that things have to change and I'd just have to get used to chemical farming.

"Then I started getting visits from my neighbors. Oh, they were polite enough—Amish are always polite —but they made it real clear that all those chemicals were runnin' off on their fields, and they weren't happy about it. Well, that did it! Clarence and I always respected our Amish neighbors—never did anything to damage the water table or to harm the soil. But then you know that, Ruth."

"Of course," answered Ruth, who was aware of how well her family was thought of within the community. For generations their farms had been surrounded by the lush Amish lands. And for just as long, they'd lived in harmony through simple mutual concern for keeping the land wholesomely productive.

"When I talked to my renter he said he wouldn't do anything different. *Wouldn't,* mind you. So I told him *I* would do something. And I stopped leasing him the farm. Just like that. Next season—no more chemical -cides." She slapped her hands together to emphasize the point. "But there wasn't any tidy rent check coming in to keep me going either. So, I started looking around to find some help. I must have talked to everyone in the county, I guess. I asked Amish farmers if they had any boys interested in working the place, but no one knew of any young men available to work off their own farms."

Mamie shook her head and sipped her tea. "And then I asked some regular farmers," she said, "but no one would work the place unless I let them use all those chemicals. Said they get bigger crops. Humpf. *Bigger,* maybe, but not *better.*"

Mamie was on the verge of one of her "healthy foods—healthy body" speeches; Ruth knew she had to do something quickly to divert her back to talking about Jacob.

"So, how did you finally find Jacob?" she jumped in.

"Oh, yes, Jacob. Well, everybody knew I was looking for help, so word got out, I guess. Then, one day in the fall, about two years ago—actually, it'll be three years this coming fall—Jacob stopped by. He said he'd like to apply for the job; said he had lots of experience in farming."

"And he told you he was Amish?"

Her aunt chuckled. "No, no, no. Never said a thing about it. Not for a long time. No. But I wondered. He was so soft-spoken, kind of shy. Well, not shy, really. Jacob's more . . . reserved, I guess. He doesn't say much. But when he stayed for dinner that day so we could talk about farmin' techniques—I started thinking he *must* be from Amish stock. And, sure enough, I was right."

"How could you tell?" Ruth found herself asking, wrapped up in the story.

"Because"—her aunt snorted—"the first thing he started telling me was about cleaning up the soil from all those chemicals the other guy had been using. Well, it wasn't any secret by that time. I'd told everybody about it. But that was the first thing he wanted to do. Get all that stuff cleaned out of the land. Jacob talks about the land like it's a feeling, breathing thing, and that was a dead give-away. Only the Amish talk like that anymore. Everybody else talks about profits and yeilds; the Amish talk about tending the earth."

"And so you hired him on the spot!"

"Yes, but I've done more than that," her aunt replied, leaning closer and whispering. "Six months ago I made him a partner, Ruth."

Ruth stared at her aunt, dumbfounded. She meant *business* partners—not working *as* partners. "He's not just hired help, then?"

"Jacob's no hired hand, Ruthie. Not anymore. There's a big difference. And I want you to understand it clearly." Taking hold of Ruth's wrist, Mamie looked her directly in the eye. "Half of this farm belongs to Jacob Yoder. He's worked hard for it, and he deserves it. Do you understand?"

"I think so," Ruth replied weakly. "You're in business with Jacob."

"Right now *I* am; later on, *you'll* be his partner."

Ruth looked at her aunt in shock.

"When I'm gone, Ruth, you'll inherit the other half of the farm, and then you and Jacob will be partners."

"But . . ."

"I won't have our family farm sold off in chunks,

Ruth. That's why I've left it to you two in partnership."

"But, really, Aunt Mamie"—Ruth gasped—"I don't even know him! And . . . well, I've never thought about what would happen when you . . . Do you think you should have done that with someone you know so little about?"

"I *have* thought about it," Mamie told her grimly. "I wasn't planning on telling you until you'd gotten settled in, but you wanted to know about Jacob and this is part of the story. So, you might as well hear it all, I figure."

"Go on."

Mamie leaned back in her chair once more. "At first, he worked the farm for a salary—just like any other hired hand. But it was like the farm was his. Do you know what I mean?" Ruth nodded silently. "He loves this place. Why, that first winter he took to mending barns and fences. He put his heart into everything he did, just like your uncle always did. Jacob loves this place, I'm sure of it. He'll help you keep it productive and well tended when I'm gone, Ruth." She smiled wistfully, satisfied with her decision. "Anyway when it got too cold to work outside that first winter, Jacob started repairing equipment—even got our old courtin' buggy and the sleigh spruced up. Do you remember taking sleigh rides when you were a little girl, Ruth?"

"You still have the buggy and that sleigh?" Ruth asked, surprised. She remembered long rides in the country with her aunt and uncle—it seemed like light-years ago. It almost seemed as if it had happened to another person, a girl who had disappeared long ago.

"We even have a horse again," her aunt informed her with a giggle. "Jacob bought him special, just to pull the buggy." Still smiling, she waved a tired hand.

"Well, he flashed through all *that* repair work the first winter," she went on confidentially. "I knew he had to be Amish. Couldn't sit still a minute; always had to be working at something. Idle hands, you know . . ."

Ruth needed no reminding. One thing she remembered acutely was the Amish work ethic. They always started early and, it seemed, they never stopped.

"Well," her aunt went on, "after a while I finally asked Jacob if he was Amish; he said he was, and he began to tell me little things about himself. That simple! When he wants to talk, I listen, but I don't feel right asking a lot of questions."

Mamie straightened in her chair. "Jacob's such a worker!" she continued. "Why, just before spring that first year, he'd fixed, cleaned, or painted everything around here. When he ran out of work outside, he decided to paint the inside—and he started with the house. By plantin' time, this farm was squared away— inside and out!" She chuckled.

Ruth was startled. "Does he live here—in the house?" she shot back, then looked toward the door, almost expecting to see him.

"No, no. He lives in the barn." Mamie giggled. "How would it look for a widow-lady to live under the same roof with an unmarried man?"

"You made him live in an unheated barn?" Ruth was teasing now, but intrigued, nonetheless, with her aunt's saga. "That sounds like the kind of gratitude I've been experiencing lately," she said wryly.

"Heavens, no. He *wanted* to live in the barn." Mamie was laughing uncontrollably now. Her small, round body quivered with delight. "He's a cabinet maker, as well as a farmer."

"He prefers living in barns? This is very wierd, Aunt Mamie. What does cabinetry have to do with living in a . . ." Ruth was laughing so hard at her aunt's reasoning that she couldn't finish.

Steadying herself in the chair, Mamie finally replied, teary-eyed. "He asked to renovate the small barn. The one across the lot." She pointed toward the porch and the kitchen door to indicate the direction. "He made the upper level into an apartment, and the ground level is his cabinet shop. Oh, for heaven's sake," she scolded cheerfully. "You ask for these minute details and then sit there laughing while I'm explaining!"

Feeling much more relieved and relaxed now, Ruth stretched her legs and arms, yawning. Travel, stress, and emotional ups and downs had taken their toll; she was exhausted. Even so, she began to think more seriously about Jacob. Mamie had only touched the tip of Ruth's curiosity.

"Where does Jacob come from?" Ruth asked.

"Originally he lived just a few miles up the road," Mamie answered. "I know his people, but I can't remember him as a child. Thought I knew everybody and their kin in this county."

"Well, Amish kids don't get around as much as their elders," stated Ruth. She didn't remember him either.

"From what I've gathered," Mamie continued thoughtfully, "Jacob left the area when he was about twenty; he decided not to join the Amish community. But honestly, Ruth, I don't ask a lot of questions. He doesn't talk about it, so I don't push.

"His own people shunned him all those years, simply because he didn't join their order." Aunt Mamie clicked her tongue sympathetically.

Ruth shrugged. "Shunning is an Amish custom. It's the way they keep their culture pure—unchallenged by individuals who don't agree or question the order's way," she explained.

"But can you imagine what shunning must be like, Ruth? Never speaking to your own child? People you've known all your life never acknowledging you even exist? It must have been very hard on Jacob—not one Amish person would even speak *about* him, let alone *to* him. Shunning's an awful thing; it's cruel, I say. How can people who believe in family, children, and gentle living ever do something that cruel?" she asked bitterly, then frowned. "Still, it's turned into an unusual situation—even for the Amish." Her nose wrinkled indecisively, as if Mamie wasn't sure she should speculate any further.

"What's *unusual?*" Ruth asked quickly before her aunt could shift to another subject.

"Well," she went on slowly, "I guess Jacob was gone from here for nearly ten years. Then he shows up and takes up where he left off. He's farming—right here in the middle of a predominately Amish county— and they're not shunning him anymore." She shook her head with genuine amazement. "He visits with his family every week. They even ask him to help out on their farms sometimes. I can't figure it out. Why would they shun someone for ten years, then act like nothing's happened?"

"I guess they found a way to make amends," Ruth responded, trying to stifle a yawn. She was getting tired; her thinking had dulled.

"Somehow I don't think it's that simple, Ruthie. I've lived around Amish my whole life, but I don't know all that much about them—how they think or reason, I mean. Still, I've never seen one of them leave the order, go through all that terrible shunning, and then be welcomed back. Once they're out, it's over."

She looked sadly toward the door. "What you said at dinner was really right. I've grown used to the Amish, but I haven't grown close to them. I know I never can. They don't allow that." It was obvious that she was thinking about Jacob and the guarded way he had reacted to Ruth.

Ruth yawned. "Perhaps the research I'll be doing will change all that, Aunt Mamie. We'll both get to know our Amish neighbors better, and maybe we'll come to understand them."

"I think it's a fine idea, Ruth. And I'm so glad you can work on it right here at home. I've missed you, sweetie." Her aunt stood stiffly. "But let's get you off to bed. You can start work tomorrow morning—after a good night's rest."

Down the main hall and up the curving stairway, Ruth followed her aunt through the house and up to the second floor. It was a path she'd walked many times before.

"I've freshened up your old bedroom," Mamie said as they reached the top of the stairs. "Oh, where is your suitcase?" she asked, stopping just inside Ruth's room as she snapped on the light.

"It's in the car," Ruth explained, examining the tiny faded flowers on the wallpaper. The room was covered with pale daisies with thin, green leaves—just as it had always been. "I'll get everything unloaded tomorrow." She walked over to the heavy trundle bed by the window. The quilt coverlet had been turned down; the pillows looked plump and inviting.

Mamie handed her a gown from the dresser drawer. "I hope this still fits you, sweetie," she said. "Now, snuggle down in bed and get some rest."

With a final hug, Ruth said good night, and as she slipped into the gown, she listened to Aunt Mamie's footsteps creaking back down the stairs to her own room on the main floor.

She turned off the light and crawled between fresh cotton sheets. A soft breeze fluttered the curtains at the window and, beyond, crickets made soothing night sounds. The world was peaceful and quiet.

Every muscle of her body relaxed into the soft mattress. But before she fell into a dreamless sleep, a picture of Jacob came into her mind—just as she had first seen him. Tall and imposing, a brawny man with swirls of short bronze hair and playful azure eyes. Anger and jealousy were erased from this impression of him, and all that was left was a wonderfully soothing glow. Too tired to concentrate on the strangely electric sensation, and too relaxed to worry about it, Ruth was drawn into sleep by Jacob's beguiling smile.

Long after the last light went off in the farmhouse, Jacob Yoder continued to pace the full length of the gravel lane. Time and again he walked the quarter-mile stretch, his own anger diminishing with each turn of the course.

He chastised himself for letting Ruth provoke his anger. She was English; they were just like that, he reminded himself sternly. Hadn't he learned anything about English yet?

But even as he thought it, Jacob felt he was wrong about Ruth. And that confused him profoundly. She'd spoken cutting words—even swung with dizzying speed from humor to hostility—still, Jacob couldn't imagine a woman that beautiful without redeeming virtues.

She *was* beautiful, he thought. Not like English women at all, really. At least not like the English he'd known before. Her tall, straight body fascinated him— she evoked power and grace with every move. Ruth was not a fragile, guilded girl; rather, to Jacob's eye, she was the epitome of every womanly attribute he'd always admired.

Ruth had the lean, self-assured look of Amish

women. And her eyes reflected a spirit that he thought only they could have. Her outspoken ways excited him.

And her face was exquisite. Yes, he admitted freely to himself in the darkness, Ruth's was the most beautiful face he'd ever seen. Shaded from summers in the sun, her skin was a honey hue, toned with deep-rose highlights. Her cheeks—finely formed, wide and comely—sheltered flashing green eyes that invited him to come closer, even as her words warned him away.

Why, then, had he succumbed to a pitched battle? Why had he hastily dismissed her and her ideas just because of her sharp words? No, he realized after hours of walking, it wasn't anger alone that had separated them into opposing camps.

It was envy.

Jacob envied all that Ruth had become—all that she'd been able to experience, and the freedom she felt in the world. She'd had experiences that he still dreamed of. Experiences he had promised himself; experiences that he'd searched for when he left his whole universe behind once, a million years ago.

And his envy had exploded when he sensed she didn't see the value of all she had—the wonder of traveling the world and being comfortable enough to enjoy it. Instead, she seemed to look at the world with clinically sterile eyes—unemotional, uninvolved.

Finally, when Jacob was tired enough to accept the truth, he positioned himself on a fence rail and stared up at the starry sky. He knew he must make amends to her. He must apologize.

He had no right to tell this English woman how to feel, but he must live peacefully beside her. He had to, if for no other reason than Mamie deserved their peaceful coexistence.

CHAPTER THREE

It wasn't the distant sound of hammering or the frantic cackling of a barnyard full of chickens that woke her. No, Ruth was resuscitated that next morning by the smell of bacon frying.

She lay perfectly motionless beneath the quilt, eyes closed to the bright morning light, arms folded under her head, concentrating on the sweet, smoky flavor in the air and picturing the feast her aunt had prepared in the kitchen. The mental picture was so clear and tempting that her stomach started to growl.

Finally her appetite pulled her out of bed, and she threw back the quilt and stepped out onto the thick braided rug.

Her cotton gown reached well past her knees. Beneath the yards of soft billowy fabric, Ruth momentarily felt petite. The gown was a monument to Aunt Mamie's sewing skill; she'd made it exactly to Ruth's proportions a decade before.

Ruth bent and touched her toes; the gown swirled with her. Then she stretched on tiptoes, fingertips high above her head, and breathed deeply. A long night of trancelike sleep had washed away every trace of physical and emotional stress. And now the warm morning sunshine promised a perfect day of fresh beginnings.

She started out of the bedroom, but stopped and turned to retrieve her clothes. With Jacob in the house, she couldn't turn out for breakfast dressed only in a gown.

Jacob. She sat down hard on the edge of the bed. The thought of seeing him again made her feel a little nervous.

Ruth frowned thoughtfully. She really must set things right between them and without delay. But how? When?

She picked up her old cut-off jeans and T shirt from the rocker where she'd tossed them the night before, wishing she'd forced herself to bring in at least one fresh change of clothes from the car. It was bad enough she'd been an absolute witch last evening, but going down to breakfast *looking* like a witch might only confirm his opinion of her.

Ruth walked to the vanity and stared into the mirror. Her dark-blond, waist-length hair, banded at the nape of her neck, looked drab, almost dusty, and the straight-cut bangs lay limp against her forehead. Ruth thought she looked like a victim of emotional jet lag.

She checked the cut-offs and smoothed out the T shirt; they'd pass until she unpacked a change of clothes. As for the drab person in the mirror—she had to hit the showers!

Crossing the hall, Ruth marched into the bathroom prepared for action. The linoleum was cold and slick, and the gigantic bathtub, standing on big, porcelain paws, reminded her that she'd have to forgo a shower.

As her stomach growled unmercifully, Ruth locked the door and turned on the taps full force. Though a luxurious bath was inviting, her appetite pushed her to expedite the matter.

While steamy water poured into the tub, she brushed her hair then worked it into a single braid that trailed down the center of her back.

"Not bad," she muttered into the mirror through toothpaste foam.

As she stepped into the tub, the aroma of bacon was overpowered by the scent of coffee beginning to brew, and her stomach reacted vigorously.

Trying to overlook her hunger, Ruth reclined in the deep, hot water, resting her head on the rim of the tub. She really must organize her thoughts about Jacob— develop some plan of strategy before they met at breakfast.

She closed her eyes, still finding it hard to believe she'd behaved so rudely to him. What had come over her? Somehow she felt that there was more to the situation than her mental state could have accounted for. She'd felt strangely off balance from the instant they met.

Maybe, just maybe, she should simply go up to him and plead temporary insanity. Wasn't that true? She'd been so emotionally unbalanced that no amount of rational explanation could explain it better.

Ruth chuckled as she lathered her body with fragrant hard-milled soap. Jacob would probably accept that, she mused, remembering his soft blue eyes and easy smile. Maybe if I tap his sense of humor, she thought, he'll see how remarkably juvenile it all was.

But even as she laughed at her own absurdity, Ruth began to worry that she'd really done more damage than even she could imagine. Her attack had been thoughtless, and now that Aunt Mamie had explained the situation clearly, it even seemed cruel.

Though Jacob's body gave the impression of indomitable strength, his kind words and actions had betrayed a kindred soul; Ruth had gravely misjudged him.

She had to find a way to prove that she was worth his trust again—that she deserved his trust. She wasn't certain why. She was still muddled from all that had happened, and the reason was wrapped in many differing emotions. But of this much she was certain: She had to earn back Jacob's trust.

Hurriedly, Ruth finished her bath. She felt a sudden urgency; she must find Jacob and find out what damage had been done. Just how she would approach him, she didn't know. But she must do it and immediately.

"Breakfast ready?" asked Ruth, breezing into the kitchen moments later.

Mamie stood doing dishes, a watchful eye on a skillet of bacon crackling on the stove. "Breakfast?" She chuckled, turning. "Why, it's nearly lunchtime, sleepyhead."

Ruth glanced at the clock on the wall. It was eight-thirty.

"Well, I'll be," she said, pouring a cup of coffee. "Do you think you could find some leftovers to feed a poor, weary traveler?" She gave her aunt a kiss and leaned against a cabinet.

"I'll see what's left." Mamie chuckled. "Jacob doesn't usually leave any leftovers."

"He's already had breakfast?"

"Oh, hours ago. He's been working since sun-up in the cabinet shop." She began setting Ruth's place at the table. "Didn't all that hammerin' wake you up?"

"No," she answered, peering out the kitchen window. She saw Jacob working in the open doorway of the barn, hammering away. "Did he mention anything about last night?"

Her aunt walked past her to the stove. "Not a word," she replied confidentially.

"Did he say *anything?*" Ruth said, continuing to watch his body swaying in time to the hammer. She watched, engrossed—mesmerized by Jacob's graceful

60

strength. His muscular arms, damp with perspiration, danced in ripples; his powerful legs, straining against the fabric of his work jeans, grounded him firmly against the hammer's momentum.

"Did he say anything about me?" Ruth asked faintly, not able to take her eyes from the window and not hearing a word her aunt had originally said in reply.

"Ruth? Are you all right?"

The tone of Mamie's voice broke the spell. Ruth blinked and focused on her aunt's face. "Sure. Why?" she replied, and took a sip of coffee.

"You're all flushed up, honey," her aunt answered, touching her forehead. "Are you feverish?"

Ruth forced a chuckle. "I just got out of a hot tub," she said, walking over to the table to lower herself promptly into a chair. Her legs were like lead, and her heart was racing unsteadily. Just watching Jacob— even at a distance—gave her the same remarkable sensation she'd experienced the night before when he first stood, outlined, in the kitchen door.

"And I'll bet you're famished," her aunt added with a look of concern. "I'll have your breakfast done in a jiffy."

Sitting down, away from the vision of Jacob's lithe body, Ruth regained her equilibrium slowly. But the memory of the sensation held her fascinated.

Sipping strong, black coffee and listening to her aunt's pleasant chatter enabled her to calm the unexpected feelings that stirred within her. If she forced herself to pay close attention to the moment, Ruth could temporarily block her confusing reaction to Jacob.

"I wanted your first breakfast at home to be real special," continued Mamie. She placed a heaping platter before her niece. "All your favorites. See?"

The plate held crisp bacon, fried eggs, and a mound of homemade biscuits, covered with buttered molasses. "Looks terrific," Ruth said appreciatively. "But I can't eat . . ."

"Of course you can," Mamie insisted. "Just pick up your fork and get started. You're going to need a lot of energy for all that research you're going to do." She paced back to the stove to get the coffeepot as Ruth began to eat. Together they sat talking until her aunt was satisfied Ruth could hold no more.

"Just how do you start researching a project?" Mamie asked with genuine enthusiasm.

Ruth swallowed a sticky morsel of biscuit. "Usually I start by setting up camp," she said. "You know, get the tents in position, make sure the place is organized and the food is safely hidden from marauding animals. That sort of thing." She took another bite, trying to look serious.

Her aunt's eyes twinkled. "I think you can skip that part on this trip," she advised. "The only marauding animal around here is Jacob, and I'm used to keeping him out of the food."

Ruth laughed. "Then I guess we can start by getting acquainted with the topography—that's the geographical area we're covering in this project, and see if we can locate any friendly natives."

Mamie nodded in solemn agreement.

"After we locate some subjects, then we'll tie them down and interrogate them," she went on with authority. "That's how Dr. Lane always got his best information. He'd just tie some natives to a tape recorder and talk them into submission. It's very scientific," she concluded with a wink.

"Well, you'd better run and get your tape recorder," announced Mamie, looking past Ruth and through the screen door. "A native is coming into camp right this very minute." Together they reached the door just in time to see a middle-aged Amish woman climbing down from her buggy in the barn lot.

"Guten Morgen, Herr Yoder," the woman called heartily to Jacob in German, while tying the horse's reins to the hitching post next to the porch.

"Wie geht's, Frau Raber?" Jacob replied in a deep voice.

"Danke, sehr gut," she called over her shoulder. Tugging at her steel-gray ankle-length skirt, the woman climbed the steps and crossed the porch.

"What brings you out on a Saturday morning, Mrs. Raber?" Mamie inquired cheerily, holding open the door and inviting the woman in.

"Baking, baking, baking, Mrs. Detweiler," she answered in perfect English. Preoccupied with untying her black bonnet, Mrs. Raber hadn't noticed Ruth, who had moved away from the door and stood quietly watching her. "I have a million things to make today, and I've run out of cinnamon and ginger."

The woman's face glowed pink with the morning's heat, but her pale skin—creamy and almost translucent—showed not a trace of sun. Shielded, for a lifetime, by the black polished-cotton bonnet, her face was as soft and unblemished as a child's.

"Why so much baking?" asked Mamie, pulling out a chair and offering her a seat. "Are you having company this weekend?"

Mrs. Raber laid her bonnet on the table and brushed the dust from her white bibbed apron. "No. No company," she replied, but shook her head, declining to sit. "We're going on a trip next week, and I'm taking some home-baked sweets along."

Her hands went up to smooth the hair around her organdy cap, and she saw Ruth. Her hands stopped, and she went silent.

"This is my niece, Ruth, Mrs. Raber," Aunt Mamie informed her.

"Ruth Mueller." Ruth stepped forward and offered the Amish woman her hand.

Mrs. Raber nodded and went back to smoothing her hair, completely disregarding Ruth's overture.

"Ruth's going to be living at home for a while," Mamie went on.

"I'm sure you've made your aunt very happy by coming home, Ruth," the woman said softly, her eyes silently appraising Ruth from head to toe. Though Mrs. Raber smiled, Ruth clearly read the disapproval in her face and made a mental note that cut-offs and T shirts were totally inappropriate for this particular expedition.

"You know, Mrs. Raber, Ruth has traveled all over the world," chirped her aunt.

"Have *you* seen the Grand Canyon?" Mrs. Raber shot back instantly, her minimal smile changing to a veritable grin.

Surprised by the woman's sudden animation, Ruth could only answer, "Yes, I ha—"

"We're going to see the Grand Canyon on *our* trip," she said before Ruth finished her sentence. "My husband and I are taking the taxi to Kansas to visit my sister's family. And on the way back, we're going to visit the Grand Canyon."

"I'm sure you'll enjoy it," responded Ruth. She wondered how the woman could believe the Grand Canyon was a natural extension of a trip to Kansas, but she didn't think it wise to question her. On the other hand, "the taxi" statement was too intriguing to pass up. "What taxi service would take you so far?" she asked innocently.

"Mr. Hamilton, I believe his name is," Mrs. Raber replied without hesitation. "He lives over by Goshen," she explained. "Well, I can't stand here talking all day." Picking up her bonnet, Mrs. Raber started back toward the door. "There's too much to do before we leave."

"Of course. Let's go on out to the greenhouse." Mamie followed her out onto the porch. "I've got some fresh-ground cinnamon you'll just love."

Ruth watched, puzzling over the conversation, as the two hurried out to the greenhouse. Jacob's hammer rang dully in the morning air, and Ruth saw he was again working away in the small barn.

"Enjoy the Grand Canyon," Ruth called to Mrs. Raber through the kitchen's screened door.

"I will," she replied.

Ruth knew the time had come to face Jacob; she took a deep breath and decided to meet the situation on his ground. She went to a cabinet, took out a heavy mug, and filled it with coffee.

Remembering they were out of sugar and honey, she poured two heaping spoonsful of heavy molasses in the cup and stirred it quickly. A moment later, before her courage abandoned her, Ruth was on her way across the barnlot, coffee in hand, a pleasant smile covering her apprehension.

"Good morning, Jacob." Determined to make the first move, Ruth forced out a bold greeting, without looking at him directly. "Aunt Mamie just made a fresh pot of coffee; thought you might like a cup."

"Plenty sweet?" he asked. Jacob had hoped she would at least be open to conversation this morning, but he certainly hadn't expected she'd come looking for him.

"Two spoonsful of molasses; is that enough?" Ruth handed him the mug, smiled, and quickly turned to explore his woodworking shop. "Aunt Mamie has been telling me that you're converting the barn into a cabinet shop," she said warmly. "And you have an apartment upstairs?" Ruth walked to a stairway in the rear of the shop, and Jacob followed.

"That's right," he explained. "Eventually it will be three bedrooms, bath and a half. But so far I've only had enough time to complete the living room, kitchen, and one bath." He took another drink of his coffee.

"How can you do all that and keep a farm this size going at the same time?" Ruth meant it as an honest compliment. The shop itself reflected hours of dedicated work. The plaster-finished walls were lined with workbenches, tool bins, and dozens of long, wide shelves full of rough lumber. Every inch of the place had been painted a pristine white; even the smooth concrete floor was spotless. And except for the tools being used for his current project, nothing was out of place.

"It's not so hard," Jacob replied, wondering if Ruth's sudden interest was as genuine as it appeared. "It helps fill in the time between planting and harvest, and it gives me something constructive to do during the winter." He came a little closer to where she stood. "It's also a good second income. Like your aunt's greenhouse."

Don't waste time in chit-chat, he cautioned himself. Before they were at each other's throats again, Jacob had to be sure a permanent cease-fire was negotiated. And this seemed like the perfect time to approach it.

He reached out and gently grasped her wrist. "Ruth," Jacob said in a clear voice, "I want to apologize to you about last night."

The impact of his simple gesture and the unwarranted apology reverberated through her body. Like shock waves, his warm hand sent dizzying flashes of heat pounding through her body. Trembling, she turned to face him, and his lush blue eyes held her in place.

"Did I frighten you?" he asked then, aware of the effect his imposing size had on others. He released her arm, but still she didn't speak.

"I'm sorry," he added quietly, now apologizing for having touched her.

"You shouldn't be apologizing to me," Ruth managed to say. She leaned against the workbench. Her legs still trembled. "I'm the one who owes *you* the apology, Jacob. That's why I came out here. I wanted to tell you how terrible *I* felt about last night."

His eyes were deep pools of blue, and, try as she might, Ruth couldn't bring herself to pull away from them. The longer she concentrated on them, the more comfortable their effect became.

"I guess we were both talking instead of listening," Jacob admitted. How could he have felt anything so ridiculous as envy toward this woman, he wondered, watching Ruth struggle with her confession. He must have misjudged her; he wouldn't let her bare the brunt of what had happened. "But I think my temper really caused it all to flare," Jacob added to take his share of responsibility in the matter.

Her apology impressed him. Those fathomless green eyes of hers were a reflection of truth. He was sure of it.

Ruth nodded slowly. Her body had begun to cool, but she relished the deliciously exotic reaction his nearness gave her. "I want to explain," she insisted. "I hate people who make rational excuses for their irrational behavior, but—"

"You don't have to explain," he interrupted, hearing her intentions as clearly as if she'd actually spoken them. "I understand." And though he didn't really, it didn't matter anymore. How could he allow her to explain, when he couldn't really verbalize the reasons for his own misconduct?

"I hope you do." Ruth sighed, glad she wasn't pressed to expose the outlandish jealousy issue that had caused it all.

"Why don't we call it a draw?" Jacob suggested. "Hard-headed Amishman, zero . . ."

"Hard-headed anthropologist, zero," inserted Ruth with a chuckle. She was enjoying the light from his eyes now; it warmed her through and through.

Just as when she first saw him, Ruth was again captivated by those brilliant blue eyes. They seemed to suspend her in time and thought. She'd never known a man like this, a man who could make her feel such delicious sensations by merely looking at her.

Jacob took a drink of his coffee, but never took his eyes from her. Ruth was even more lovely this morning, he thought, than she had been the night before. The sunlight from the shop window caught the highlights of gold and copper in her hair.

"Would you like to see my apartment?" he asked, wanting to detain her as long as possible.

But before Ruth could answer, the spell between them was broken.

"It's about time for lunch," Mamie announced, bustling into the cabinet shop.

Jacob lazily pulled away from Ruth's gaze. "Must be," he said while giving Ruth a reassuring wink. "I'll give you the full tour later," he promised.

"I guess the Rabers have finished plantin'," Mamie continued to Jacob. "They're takin' off on a long trip this week."

"They're going to Kansas to see the Grand Canyon," Ruth added with a puzzled look.

"Uh-huh," Jacob replied, picking up his coffee mug. "I knew an Amishman who went to visit family in

68

Missouri once and ended up seeing Carlsbad Caverns in New Mexico."

"Oh, Jacob, don't tease Ruth. Explain it to her," insisted Mamie.

Ruth had caught the playful flicker in Jacob's eye. "Go ahead," she prodded. "See if you can come up with a reasonable explanation, Jacob."

"It's all *very* reasonable," he informed her proudly. "The Amish love to travel, especially to see natural wonders like Yellowstone Park and the Grand Canyon. But they just can't announce they're taking a vacation."

"Why?"

Jacob tapped the worktable to help make his point. "Vacations are *worldly,* frivolous. And not a practical use of time."

"Ahhh," Ruth said, understanding. "So they work a little sightseeing into family visits."

"I think she's got it!" Jacob was delighted. "You see, keeping family ties strong—even if family members live at great distances—is very important to them. So visiting isn't frivolous—it's practical. It holds family bonds together."

"So if you're visiting family in Kansas . . ."

"You get to see the Grand Canyon because it's in the neighborhood, so to speak."

"Exactly."

"I think your research has started," said Mamie, glowing with excitement. "Now tell her about taxis, Jacob," she insisted.

"Go on," Ruth pleaded, pulling her legs up under her chin. Her enthusiasm peaked as Jacob's warm nature resurfaced once more.

"Whenever the Amish have to travel any real distance—let's say more than two hours from home by buggy—they hire English to drive them. An English," Jacob continued, "is anyone who isn't Amish."

"Well, I know one English who's not unpacked yet," Mamie reminded Ruth. "Why don't this Amishman give her a hand?" She patted Jacob on the shoulder. "And by the time you've unloaded the car, I'll have lunch ready."

Ruth groaned. "I'll pass on lunch." Her breakfast had barely settled, and she struggled to her feet. "But I could use some help, if you don't mind, Jacob." The powerful attraction he induced had simmered to a cheery glow that magnetized her; Ruth felt good just being close to him.

Willingly, Jacob followed out to where she'd left her car.

"So you drive a new minivan," he said as she unlatched the tailgate. "Get good gas mileage?"

"Not as good as a horse," she answered, beginning to pull out the boxes and bags containing the sum total of her personal possessions. "But I like it."

"Sure holds a lot of cargo." Jacob effortlessly lifted out two large cartons. Ruth took a lighter box, and they carried them through the house and up to the spare room.

"I'm going to need a desk if I'm going to do all my work in here," Ruth thought out loud, surveying the bare room.

"And two full walls of bookcases," added Jacob, wiping his forehead with his shirt cuff. "Are you going to read all these books for your dissertation?"

"Most of them," she tossed back, absorbed in mentally arranging her study.

He picked up a thick volume and read the cover: *The Dawn of Man.* "Do you think it's really necessary to go back to the beginning of time to explain Amish culture?" he grumbled, and picked up another book.

"What?" Ruth asked absently.

"Now, here's a real winner: *Understanding Cults in Twentieth Century America.* Where does this fit in to studying the Amish?"

"It doesn't," she told him, taking the book out of his hands.

For nearly an hour, they marched through the house with Ruth's belongings.

"Didn't you bring anything but books?" Jacob complained as he set the last weighty container down in the spare room.

"I like books," Ruth said. She felt a little uncomfortable at admitting her furnished campus apartment had only been big enough for herself, her books, and a few prized souvenirs from past research expeditions.

"But did you need to bring *all* of them?"

"I'm here to do research, remember?" Ruth said, not bothering to admit she'd given up her apartment.

"So you bring all these books, so you can read what all the so-called experts have ever written about the Amish. That's real independent research," he grumbled.

"I've got to get a background in the subject," she retorted. "Don't you like books?"

"I like to read," he said as he sat back on a stack of boxes. "But I don't get all my ideas from books. I like to think on my own once in a while."

The accusing tone in his voice was irritating. "Are you saying I *don't* develop my own conclusions?"

"I don't see much evidence to the contrary," he advanced. "What do you plan to do? Read everything ever written on the Amish so you'll be able to keep your ideas in line with everyone else's?" Before the words were out of his mouth, Jacob regretted having said them.

"Do you really believe I'd waste a year of my life

just paraphrasing other people's opinions?" Ruth demanded, her eyes flashing as she swung to face him. "Maybe you're just anti-intellectual," she diagnosed, barely keeping her anger in check. "You sound like a man who's not willing to look beyond his own set of accepted opinions. Are you against science in general, or is anthropology your pet peeve?"

Jacob held up his hands and shook his head. "Let's stop now. Before this gets out of hand again." He didn't want to argue with her, but she kept touching a hidden resentment in him that no one else had ever contacted before. "I'm not angry at you, Ruth. Please believe that."

She stared at him, remembering what he had asked her just that morning. Before she realized it, Ruth handed his question back. "Jacob, do *I* frighten you?"

Looking up at her body—so fragile in comparison to his own mass—Jacob had to grin. "You're not exactly a heavyweight, Ruth."

She wanted to reach out and touch him, but Ruth was certain the contact would overturn the delicate balance of emotion she was barely maintaining. "You don't approve of what I'm going to do, is that it?" Ruth asked carefully.

"That's not for me to approve or disapprove. It's what you're going to come out with that concerns me." Something about her—no, *everything* about her —stimulated him. One minute her presence tempted his body, but the very next minute she made him feel defensive. Jacob lifted up from the book carton and walked to the window as if the little distance could restore his emotional equilibrium. "I'm just tired of *experts* churning out the same old tourist bunk about the Amish. Just once I'd like to see somebody take the time to do an honest portrait of them."

"And you don't think I'm capable of doing that?"

He turned back to her, leaning against the window frame. "Yep, I think you could probably do a good job at it, if you had the right motivation," he answered with unmeasured honesty.

"What do you mean, Jacob? Why would my motivation be any different from what it has been in the past?"

"Because you aren't working with the same set of rules that you're used to doing research under. This isn't some grant job where you're being paid to be open-minded and observant. You're writing a doctoral dissertation, Ruth. And if the university doesn't like what you come up with on the Amish, you might not get that Ph.D. There's a lot at stake. How honest and objective can you afford to be?"

Jacob's reasoning was impeccable, and for a moment Ruth was amazed that this supposedly simple farmer was able to see things so clearly. He'd handed her something to think about that she'd never even considered before.

Seeing that she'd accepted his idea, Jacob gained new energy on the subject. "Tell me," he said to her, climbing back over the boxes to sit beside her. "Why did you choose the Amish for your research?"

"Well, it's a unique topic," she answered slowly. Jacob was so close to her, and Ruth was all too aware of his body's heated scent again. Her thoughts suddenly split into separate tracks—one trying to respond to his questions, while the other tried to absorb his powerfully sensual aura.

"That's not much of an answer."

She looked at him, confused. "What are you getting at?" Ruth could barely concentrate on his words.

"Last night didn't you say you planned to interview Amish people?"

"Of course. I want to talk to as many Amish as I can."

"All right. The first thing they're going to ask is: *Why do you want to know?* I guarantee it." He held up one great hand as if to swear the truth. "Everyone you try to talk to is going to say, why are you asking me all these questions? Why should I tell you anything?"

Ruth forced herself onto his wavelength again; her fragmented mind gathered again on Jacob's words. His was a valid point that deserved her honesty and forethought.

"I'd just have to tell them the truth," she admitted as his hand lowered and grazed her bare leg, causing her to emit a little gasp. "And the reason isn't the least bit academic or scientifically rational."

"Good." He grew more confident. "Now, *why* did you decide to spend the next year of your life researching the Plain People of Elkhart County?"

"Because I just want to know. I've always wanted to know about them. Personal curiosity. Pure and simple. Now, how's that for scientific purpose?" she asked, looking once again into his clear blue eyes.

Jacob laughed loudly. "I like it." He roared, the laughter relieving some of the renewed emotional tension he felt being next to Ruth once more. "It makes sense."

"Dr. Lane wouldn't have thought so," admitted Ruth, grinning. "Personal satisfaction doesn't get research grants."

"And it probably won't buy a Ph.D. either," Jacob assured her. "But it may get the Amish to talk to you. They'll trust you if you tell them the truth, Ruth. Just say: 'I'd like to ask you about being Amish because I've always wanted to know more about the Amish.' "

Ruth shifted and crossed her legs. "You know, I've

74

wanted to do this research for years. Want to know why?"

"Sure." Jacob crossed his legs as well and settled down to hear her story. He wanted to know *everything* about her—this beautiful woman who attracted him so.

"Remember last night when I said something about people not seeing change in the Amish because they're used to them—like background scenery?"

Jacob nodded.

"Well, I fit in that category. I grew up in this county, even went to grade school with Amish kids. That was before they built separate schools," she clarified. "But I never really knew anything about them. They were just there. Nothing special. I thought the whole world was like Elkhart County. My father and uncle farmed with tractors; the Amish used horses. Contrast was the norm for me. But I never realized how unique this area really is until I left and went out into the outside world. Isn't that strange?"

Jacob gave her a sly grin. "I don't think it's strange at all," he answered slowly. "I had an experience like that myself."

"Of course," she confirmed. "Aunt Mamie told me you lived away for a long time." Beyond that slight admission, Ruth judged it best not to comment or ask questions.

And when Jacob didn't offer any more information, she continued. "When I settled on anthropology for my career, I knew that some day I'd come back home and learn all I could about the Amish. I made it a goal. Isn't it remarkable how we overlook the most obvious things? It's as if we're always looking for the unique or exciting someplace else."

"Can't see the forest for the trees?" offered Jacob. He was thoroughly satisfied that Ruth's intentions were honorable. "I'd bet money that you'll find the forest this time." Unfolding his legs, Jacob stood and stretched. "I'll build you some bookcases for storing these gems of wisdom," he said, eyeing the unopened boxes.

"Thanks, Jacob."

She watched him disappear down the stairway in summons to Aunt Mamie's lunch call. But for the next hour, Ruth could only really think about Jacob and the recurring waves of excitement he caused within her.

Home *had* changed, it occurred to her. It was even better than she remembered.

CHAPTER FOUR

In the two weeks that followed, Ruth settled into the restful, unhurried rural life-style she'd grown up with. It was quite a contrast to the hectic, stress-ridden pace she'd been accustomed to while working for Dr. Lane. The constant pressure of deadlines, schedules, exams, and preparation no longer existed, and Ruth experienced subtle yet noticeable shifts in the way she responded to the world around her. Released from her anger and without Lane's erratic pressure, she found life's tranquil dimension again. And, thanks to Jacob's intervention, her approach to research found a fresh dimension too.

The farm had settled down. A cool breeze appeared from the west, and the sun hung low in the sky. Sitting in the porch swing, legs crossed demurely beneath the folds of a modest summer skirt, Ruth studied the notebook she'd been making since her arrival. She could hear Aunt Mamie busy in the kitchen, humming as she worked at preparing dinner. It's Saturday night, Ruth thought idly, smiling to herself. We must be having fried chicken.

She stretched, her mind unable to concentrate on her research diary. Her eyes kept wandering from the cramped handwriting of the page down the lane and into the blurred distance beyond. Despite herself, she'd missed Jacob a great deal. He had been gone for quite some time, but he was due back any time now, and the waiting was almost unbearable. There was so much she wanted to talk to him about; so much had happened, or so it seemed. Ruth was so glad Jacob was finally coming back today. She'd missed him a great deal.

In the two weeks Jacob had been gone, thoughts of him had infiltrated her daydreams. Ruth found herself talking to him in her mind, because she couldn't speak to him in person. And at first her fantasy conversations were purely academic; she set up ideas and questions to ask him when he returned. But for days now, her mental conversations had been anything but academic.

At night, she would lie in the soft darkness, alone, indulging in reverie. And when she gave her imagination full charge, Ruth found there was no stopping the vivid, sensual delights she could conjure up about Jacob and herself. Fantasizing about Jacob had become far more satisfying than working on her research. With each day that passed, Ruth grew more eager to

77

see him, to be near him and feel that tempting energy that flowed so effortlessly between them.

Laying the notebook aside, Ruth got up from the swing and paced to the far end of the shaded porch, straining for any sign of Jacob's return. But she saw nothing. She leaned against the house and toyed with a sprig of the lilac bush that grew next to the white painted railing.

Hers was a new and mysterious feeling, vague and exciting at the same time. Ruth had never longed for a man; she couldn't remember ever feeling this way before, and it was a fearfully delicious sensation. When her mind first stubbornly fixed on him, it was like a song she couldn't stop hearing. Every replay of the song was more compelling than the one before. Ruth tried to talk herself away from Jacob's song. Sternly she reminded herself again and again that she didn't really *know* this man—that they'd hardly spent any time together—that there was no logical reason for her to be absorbed in thoughts of him.

She'd tried her best to convince herself that her fixation was adolescent, at best. But Ruth blissfully failed in every attempt to reason herself out of the fantasy. The total experience was just too indescribably foreign and intriguing.

Ruth examined the lilac sprig—hundreds of tiny, perfect buds clinging together to form a single blossom. It was a model of her life; she was made up of hundreds of parts, each one wanting something different from life. But in her twenty-eight years, Ruth had concentrated on only one part—intellectual pursuits. She had worked to satisfy a commanding need to explore the world and understand as much of it as she could. And, in doing so, she'd forgotten to nurture her emotional needs. Clearly, Jacob Yoder had introduced a totally unexpected emotional color to the dull canvas of her life, and she hungered for more.

Ruth sat back down in the swing and rocked slowly, smoothing the drape of her skirt. There wasn't any doubt that her years of research travel and scholarly discipline had been exciting, but they had also been limiting. In retrospect, Ruth wondered how she'd missed finding a balance in her life. Why had she allowed her world to develop into a monotone? Perhaps she'd never given herself permission to look for someone like Jacob to brighten the picture.

The swing squeaked back and forth. Ruth closed her eyes. The truth was that she'd never given priority to anything or anyone aside from her work. There had never been time before, she reasoned. Relationships took time, and all her time had been allocated to Phillip Lane and the university.

But now things were different. These last two weeks had given her a chance to rethink her life priorities.

Fantasies of Jacob had been allotted a fair measure of her time. Whether her daydreams of him would remain just that didn't really matter then, because the possibilities alone colored her time with extraordinary energy and a feeling of well-being that she'd never experienced before.

Yet, while Ruth delighted in her fantasies, the idea of actually seducing Jacob never really formed as a conscious thought. Her attraction to him was far too complex and all-encompassing to be reduced to a purely physical dimension. Her desire had been roused by more than the thought of Jacob's hard, tempered body; every component of his complex, alluring personality inspired her.

Returning to her notebook, Ruth flipped through the pages. She was looking for a common thread to link her meager observations into a logical sequence.

Not only were her daydreams of Jacob confusing, her observations had yielded little more than a hodge-podge of rural trivia. Perhaps she'd be able to concentrate on her work with Jacob back at the farm. Or maybe she'd be more willing to work with him assisting her.

During the first Saturday afternoon while Ruth sorted out her belongings, she decided to take Jacob's advice to heart and research the Amish people in a more direct way. The data she intended to use in building the meat of her paper would come mainly from interaction and observation.

By the time Mamie shouted for her to come down to dinner, Ruth had her research method well in mind.

"All unpacked and settled in?" her aunt asked as she set a heaping platter of fried chicken between Ruth and Jacob.

"Not yet," Ruth replied. "But I did get my clothes and miscellaneous stuff organized."

"I have to build her bookcases before she can unpack her library," reminded Jacob, winking.

"No need to hurry with that project, Jacob," Ruth replied. "I really won't need a study until I'm ready to put everything down on paper. And even then I won't be needing all my books."

Mamie sat down and began passing bowls and platters. "How long before you start actually writing your dissertation?"

Ruth drizzled thick gravy on her mashed potatoes and handed the bowl to Jacob. "I probably need about eight or nine months of research, which means I should probably start by March," she told her. "If I do my research right, it should only take a couple of months to do the writing." She looked up at Jacob. "I've taken your advice a step further," she informed him. "I'm not going to read *any* background data just yet. I want to see what conclusions my own observations yield first."

"That should be very interesting," he said solemnly, but Ruth could see a look of pride in his eyes, a look she found infinitely endearing. "Where do you plan to start?"

"I'm starting right here," she said, tapping the table with her index finger. "I need to get back in the flow of normal country living again. You know, the seasonal routine—so I'm actually a part of that world, not just an observer."

Mamie nodded. "That's a good idea. I'm sure you've been on a different schedule living in Boston for so long. Hectic, hectic, hectic."

Jacob laughed and buttered a yeast roll still warm from the oven. "And you think your pace *isn't* hectic, Mamie Detweiler? Let me tell you, Ruth." He leaned closer and whispered loud enough for both of them to hear. "Your aunt is speeding up in her old age, not slowing down. You might find living with the rural whirlwind every bit as hectic as your university in Boston."

Now Ruth laughed. She remembered Aunt Mamie as a woman on the go; she had always been able to work harder and longer than any one Ruth knew, including Ruth. Apparently that hadn't changed during her absence.

"This," said Jacob, indicating the sumptuous dinner, "marks a downshift from high gear each week. Whenever we have fried chicken, it must be Saturday. And the day after Saturday is the only day of the week your aunt slows down. Remember, fried chicken day. It marks twenty-four hours of less work!" Stuffing more mashed potatoes into his mouth, Jacob just grinned.

"You two are wicked, just wicked," grumbled Mamie, amused. "If you'd put more energy out, you'd have more energy to spend."

"Does she still get up at three A.M. every Tuesday to head for the Shipshewana market?" teased Ruth. She remembered, all too well, her aunt's unwavering work week.

Jacob nodded. "Mondays are laundry; Tuesday's market day—*all* day," he emphasized, counting the days down on his fingers. "Wednesday and Thursday, she cleans, gardens, and has the greenhouse open for business . . ."

"Friday is shopping in town," added Ruth, now counting too. "Saturday we bake . . ."

"And have fried chicken for dinner," interjected Jacob.

"Heavens, don't forget that boy's fried chicken," Mamie remarked. "But that's the winter schedule. Now that summer's here things will change a mite. I go into town on Thursday to shop instead, then I have the greenhouse open Friday and Saturday for the tourists." Her nose wrinkled at that last thought.

"But Sunday we still start cookin' real early, just in case somebody drops by for dinner." Ruth giggled. Her aunt usually had at least one unexpected guest for Sunday dinner. She had always suspected that the non-Amish farmers of the county got together and decided who would drop in on Mamie each Sunday. Her cooking was that well known.

Mamie stood, huffing, and went for the coffeepot on the stove. "I hear you two laughing," she threw back at the table. "But I'm quicker than any two your age!"

Jacob sat back chuckling, his eyes dancing at Mamie's feigned indignation. "I should have married you years ago, Miss Detweiler," he told her. "Think of the work we could have done together."

Now that Ruth's jealousy had disappeared, Jacob's teasing only added to her pleasure. She saw why Jacob made her aunt happy, and she was beginning to appreciate the magic his warm, easy manner had brought back to the farm.

"Work isn't the only thing in life, Mr. Yoder," Mamie reminded, pouring more coffee. "That's where you two still have some learnin' to do." She set the pot back on the stove. "You tease about my working, but you take your own much too serious. You see, the difference is that I enjoy a little pleasure with my work. A little socializing. Makes the days rush by. I don't get tired, and I never get bored." Mamie wagged a finger accusingly at them both.

"Don't talk to me," Ruth argued gently. "Remember? My business is *all* about people."

"That may be true," recanted Mamie. "But Jacob here definitely needs more socializing. All he thinks about is how much he can get planted, built, harvested, painted . . ." she insisted, taking a deep breath. "All work and no play makes a young Amishman . . ."

"Financially independent," finished Jacob, tipping his coffee cup to the air.

"Humpf," Mamie snorted. "You have plenty of time to reach financial independence." She turned to Ruth. "Did he tell you about the restaurant job?"

"You *cook* too?" She giggled to Jacob. He winked, but Mamie had the floor.

"He got a big contract for a new restaurant going up over by Goshen. All winter he was buildin' tables, chairs, booths—that sort of thing. And Monday he's going in to finish the interior work. Doin' all the finish work," she informed Ruth, who was impressed. "Hardly had time to finish the plantin'—had to get on with more work. I tell you, this boy will work himself into the ground!"

"Two weeks of finish work and it's done," explained Jacob, as if the job were a small matter.

"Sounds like you're quite a businessman, as well as a farmer," responded Ruth.

"Oh, his work is the talk of the county. He probably could quit farmin' and make more with his woodworking," Mamie commented proudly. "This is a big restaurant too. Seats . . . how many, Jacob?"

"Only five hundred," he said modestly.

"Too bad it's one of those tourist traps." Mamie made a face and shook her head. "Maybe I ought to take my sign down this summer," she added.

"We're not taking your sign down," Jacob insisted, looking over at Ruth, who nodded her confirmation. "You enjoy meeting the people. And it doesn't bother the Amish around here."

"Well . . ." her aunt began, uncertain if he was right.

"Where is the restaurant?" Ruth broke in, sidestepping the sign issue.

"South of Goshen," answered Jacob. He pushed back his plate and leaned back in the chair. "I've got two full weeks to finish; it opens July first. The company's putting me up in a motel, so I won't waste time commuting. Won't take long."

Ruth smiled, but her stomach tightened slightly. She didn't like the idea of Jacob not being around for two whole weeks. Now that they'd started to get acquainted, she was looking forward to his company daily. But, she reminded herself as she and Jacob went out to the back porch to relax after supper, she really had a lot of work to do too.

"You never did say how you're planning to do your research," Jacob probed, settling into a chaise longue.

The big recliner was a snug fit for his large body; his feet hung inches over the end.

Ruth settled Indian fashion next to him on the wooden planks of the floor. "Diary and informant method," she announced.

"Talk up, so I can hear you!" Mamie called through the kitchen window.

"Want some help with the dishes?" asked Ruth, slightly embarrassed that she hadn't offered to help.

"Don't need any help," her aunt replied. "Just speak up so I can hear the conversation."

"Did you hear that I'm going to use *the diary and informant* method for my research?" Ruth asked loudly.

"I'm not deaf! I heard that part." Dishes rattled into the sink. "What's that mean?"

Ruth and Jacob chuckled quietly. "It means," Ruth went on, resuming her normal tone of voice, "that I'm going to keep a day diary of my Amish meetings, my impressions—that sort of thing."

"Oh," Mamie murmured. More dishes went into the sink; she was really too busy to listen.

"And the informant part?" asked Jacob.

Since the idea had come to her earlier that afternoon, Ruth had been wondering how to approach him with it. *Truthfully,* she reminded herself, deciding the time had come to ask him.

"I've been thinking about our conversation this morning, Jacob. I agree with what you said—about not running over the obvious again. I mean, I want my dissertation to say something meaningful about contemporary Amish life. You know, I *might* end up with the same conclusions that other experts have had . . ."

"But at least you'll come by them honestly—

through your own eyes." His voice was smooth and deep against the comforting night sounds of the farm.

Ruth smiled up into his eyes. "That's what I'm aiming for," she told him, suddenly wishing she could touch the fine texture of his skin. Looking away, she leaned back on her elbows. Being too near Jacob caused her mind to wander in dangerous directions. "I want to get out and reacquaint myself with the area," she went on slowly. "Start getting the feel again, start talking to people, start living the country life again, as I said."

"That's a good place to start," Jacob told her, one hand dangling close to the curve of her hip. She could feel the heat of his fingers glowing through the fabric of her cut-offs and spreading down to her ankle. "This might be something to think about," he went on, now rubbing his hand along the smooth surface of her knee.

He stroked her knee again, then draped his arm along the metal edge of the chair and leaned within inches of her. "You might consider modifying your work dress," he suggested in a husky voice.

Ruth was drawn up to him. For what seemed an eternity, they sat, both immobile, just looking into one another's eyes. She wanted him to kiss her—she somehow *needed* him to kiss her.

But thoughts do not necessarily give courage. Frightened by the power of her desire, Ruth hesitated, and Jacob slowly pulled back.

"I think you should wear something a little less provocative than cut-offs," he continued, as if nothing had interrupted his thought. "*I* think cut-offs are fine, but your Amish research subjects . . ."

"Oh, yes. Of course." Ruth quickly shifted positions, stretched her legs out under his chair, and took a deep breath to steady herself. "Mrs. Raber gave me quite a once-over when she came to visit."

"I don't mean to be critical," Jacob added with a wry smile. "As a matter of fact, I like the way you look. But my opinion doesn't count."

"Oh, but it does. Your opinion is very important. That's what I'd like to talk to you about. I've decided that what I really need is someone who is close to the Amish to help interpret the information I get from them. That's what an informant does: He explains and interprets from an objective point of view." Sitting up, she looked Jacob directly in the eye. "I'd like you to work with me—serve as my research informant. Would you do that, Jacob?"

He did not answer her immediately. Rather, Jacob stared out into the dusk, his chin tilted away from her in thought. "I don't know if I can help," he finally answered quietly. "I doubt my presence would be an asset."

"Oh, but I know you would," Ruth insisted. "You've lived in both worlds; you understand how it feels to be on both sides of the issue."

"And just what is the issue?"

"How the Amish view the world beyond them. And how their view is changing. Someone like you could read the smallest change in thought or attitude, because you understand how Amish think."

He drew one leg up to his chest and wrapped both arms around it. "Maybe so," he said thoughtfully. Jacob didn't want to become involved in Ruth's research. The very idea of it bothered him. But if he did help her in some small way, at least he would have an opportunity to spend time with her, to learn more about this fascinating woman. "But you can't tell anyone else about our arrangement."

"I know," she assured him. "That's fundamental to

using an informant in research. We never divulge sources; we never take a chance on embarrassing the informant."

"It's not embarrassment that concerns me. Just take my word for it. This idea of yours can't go any further than the two of us. Well," he amended, "you can explain it to your aunt. But make sure she understands that no one else can know about it," he added firmly. "I want to help your work, Ruth," he went on, gazing into her eyes, "not damage it beyond repair."

"Thank you. I really appreciate it." But Ruth had found his words a little unnerving. Her research expertise hadn't prepared her for Jacob's imposed secrecy. Reluctance was a normal reaction; secret pacts were not—or, at least, they hadn't been a part of any informant-based research she'd done before. But she dismissed his strange demand. In light of Jacob's agreement to help, it seemed unnecessary to worry about it. "Is there anything else I should know before we get started?" she asked, trying to lighten the mood between them.

Jacob relaxed and smiled cagily. "Just one more thing," he told her, his features caught in the faint light from the kitchen window. "I assume that as your informant, I will be expected to answer any and all questions you ask to the best of my ability. Is that true?"

Ruth nodded solemnly.

"Even questions about my own background, right?"

"Yes."

"How personal do you intend to get?" he said, leaning closer.

Shaking her head, Ruth reassured him. "It will be strictly scientific in nature. If my questions seem too personal, just tell me. I'll back off."

Jacob grinned at her. "Good. I'd like to see how *personal* you can get."

She knew her skin was burning crimson; his lusty meaning was all too clear. And though she'd not admit it to him, the idea set her mind whirling.

"I can see you blushing, even in the dark," he teased her in a whisper.

"You're taking unfair advantage of my situation," she threw back at him, shifting on the hard surface of the porch.

"Never, Ruth." His words came clear and strong. "But I expect something in return for helping you." Eyes wide, Ruth could only look at him, wondering. "If I help you—tell you all you want to know about myself and Amish life—then you have to answer my questions too."

"What questions?"

"I want to know all about Ruth Mueller. I'm doing some research on my own. I'm studying beautiful anthropologists, and you're going to be *my* informant." His hands reached over and touched her shoulder. "Doesn't that sound fair to you?" he asked, nudging her closer.

She was terribly unbalanced again. His touch was doing strange things to her. She felt as if she were weightless, she seemed to float nearer his inviting lips, guided by his strong hand.

"I suppose that's fair," she whispered.

"I can't hear you out there!" Mamie's voice rang out from the window. "Why don't you come in for dessert now?"

Jacob smiled, and Ruth heard him sigh. His hand moved away slowly, and reluctantly they stood to go in. A moment more, Ruth thought, pulling herself to her feet unsteadily, a moment more and he would have kissed me. A moment more, she realized, following him into the kitchen, and she would gladly have let him.

That following day dawned bright and promising. Ruth awoke early and was downstairs planning breakfast, before Mamie began to stir in her bedroom adjacent the kitchen.

Ruth had the day already planned in her mind. But before her ideas for a lazy Sunday with Jacob could be set in motion, they were derailed.

"Morning, sweetie," her aunt sang out in greeting. "What are we fixing here?"

"One of *my* favorites," Ruth announced. "Biscuits and sausage gravy."

"Oh, good. Jacob loves biscuits and gravy. Can I give you a hand?"

Ruth motioned to her initial attempt at making biscuits—a gooey bowl of limp flour paste. "I've got the gravy under control, but the biscuits . . ."

"I see," murmured Mamie. "I'll mix up a batch." She set to work quickly, trying to get the biscuits in the oven before the gravy was ready. "I'm glad you got things underway," she told Ruth. "I overslept, and Jacob needs to get on his way shortly. He might have had to leave without breakfast."

Ruth gave her aunt a surprised look. "He doesn't leave for Goshen until tomorrow," she exclaimed.

"That's right, but he always visits family on Sunday. It's quite a trip by buggy, and he likes to get started early."

"Why does he use the buggy?" she asked, disappointed.

"Oh, I don't know," her aunt went on. Her small hands twisted the biscuit cutter into the elastic dough and notched out the circles quickly. "It gives the horse some exercise, I guess, and it's a nice change from

90

driving a truck. I don't know; he just does. Takes the sleigh when it's snowy. You ought to get him to take you out ridin' too," she added. The biscuit pan full, she stooped to slide it into the oven.

"I'd like that." Ruth tried to sound cheerful. "But I might have to wait, if he's going to be in Goshen for two weeks."

Jacob arrived for breakfast dressed quite differently than she'd seen him before. The pale-blue denim shirt and snug jeans had been replaced by fuller-cut black slacks and a white dress shirt. Except for a black belt he wore in place of traditional black suspenders, Jacob could have been any other Amishman, dressed in his Sunday best.

"You look very Amish," Ruth told him as she served his breakfast.

"Courtesy," Jacob replied knowingly.

Ruth understood. "And the buggy?"

"Pleasure." He sampled the gravy and nodded. "Every once in a while I get lucky and find an Amish fellow who's interested in a friendly buggy match." He winked at her.

"You race that old buggy?"

"Oh, no," he answered slyly. "Buggy racing is a sure sign of vanity. And vanity is a worldly trait."

Mamie laughed at him. "They just match up to give the horses a run."

"And keeping a horse in shape is practical," Ruth added, getting the drift at last.

"You'll soon know the Amish mind," he assured her.

But as Ruth watched Jacob drive the shiny black buggy down the lane, she wondered if she would ever harness enough of his attention to really get to know him.

Jacob came in after dark that evening; Ruth heard the buggy rumble into the barnlot after eight. But he didn't come to the house, and she wasn't able to go out. Mamie's Sunday dinner company—a farmer named Oland Hardy and his wife, Virginia—were absorbed in the stories about Ruth's expedition to New Guinea that Mamie was promoting in the living room. Ruth was the evening's entertainment, surrounded by an admiring audience, unable to escape until her aunt's guests were thoroughly saturated.

The next morning Jacob was gone before sun-up. Even Mamie didn't get to say good-bye to him.

During his two-week absence, he phoned only twice, and both times Mamie got to the phone before Ruth. The work was going well, he told her, but he had to work twelve hours a day to meet the restaurant people's deadline. In his second call, he assured Mamie he'd be home to stay the next Saturday; he was looking forward to her fried chicken, he said before hanging up.

Well, here it is—Saturday night, Ruth said expectantly under her breath. Her eyes scanned the near horizon for the hundredth time. A cloud of dust was rising in the still summer air at the end of the lane.

She stood up and saw Jacob's truck coming toward the house—even before she heard it.

"Jacob's here!" she called to her aunt.

"Tell him dinner's about ready," Mamie answered from the kitchen.

Ruth walked toward Jacob as he got out of the truck. "How's the carpentry business?" she asked, chuckling to camouflage the excitement of seeing him again.

"Finished!" he replied, walking toward her with long rapid strides. "Another tourist eatery added to my list of accomplishments." They met halfway to the house. "How's the social anthropology business?"

He reached over and gently tugged the end of her single braid where it lay against her breast. His hand brushed along the thin blouse she wore, trailing invisible sparks and firing her imagination anew.

"Slow. Very slow," she answered, feeling breathless and slightly dizzy. "I *haven't* made a lot of headway in research, but Aunt Mamie has thoroughly retrained me in farm routine."

When they turned to walk to the house, Jacob laid his arm across Ruth's shoulders. She had to fight off an instant desire to pull him closer.

"Well, I've been thinking about you," Jacob suddenly remarked.

Ruth flushed with mounting heat. "You have?"

"Yep. And I've got some ideas that might help you get this research off the ground." But before he could explain any further, Mamie rushed out to greet him.

"My, my." She cackled, giving him the hug Ruth would not allow herself. "You're lookin' awful sharp for a hardworking carpenter." She kissed him on the cheek and pulled him toward the house.

"I thought I'd better shower and shave before I left Goshen for home." Jacob laughed. "I wasn't in any shape to honor your fried chicken, Miss Mamie." In one broad sweep of his great arms he squeezed the old woman and Ruth to his sides. Ruth felt his warmth penetrate the entire length of her body. She closed her eyes briefly, savoring the pressure of his strong, lean frame.

That night Jacob provided the entertainment. Well into the wee hours of the morning, Mamie and Ruth sat listening to his humorous stories of the successful Goshen job. And later, as Ruth tried to sleep, she knew why Mamie loved Jacob so. He was affectionate and charming; but, most of all, he'd brought a feeling of *family* back to the Detweiler farm.

It was a long time before Ruth fell asleep that night, and then it was to dream of Jacob.

CHAPTER FIVE

T. Monroe Sullivan was a pudgy, hawk-nosed farmer with tobacco-stained teeth and a sandpaper voice that made Ruth's skin crawl; T. Monroe's whole personality was like fingernails scratching a blackboard. The only positive habit he appeared to possess seemed to be promptness; T. Monroe arrived exactly at one o'clock—the regularly appointed hour for Mamie's Sunday dinner to begin.

But when Mamie suggested they wait to eat, just in case someone else planned to join them for dinner, T. Monroe also exhibited the quality of patience. Ruth suspected, however, from his stiff, strained compliance, that the half-hour delay tested the outer limits of T. Monroe's personal patience quotient.

No one else showed up that Sunday for dinner; Ruth assumed that everyone in the county must have known it was T. Monroe's turn to sample Mamie's hospitality, and even Mamie's cooking couldn't tempt them to share the occasion with someone like T. Monroe Sullivan. Ruth wished she, too, could abdicate her place at the table; T. Monroe was a sour companion.

"I'm tellin' ya, Mamie, they're squeezin' us out bit by bit. Regular modern-day farmer can't make no progress for them Amish," T. Monroe grumbled over his second helping of apple strudel. "Can't pick up an extra chunk of land these days to expand a good operation. Them Amish gobble up every scrap that comes up for sale before any real farmer can get to his banker."

"You need to be quicker on your feet, Monroe," Mamie soothed. "More strudel?"

"No, thanks." He passed his hand beneath the bib of his overalls. "If they have their way, this county's gonna be owned by the Amish one day. Why, look at you, Mamie. Surrounded by 'em—for miles in all directions," he pointed out, pushing the tight denim out and away from his expanded stomach. "Over my side of the county, we've been tryin' to hold 'em at a distance, but every once in a while a farm comes up to auction, the real farmers can't get financing quick enough—you know, things are gettin' tighter," he mourned into his coffee cup absently, "and them Amish bid themselves into a bargain. Sad, real sad."

Though Mamie shook her head politely, Ruth knew she wasn't that sympathetic to Sullivan's viewpoint. Still, Ruth was too preoccupied to counter his stand personally. It was hard enough to stay seated through his incessant complaining. So far that afternoon T. Monroe had bemoaned the weather, taxes, government aid, and the price of corn. Now he'd turned to the Amish for fresh material. And Ruth had more promising thoughts than this sour little man to occupy her mind.

"Did you hear what happened when they auctioned

off the Porterfield farm last week?" continued Sullivan.

Mamie sipped her tea, shook her head again, and looked at Ruth, who was peering out the kitchen door. "Porterfield went bankrupt," she explained to Ruth, a raised eyebrow pleading with her niece to at least look interested in the conversation.

"Yep. Belly up," confirmed Sullivan with more satisfaction than sympathy in his gruff voice. "Nice little place—only 'bout one hundred sixty acres. Old Porterfield liked a small operation; never did compete much in the market. Can't grow much profit these days with a dinky patch like one hundred sixty acres. Still, land's land—and it's hard to come by." He continued to push out the bib of his overalls; the brass clasps, taut against the strain, seemed ready to tear through their fabric straps at any moment. "More coffee?" he asked.

"What did you want the Porterfield place for?" Mamie asked as she got up to refill his cup. "That place is miles from yours."

"That's not the point, Mamie," Sullivan retorted with marginal courtesy. "A lot of us have to work scattered acreage; if you want to keep those profits up, you got to buy what you can, where you can find it. Anyway, me and a couple of other farmers decided to check out the Porterfield auction. See what it'd go for and who'd—"

"And see who'd risk another mortgage payment," countered Mamie with sharp accuracy.

Her aunt's crisp reply pulled Ruth back to the conversation for only a second. She just couldn't get interested in this squat man, who obviously enjoyed the squeaky sound of his own voice. But as his brusque, disjointed conversation monopolized the afternoon, Ruth saw one positive side to having T. Monroe Sullivan as a Sunday guest: As long as he provided the entertainment, she wouldn't be expected to fill the time with extemporaneous anthropological travelogues.

With that thought in mind, Ruth forced herself to look over at T. Monroe with a reassuring smile.

"Now, Mamie, that's all you ever think about," argued Sullivan, ignoring Ruth. "Mortgages are a cost of doin' business. Farm overhead."

"Big mortgages are a weight hanging over your head," Mamie retorted, pecking the table with a gnarled forefinger.

Mamie didn't need any help in fending off Sullivan, thought Ruth, so she again turned her attention to the barnlot beyond the kitchen door. Jacob had said he'd be back early this afternoon, and Ruth wasn't about to miss his return.

"Well, it's the *normal* way of doin' business," insisted T. Monroe as one hand flew out from behind his bib to flutter in the air over the table emphatically. "Well, anyway," he resumed, going back to his original topic, "went over to the Porterfield auction, and damned if a half dozen of them young Amish didn't come in and buy the place. Paid *cash.*" T. Monroe's weathered face began to color. "Cash," he repeated angrily. "I ask you, Mamie, where'd those boys come up with that kind of money?" He didn't wait for a reply, as he obviously planned to answer his own question. "It's some kind of conspiracy, I tell ya. Them Amish never spend a dime; save everything. Won't even pay to educate their kids, mind you, 'cause they're too damned busy sockin' money away so they can buy up every scrap of land and force us real farmers *out!*"

Ruth had had enough of T. Monroe Sullivan. "Excuse me," she said quietly, getting up and walking out onto the porch.

With the reins held loosely in his hands, Jacob relaxed on the hard buggy seat and gave the horse its head to follow the last miles of their trip back to Mamie's farm.

With eyes cast to the asphalt pavement, Jacob was trying to readjust. It was like this every Sunday. During the long drive to his family's farm, he'd pull himself away from thoughts of the outside world and return to the world of his youth. For a few short hours each Sunday, Jacob Yoder was Amish again.

On the return trip, he always had to force himself to shift again; until his next visit, Jacob Yoder was . . .

Was what? he asked himself. He certainly wasn't English. And he wasn't really accepted as Amish. What was he?

The question nagged at him constantly. His life seemed to revolve around that single question which formed an endless circle of doubt in his head—a mental loop Jacob Yoder had been unable to bypass for twelve years.

Twelve years; nearly one third of his life. One third of his life spent not belonging, not fitting in. Yet, since his return to Elkhart County, Jacob had been more comfortable with the question. At least here he'd been able to start putting the pieces of his life back together, and the answer to his question was finally coming into focus. He'd always suspected what the final answer might be, but, even so, he was surprised when it was finally presented to him.

Today an answer had been offered. All that was required was his decision. The endless loop had returned to its starting place; this was where he had been twelve long years ago—on the verge of decision that would change his life.

Jacob flicked the reins in his hand. It had been a memorable day.

He let his mind slip back to recapture it. This was one Sunday that he could not quickly divorce from that part of him that was Amish.

Two of Jacob's sisters, Jemima and Mary, had been busy setting up long tables in the yard when he arrived; his sister-in-law, Cora, was in the kitchen with his mother.

"Ah, it smells good in this kitchen!" Jacob greeted them in German, above the noise of small children in the yard. He took a sweet pickle from one of the many heaping bowls lined up on the kitchen counter.

"Stay out of that, Jacob," warned Cora, taking pies from the kerosene oven. "We'll eat soon enough."

"Don't be a bother, Jacob," said his mother.

Pickle in hand, Jacob knelt down beside his mother's chair. "How are you feeling, Mother?" he asked, kissing her forehead.

"Fine. I'm fine. But you look thin, Jacob. Have you stopped eating these past two weeks, huh?" She smiled at him, but her hands continued to work at slicing the head cheese before her on the table. "And how did your job in Goshen go?"

Mrs. Yoder's plump form hid her body's frailty well. She would be seventy soon, and had retired from the more demanding duties of the farm, to live out her years in relative leisure. The farm was now run by Jacob's youngest brother, Enos, and his wife, Cora.

"The job went well," Jacob told her. There was no need to go into detail. His mother was not interested in the outside world; she only asked to show interest in his productivity, not the product.

"And the farm?" She stood and carried the platter

99

of sliced head cheese to Cora. From the hesitation in her step, Jacob could tell her arthritis was worse.

"Why don't we go out and sit down," he offered, taking her arm and guiding her toward the door. "It's cooler there." Without objection, she let him help her outside. Her favorite rocker had been brought from the house and placed under a spreading shade tree—a vantage point from which she could see the children playing, while still being in the center of the adults' conversation.

"And, now, your farm?" she asked again, slowly lowering herself into the rocker.

"I'm in partnership with Mrs. Detweiler," Jacob ex- lained again patiently. "Planting was finished early," he went on. "Now that this business in Goshen is fin- ished, I can get started on the back orders I have for other cabinets. Need to get caught up before harvest time."

"Don't neglect your field work for this cabinet busi- ness, Jacob. Good land like yours deserves tending." She looked at him over the top of her wire-rimmed glasses. "How many acres, do you say?"

To his mother, the partnership with Mamie Det- weiler was as good as a deed to the land. Jacob didn't want to press her into acknowledging the fact that he didn't actually own the land he worked. "There's a total of two hundred acres, Mother," he told her again.

"And how is Mrs. Detweiler and her arthritis?" his mother asked with genuine interest.

"Not too bad," Jacob said. "She's really feeling much better. I think her spirits are up because her niece has come back to live on the farm. Ruth is like a daughter to Miss Mamie."

Jacob's mother rocked slowly in her chair, her white hair shining in the sunlight. "A mother's happiness is

100

not complete without her whole family near," she said softly, looking up at him with gentle blue eyes. "Only one thing I can think of would make that happiness even better," she told him, a glimmer lighting her face. "And that's to have all her children living the right life."

Without reply, Jacob sat down on one of the long benches next to his mother's rocker. He stared out at the children playing tag near the barn, but his mind was not on their game.

This was the first time since he'd come back that anyone had broached the subject of his rejoining the Amish community. The implication in her words was more than clear, and they shocked Jacob.

Jacob was truly surprised. He never thought the option would ever be offered to him again. And after the difficulty he'd had resolving those ten years of being shunned, he'd never seriously considered the possibility of joining the community, though it crossed his mind occasionally. He had been satisfied with simply having family communication restored.

"Lizzie's in a family way again, Jacob," his mother went on, using family gossip as a different tack to the same goal. "She married late—all that sickness, you know. But the doctor says she'll have a fine healthy baby now." She rubbed her knotted hands together, warming them in the sunlight. "Now that you have settled down and have a good piece of land, you could have a family too. You'll need lots of children to help you farm so many acres."

Jacob turned back to her and smiled. The one hundred acres he would inherit from Mamie was small in comparison to modern farms, but by Amish standards it was a substantial holding—one that would require a large family to do the work by Amish methods.

Together they sat in the sunshine until Cora called

101

everyone for dinner. No reply was necessary; his mother knew he'd understood her every word.

The buggy lurched off the smooth asphalt of the county road. With his barn in sight, the horse began to trot; his hooves stirred fine gravel dust into the air. Jacob, abruptly drawn from his thoughts by the buggy's sudden jarring, hauled in the reins, and they continued down the farm lane at a more respectable pace.

Ahead, on the porch, Jacob saw Ruth, and in that instant all other thoughts were set aside.

She waved and ran to meet him. "I hear you give Sunday buggy rides, sir," she teased.

"Climb right on up here, missy," Jacob replied, stopping the buggy so she could get in. "Settled?"

Ruth nodded. The small enclosed buggy was like a great black box set on wheels, its roof scant inches above their heads. "Cozy," she commented, arranging her legs within the narrow space between the dash and the seat. It *was* cozy; Jacob's broad shoulders required a lot of room. She could sense his body heat radiating across the confined inches between them.

Jacob slapped the reins and the buggy creaked around in a wide circle and headed back down the lane.

"Who came in to dinner? Don't recognize the car," began Jacob, having to shout over the sound of the rocky lane.

"T. Monroe Sullivan," Ruth answered, loudly imitating Sullivan's voice.

Jacob gave her a worried look. "Do you think we should leave Mamie alone with T. Monroe? Think she'll survive?"

"She was doing just fine all by herself," Ruth shouted an assurance, grinning. "The last thing I

102

heard before I retreated to the porch was Aunt Mamie giving him a lesson on farm finance."

"Oh? Was that Sullivan's beef for the day?" The buggy wheeled out onto the smooth road, and the violent vibration and clatter of gravel gave way to a steady click of horseshoes and a gentle swaying. "What was Sullivan griping about today?" Jacob rephrased his question in a normal tone.

Ruth laughed. "First he started in on taxes, then he growled about wheat futures, and finally he went into gossip about the Porterfield auction."

Jacob tensed. "What about Porterfield's?"

"He has this theory that there's an Amish conspiracy, that they're buying up all the land to force regular farmers out of the county." Ruth laughed, because the idea sounded even more ridiculous when repeated, but Jacob didn't respond lightly.

"Did he happen to mention that twenty Amish families had to uproot their lives just last summer and move to Missouri, because there wasn't any land left around here for them to buy?" Jacob asked, an unmistakably sharp edge to his voice.

"No, he didn't," Ruth replied. "But he did say that six young Amishmen went together and bought the Porterfield farm. Paid cash, I guess." She noticed the muscles in Jacob's neck tighten. She'd upset him—not at all what she'd intended.

"You know how those young men got the money together to buy that little parcel of land?" he asked her, barely controlling his agitation.

She shook her head. "No, but T. Monroe Sullivan says it's unnatural to pay cash. 'Financin' is a regular cost of doin' business,' " she answered, again imitating Sullivan, but with much more comic flare this time.

Jacob looked over at her. A grin formed slowly. "Was I sounding like T. Monroe?"

103

"Just a smidge. I'd hate to see the two of you alone in the same room without a referee," she teased.

"Oh, we were—*once,*" said Jacob with a laugh. "And that was enough for me. I'm glad there aren't too many T. Monroe Sullivans in the world. I don't think the rest of us could stand it."

He propped one foot up on the buggy's dashboard and checked the rearview mirror.

"I know that *I* couldn't stand it," Ruth replied, relieved Jacob had relaxed once more. "So let's not mention Monroe again."

Jacob smiled and flexed his foot on the dashboard. "Sounds like a good idea to me. I can think of at least a dozen more interesting things to talk about." But at that moment, only one topic was on his mind and that was Ruth.

She'd worn a light cotton skirt that draped in layers over her long, tanned legs. Her blouse was a lighter cotton that revealed the full, fine curves of her breasts and framed the delicate skin of shoulders and neck in a half circle of pale summer color.

A car passed their buggy from behind, and Jacob's attention was diverted from Ruth. He held the reins tight as the horse shied at the sound of the car's engine.

The car moved on ahead of them, trailing a cloud of dust, and Jacob swung the buggy onto another side road.

"Hazard of buggy travel." He chuckled, not to show his concern. "Awful dusty in the summer and bitter cold in winter."

"I'd be more worried about English traffic more than dust," confirmed Ruth, now watching for traffic through the back window.

"Don't worry, Ruth," Jacob answered. "This road doesn't get much motorized traffic."

His comment reassured her, but she didn't turn around in the seat. Rather, she put her elbow on the back of the seat next to Jacob's shoulder and leaned her head on her hand. She was drawn to him; his nearness made her tingle with energy.

Ruth watched his muscular leg flex and push on the dashboard as he balanced himself against the rough motion of the carriage. The polished black fabric of his pants molded around the sharp detail of his thigh and knee. The large muscles rippled and tensed in time to the buggy's rocking.

More than anything Ruth wanted to touch him—to feel the outline of his muscles rising and falling beneath her fingers. And just as her mind pictured the thought, the buggy wheeled through a shallow chuck-hole, and Ruth was forced to steady herself—one hand on Jacob's thigh, the other on his shoulder. She was instantly magnetized in a completed circuit of his body's energy.

She held her palm against his shirt sleeve, hard enough to contact the solid form below and feel it quiver to action as Jacob slapped the reins again. Her fingers clutched the heated fabric of his trousers, and she touched the layers of hard, bulging muscle that strained to hold him in place against the dash. Both her hands were instantly hot—charged with some strange, riveting voltage. Quickly she pulled herself upright and straightened in the seat.

"Sorry," Jacob said calmly. "Road's rough in spots."

"That's all right. No apology necessary," Ruth answered quietly. It was as if she were still touching him even though her hands were now on the cotton fabric of her skirt.

"I have an idea." Jacob grinned, took his foot from

105

the dashboard, and turned to her. "How would *you* like to drive this buggy?"

"I'd love to," responded Ruth. She held out her hands, expecting him to hand her the reins. Instead, Jacob slipped his right arm over her head. Never letting go of the leather straps, his arm dropped across her shoulders and down around her waist in a single, precise movement.

His great arms now circled her, and his hands slowly slid down from her elbows; his folded fingers lightly grazed the surface of her skin, leaving a path of warmth. Placing the reins firmly in Ruth's grasp, Jacob took hold of her wrists, his hands forming supple bracelets. With his arms extended parallel, the full form of his chest pressed against her back; his body's heat danced through the light cotton of her blouse.

"Lean back on me," he suggested softly in her ear, the words a warm breeze along her neck. And Ruth eased back into Jacob's embrace.

Every nerve in her body responded with heightened awareness. She felt Jacob's pulse throbbing at her wrists; she heard the whisper of his breathing and felt the slight pressure of his curly head at her temple. Ruth closed her eyes and just centered on the feel of him.

A moment passed silently, and, strangely calm, she opened her eyes. Ruth knew that she had been yearning for just such a moment with Jacob. Where her desire had once frightened her, it now provided her courage.

"Getting a feel for the reins?" he finally asked.

Tilting her head, Ruth smiled at him. "I don't think so," she replied, afraid he was considering moving away from her.

The road twisted and turned through dense woods now. Evening approached as an orange sunset, streaked in vibrant pinks and golds, and quietly they drove along watching the sun's display through the trees.

"Do you know where you are?" Jacob eventually asked.

"I'm not sure," Ruth admitted. She hadn't been paying attention to anything beyond Jacob's touch. "Is this the Stutzman farm?" she ventured, vaguely remembering the dense woods as an old landmark.

"It used to be Stutzman's place," Jacob told her. He shifted in the seat and moved even closer. His leg now pressing Ruth's. "It's an R.V. campground now."

"You're kidding," she answered amazed. "Stutzmans are *Amish,* aren't they?"

"They *were* Amish. A few years ago old man Stutzman got into a disagreement over Amish rules and regulations with the local bishop, and the group put him under the ban. I guess there was a terrible fuss, and the old man got so angry that he sold his entire farm—woods, ponds, the whole ball of wax—to a guy from Chicago who wanted to start an R.V. park for tourists. He left the order, took his family and his profits, and went off somewhere."

"Wasn't that an awfully drastic reaction?"

"Sure was. But he certainly got the last laugh on the Amish and their ban. He threw some fantastic farmland away, just to get even. . . ."

Before Jacob could go on, an open buggy came racing up behind them, careening wildly. Whipping his horse to top speed, the young Amish driver passed them, running wheel to wheel with their buggy and spooking their own horse. Jacob grabbed the reins from Ruth.

"Ho, Rainbow," he bellowed to the shying horse, and pulled back hard on the reins. "Down, down." Rainbow responded, skipping nervously in the middle of the road. "I'd better take it from here," Jacob advised. He hoisted the reins over Ruth's head and slid a few inches away from her.

"What was *that?*" she asked, still shaken.

"That's part of our research for this evening."

Advancing from a farm lane ahead, three more buggies full of young people pulled out onto the road. They quickly picked up speed, and Jacob followed them at a distance.

"What's going on?" Ruth asked him. "Where is everybody going? What's going on?"

"Rumspringa," he said in German, then laughed at Ruth's puzzled expression. *"Running around,"* he clarified. "And I thought you'd like to see it. Look up there!" he whispered excitedly.

They were approaching a T in the road, and standing next to the stop sign, Ruth made out the form of an Amish girl. Jacob pulled their buggy off the road and stopped in the shadow of a big tree where they could watch discreetly.

"Okay," Ruth whispered. "Explain what I'm watching." She knew that the Amish started courting young, but "running around" didn't sound prim and proper enough to describe Amish premarital ritual. Then again, reckless buggy rides weren't exactly what she would have pictured either.

Jacob put his arm around Ruth and leaned over to speak quietly in her ear. "The boys in those buggies are probably heading over to the campground. Of course, their folks have been told they're going to a singin' at another Amish farm, but most of the older ones are headed for their weekly rendezvous at the campground," he explained. "By this time on Sunday, all the weekend campers have gone home, and the kids have the grounds pretty much to themselves."

"Doesn't the owner mind them using his place?"

"I doubt it. He's probably never seen anything like it and gets a kick out of watching their antics. Amish kids don't usually get involved in vandalism so his property's safe enough." Jacob straightened beside her and pointed up ahead. "Here we go. Watch this."

Another open buggy rolled down the cross road at a canter. As it approached the girl standing by the stop sign, the boy driver pulled over and got out. They spoke for just a moment, and then both climbed into the buggy and drove away.

"Now they're going to the campground?" Ruth asked, feeling like an excited teenager herself. Had Jacob brought her here for research? she wondered. Or were they really sharing in the *rumspringa* too?

"Those two are probably going to the singing," Jacob mused. He slapped Rainbow with the reins and they started moving forward again. "That looks like a serious relationship in the making."

"How can you tell?" she asked, probing for clues as much to interpret Jacob's thoughts and actions as to satisfy her own curiosity.

Jacob looked over at her and chuckled. "They're keeping it a secret." He winked. "When it's the real thing, as they say, Amish maintain strict secrecy. Their parents don't even know what's going on, and they wouldn't think of asking."

Ruth smiled at the revealing remark. "Is that why they met way out here in the middle of no place?"

"Well, a couple's not going to advertise their intentions, and if he picked her up at home, everyone in the family would see who's courtin' her, right?"

"Of course."

"And what if they decided to quit—start seeing somebody else? Think of all the explanations they'd have to come up with if a lot of people knew about them." Jacob gave her a wry smile. "Total privacy and confirmed secrecy—that's the way. Makes the whole 'courting' thing easier on the two people involved."

Now Ruth smiled again. *Privacy was a very good idea.*

Jacob turned at the T and they followed the couple for another mile.

"Do they quit relationships a lot? Or do they usually stick once they start running around with one person?" she asked, trying to imagine Jacob as a handsome, young Amish boy, courting girls in this strange fashion.

"Usually they quit a lot, before finding one who's right," he remarked. "That's why secrecy's a good policy. They can look around as much as they like."

"What happens if they're discovered? What if they can't keep the secret going?" She tried to keep her words casual, but she really wanted to know how much looking around Jacob had already done.

He shook his head solemnly. "That's rough," he told her. "Everybody makes fun and teases you, if you aren't clever enough to keep your dating secret. Being the object of ridicule can break up a couple. Amish have a lot of pride, you know; can't stand being laughed at."

That, Ruth vowed, *was something she had to remember.*

Up ahead, a huge, brightly painted sign read: AMISH COUNTRY CAMPGROUND.

Yet another carriage, containing more young boys, turned ahead of them into the camp's entrance.

"Is that rock music?" Ruth asked Jacob. She would have sworn that a radio was blasting from the buggy ahead.

"*Hard* rock," Jacob answered with a smirk. "The owner of that buggy has an AM/FM stereo with cassette player installed in the dashboard." He thumped his foot against their own dashboard. "Speakers fit in under the seat."

"That's too much. Do you think his parents know?"

"I'm sure they do, but they won't say anything." He looked over at her. "I hear your wheels turning, Ruth. And rock music and stereos don't mean the Amish are changing."

"Then what does it mean?"

"It's *allowed*—for a few years when they're young. The kids experiment with all kinds of things. One kid I know put a regular car license plate and a Chrysler hood ornament on his buggy. They soon see that the things of the world aren't all that great. They get the fascination out of their systems, join the order, and end up appreciating their Amish world a lot more."

"Amish version of reverse psychology?" Ruth said, and Jacob just smiled.

Jacob passed by the dozen or so buggies and their rowdy occupants at the camp entrance to drive Ruth around the campground. Miles of broad unpaved tracks now criss-crossed old Stutzman's woods; metal hookups for electricity and water access pipes sprouted like oversized iron wildflowers at twenty-foot intervals throughout the dense hardwood grove.

"I can't believe it," Ruth exclaimed, as they approached the once-secluded pond where her uncle had often taken her to fish. "That's a concession stand!" She pointed to a lime-green concrete building perched at the edge of the pond.

"Over by the entrance, they put in an Olympic-sized swimming pool and a souvenir shop," Jacob added with equal chagrin. All Ruth could do was shake her head in reply.

"Would you like to stop?" Jacob asked her as they

reached the end of the camp road. Ahead she could hear young voices clearly in the air.

"I'd like that," she told him. Ruth wanted to experience more of Jacob Yoder. "Find someplace where we won't be seen."

Deep shadows formed in the twilight, creating hidden blinds shielded by the dense trees. Jacob stopped the buggy in one such shadowy spot a hundred feet from the congregation of buggies and draped the reins across the dashboard.

"We got here at just the right time," Jacob said. As soon as he let loose of the reins, his arm wound around Ruth's shoulder again.

Up ahead some of the boys sat smoking, while others just milled around. Their excited voices rang out in frequent, boisterous laughter.

"What are they saying?" she asked, not able to make out their German slang.

"They're telling very old, very dirty jokes. You aren't missing anything exciting," Jacob said with a chuckle.

"How long will this go on?" She moved closer at his invitation and cautiously maneuvered into his arm's warm shelter.

Jacob lay his head against her hair. "Oh, they'll stay until the cigarettes run out or it's time for the singing to be over." His fingers ran lightly along the fabric of her sleeve. "Then they'll be off to pick up their sisters from the singing or . . ." His lips brushed her cheek in a feathery kiss. "Some will just drive around looking for a special girl to court on his own."

Her heart beat with anticipation, and Jacob nestled her more securely in his embrace. "And what about the couple we saw at the crossroads?" she murmured. "Will they come *here* after the singing—when all the others have gone?"

"Maybe," he whispered softly in her ear. "If they're sure no one's around to see them."

Ruth turned to him. "And if it's completely private, what then?"

His eyes met hers. Widely blue and intriguing, they drew Ruth closer. She reached out and curved a hand around the nape of his neck. Her fingers ran beneath the bronzed curls.

"What would they do, Jacob?" Ruth whispered breathlessly.

The answer was unspoken. His arms engulfed her, and they gave in to silent desire.

Urgently, powerfully, his smooth, full lips kissed her, pulling the last measure of breath away from her in a low hungry moan. He urged her closer, and Ruth drew up against his chest. Both arms wrapped around his neck and she clung, magnetized, as his lips opened full onto her waiting mouth.

White hot, she glowed incandescent in his arms, tasting his tongue as it circled the moist interior of her mouth. Willingly she replied to his invitation, her tongue copying each intimate gesture with subtle accuracy.

The world—their world—was instantly transformed. There were no rowdy voices or rock music in the distance, only the thunderous pounding of heart upon willing heart.

Breathless and weak, Ruth kissed Jacob's jawline and neck. She held him, her head pressed against his, clinging with faded strength to his generous form.

"Oh, Ruth," he whispered. "You don't know how I've wanted to hold you like this."

She wanted to speak, to tell him how she'd longed for him too. But her mind could not find the words to convey her feelings. Yet, had she found the words, her voice could not have carried their rightful meaning.

Nothing could express the desire she felt for him or the impact that his admission had made on her.

Still, her response came through to him without words. Jacob felt her body trembling against him. He heard her broken, shuddering breath as Ruth's arms tightened about him, and he knew that she had wanted him just as much.

Jacob's left hand went down to her thigh; it tightened on the skirt fabric and slowly inched the material up until his hand met the bare flesh of her leg.

His broad fingertips floated along the skin of her inner thigh and sent new waves of white-hot energy surging through her veins. She parted from his pulsing kiss and clung to him, her head pressed to his shoulder.

"Your skin's so soft, Ruth." Jacob sighed, continuing to stroke her leg as he cradled her with one arm. Her long braided hair brushed against his shirt sleeve, and he extended a finger to feel its texture. "And your hair's like cornsilk—so fine, so sleek."

She lifted her head. Jacob's face was highlighted in the pale glow of the rising moon. "I missed you so much these last two weeks," she managed to confess.

"And I missed you," he murmured. "More than once I wanted to drive back and see you, but I knew if I came back, I might never go back and finish the job." Jacob kissed her forehead. "I couldn't get you off my mind." His hand rested on her thigh, kneading the warm skin.

Ruth ran her fingers through the thick curls above his ears. "And I couldn't stop thinking of you either." She kissed him. His enormous body quivered against her, and his hand tightened on her leg again.

"I must have picked up on your thoughts," he offered, hugging her.

The rowdy clamor of the Amish boys grew louder

114

just then; heavy footsteps and giggling seemed to surround them in the darkness. Ruth stiffened, thinking the teens had discovered them.

"Shhh," Jacob soothed. "The girls are walking home through the campground. Listen."

Though Ruth couldn't understand their language, Jacob concentrated on the chaotic chatter from the buggy gang. Motionless, they sat while the footsteps came closer.

Finally they made out the silhouettes of three Amish girls walking down the camp trail, giggling and punching each other. They passed within a few yards of their buggy, never noticing Ruth and Jacob; the tallest of the girls kept angrily repeating a phrase while her comrades giggled.

"What are they saying?" Ruth asked quietly as soon as the girls were out of sight.

Jacob hugged her close and chuckled. "The boys were accusing one of their pals of courting that tall girl, and she was setting her girlfriends straight on the matter." He kissed her again—a lingering promise of a kiss that shook her. "We'd best be going," he added with reluctance.

"Do we have to?" she murmured invitingly.

Jacob smiled down at Ruth and took her chin in his hand. "This will be the last time *our* privacy is disturbed," he promised, gazing into her eyes. "But now my first concern is getting you home on time." He gathered up the reins and slipped his arms around her as before for the return trip home.

CHAPTER SIX

Wheels rumbling, the old buggy swayed in steady motion behind the heavy clip-clop of horseshoes hitting the hard pavement. For miles the gentle rhythm, beating in concert with the sounds of crickets and bullfrogs in the distance, lulled Ruth and Jacob into a feeling of peace and serenity.

Wrapped in his arms, her head resting easily on his shoulder, Ruth listened to Jacob's heart as it pounded rapidly against his shirt. Its eager cadence told her that he shared her excitement at having acknowledged their desire for one another.

Deliberately she rested one hand on his leg and nestled her head to his neck. In return, he hugged her closer, slapped the reins evenly, and kissed her temple.

"Are you warm enough?" he asked, then kissed her again.

Ruth's fingers pressed into the wide muscle of his leg involuntarily. "Mmmm." She sighed, sensing the heat of his arms radiating around her.

Jacob Yoder smiled to himself; he and Ruth were of one mind, he was sure of it. The way her body slightly trembled as he held her to him between the reins. The subtle pressure of her slender hand on his thigh, and the way she melted into the curve of his shoulder assured him of her consent.

Now they approached the lane; he sensed her body

tensing ever so slightly. Could she be thinking what he was thinking? Was she hoping that Mamie hadn't waited up for them?

Again Ruth's body answered him. Only the porch light illuminated the night; the farmhouse was dark. Her body relaxed again as they drove past the greenhouse to the main barn beyond.

Mamie had gone on to bed, and Jacob silently blessed her thoughtfulness.

The barn's interior glowed eerily, illuminated by a few dim yellow light bulbs, and it smelled of fresh grass. Jacob's reputation for spotless order prevailed, even in the barn. Ruth moved to a corner next to Rainbow's stall and settled onto a mound of fragrant hay to watch Jacob work.

"This won't take long," he assured her, removing the horse's bridle. "Why don't you tell me about your research? What have you been up to while I was gone?"

A brilliant vision that seemed to draw the dim half light to her, Ruth sat before him bathed in the saffron glow. The tightly braided hair—barely darker than the haymow—framed her flawless face, in contrast to the deep sea-green of her eyes.

"I'm afraid I haven't been making much real research progress," Ruth replied. She kicked off her sandals and leaned back on her elbows. "I've just been thinking about things since you left for Goshen."

While her eyes followed his every move, devouring each simple gesture with sensual delight, Ruth tried to concentrate on telling Jacob about the time they'd been apart. So much had gone through her mind and she truly wanted him to know all about it all. With all the effort she had left, Ruth forced herself to begin again.

"It's been very hard for me, Jacob," she said slowly.

117

"I don't know how to explain it, really. Everything *seems* familiar—the farm, the people. But, then again, it's like I'm in a dream. No, no, that's not what I mean." She frowned and stabbed her toes down into the hay. "I feel like an outsider, somehow. Oh, Aunt Mamie's still the same; she'll never change, I hope. And the farm—well." She smiled up at him. "It's even better than I remember. And the family friends, people I grew up knowing, they've been wonderful." She stretched her legs and stared down at the hay. "We went into Shipshewana for market that first Tuesday and didn't get home till nine that night. Aunt Mamie took me from market stall to market stall, reintroducing me to everybody. I'll bet I recited over five hours of travelogue details before we got out of there." Ruth laughed. "When the market closed at three, she insisted we walk all over town—visiting the hardware store, the drugstore—you name a shopkeeper, and I got reacquainted with him. Mr. Olin—owns the hardware store—do you know him?"

Jacob nodded and continued brushing Rainbow's back.

"He had me *autograph* his copy of *National Geographic* with that New Guinea article in it. Aunt Mamie says he's kept that magazine under the counter for two years—just waiting for me to come home, so he could get my autograph. Do you believe that?" She chuckled.

"I told you, Ruth, you're quite a celebrity around here. People talk about your travels and *you* all the time. It's like you've never really left. Not many people could hold on to hometown ties like that."

Ruth sighed. "Do you know it's been over three years since I came home for a visit?" She shook her head, looking wistful. "I don't know how I stayed away so long."

118

"You've had quite a schedule to keep going," he reminded her.

"I really feel guilty about it now."

Jacob put down the brush and walked over to where she sat. "Don't let guilt destroy your homecoming," he told her softly, sitting down in the hay beside her.

"I won't, believe me," she said honestly. "No, that part of the problem is resolving itself. It's this research that has me baffled." Ruth looked over at Jacob, who sat mere inches from her. His eyes, so gentle and inviting, urged her to go on. "While you were gone, I tried to get reacquainted with the few Amish I used to know," she mused softly. "Half the produce vendors at the market were Amish. Some of them I recognized right off. But when I went over to visit with them, I couldn't talk. Me, the great global anthropologist! Me. I couldn't get beyond: Good morning—Remember me? I'm Ruth Mueller, Mamie Detweiler's niece."

Laughing softly, Jacob lay back in the hay.

"It's not funny," Ruth came back, unperturbed by his lack of empathy. "I was intimidated by them."

"You aren't intimidated by me," Jacob said to her.

"*You* don't look right through me, as if I'm not really there, then smile angelically and pretend to be mute. Oh, a few of them would nod politely and say something like: You must be very glad to be back with your aunt. Then nod again before they went silent. What was I supposed to do—go on like a census taker? *Yes, I am glad to be back, and I'd like to ask you what it's like to be Amish.*"

The haymow shook with Jacob's uncontrolled laughter. Ruth collapsed next to him and playfully nudged him with her elbow.

"I'm confessing that my efforts have been ineffective —that I'm tongue-tied and overpowered by some invisible barrier these people put up—and you're laughing."

Jacob rolled over on his side and looked down at her. "I'm not laughing at *you,* Ruth. I'm laughing because you just described the Amish style. I guess it works on trained anthropologists as well as it does on the regular, unsuspecting English."

She smiled, understanding. "You mean they politely stop a conversation before it can get started?"

He nodded. "Remember, you're English, Ruth. Whether you grew up here or not, whether they remember you since childhood or not, you're English and they're not really interested in talking to you or knowing about you."

"That's why they don't offer any more than the absolute minimum—not even: How have you been?"

"That's right." He reached over and rubbed her arm with long, luxurious strokes. "You'll have to find a way to work around their natural suspicion."

She touched the side of his face and looked into his eyes. "They make me feel like a stranger," she murmured. Her thoughts began to vaporize as her blood warmed under Jacob's compelling gaze. "I've traveled all over the world . . ." Words formed slower now. Her fingers inched along the curve of his jaw and traced the sensitive ridges of his ear. ". . . but I've never felt so much like a stranger as I do when I'm with the Amish."

"There's a saying," Jacob reminded her quietly, slipping his arm under the hay and effortlessly moving her to him. *"You're only a stranger once.* When you first meet someone; after that, they never think of you as a stranger again."

She looked into his eyes, seeing the warmth there, knowing the desire he felt for her was strong, as strong as the yearning that filled her each time she was near him. "Were we ever strangers, Jacob?" she whispered.

"No," he answered, "I don't think we ever were."

And then he kissed her. It was not the questioning kiss of a man unsure, but the devouring kiss of a man certain of the response he would receive. His determined mouth pressed hers, smothering any verbal reply. Mere words had lost all meaning now. Their bodies and minds entwined—one form, one mind—overwhelmed by a need so compelling that it refused to be denied one moment longer.

His fingers ran hard along her spine. Slowly, from the base of her neck, they moved between her shoulder blades, down the length of her torso, down to the waistband of her skirt.

She tried to shift from his embrace, to reach behind and help unhook the garment. But Jacob held her hand away.

"Let me," he whispered. "I want to." The words seared along the hollow of her neck and vibrated through her breasts. She kissed the crown of soft curls that brushed her chin and placed her hands on Jacob's massive shoulders.

Ruth felt his fingers press between her back and the skirt band, urging the button free and then slowing tugging at the zipper. Impatient now to have his flesh against her, she felt the seconds pass like hours.

She closed her eyes. "Hurry," she whispered, her fingers clutching at the hard muscle of his back.

Finally the skirt was free and Jacob slipped it down along her legs. Night air briefly cooled her skin.

Rising to her hungry mouth, Jacob kissed Ruth again. His body nearly covering hers, Ruth held him to her and arched upward into his embrace. Her breasts ached and she rubbed against his strong, broad

121

chest trying to soothe the pain. But that was not enough.

She moved her hand along his body and one by one the buttons of his shirt gave way to her nimble fingers. At the last button, she came to his belt and forced it open.

"Ruth?" she heard him whisper breathlessly, as he reached down to hold her eager fingers still. "Are you sure?"

Smiling, she kissed him and his hand moved away.

She pulled his black trousers down along his legs and slid the white shirt from his arms, as Jacob slowly unbuttoned the front of her blouse.

"Hold me." She sighed, and Jacob took her back into his arms.

His chest, soft with tiny bronze curls, was pressed against her breasts. He kissed her again, then slowly moved away, his hair brushing delicately along her abdomen and her long legs.

He kissed the flesh of her inner thighs, and Ruth felt a fire ignite within her. She was lost to reason, consumed by a wondrous compulsion.

He nipped at her flesh, taking tiny invisible bites and creeping immeasurably higher with each one.

Caressing her breasts tenderly, his large calloused hand covered the ample flesh, firmly but gently kneading her hardening nipples.

There was nothing but Jacob then. Ruth felt nothing save his touch; she heard only his labored breathing. The night air was flooded with the essence of him: the heady scent of his body, the light herbal fragrance of his hair. And his kiss still lingered heavy on her mouth. Eyes closed, she watched him love her through her mind's eye.

"Let me make love to you, Ruth." The sound of his

husky voice pulsed in her ears, and she sensed the weight of his body poised above her. "Let me."

"I need you, Jacob," she answered in a voice that seemed not her own.

Reaching out to him, Ruth touched the fullness of his desire. Jacob moaned. She continued to stroke him, until, at last, they joined as one.

"Cold?" she heard Jacob asking softly.

Ruth opened her eyes slowly against the eerie glare of the barn lights. "A little," she admitted, smiling at him. Although Jacob's arms and legs wound around her snugly on their bed of hay, the cool night air sifted through the walls of the old barn.

"Let me get a blanket," Jacob offered.

Reluctantly Ruth allowed him to slip from her embrace. He rose from the haymow, the dim yellow light adding depth and contrast to his tanned skin, and crossed to where the buggy had been parked.

His thick, powerful legs held her fascinated as they stretched across the straw-covered floor, and his broad back, layered in tight folds of muscle and tendon, flexed in time to the unhurried motion of his step.

Ruth's eyes caught every small detail of him as he removed the buggy blanket from under the seat and reached to turn off the light. Now only moonlight, filtering through a small window above the hay, cut the darkness.

"This blanket is fresh," Jacob made a point of telling her as he returned and once again reclined beside her. The old carriage blanket was a wide square of downy wool, and Jacob meticulously arranged it around her before crawling under to join her.

The hay—still tempered from their body heat—and the downy blanket formed a warm, comfortable cocoon, and Ruth snuggled back into Jacob's grasp.

"Better?" he asked as his hands rubbed her back and leg. Ruth just sighed and held him tight. A moment later she felt his body begin to shake. Jacob was chuckling.

"What are you thinking?" she demanded with a loving squeeze.

"I was wondering if you still feel like a stranger."

She chuckled too and rubbed her head against his chest. "After a welcoming like this," she told him, "how could I?"

"You know," he went on, "if you'd come back three years ago, I could have *welcomed* you that much earlier." He kissed the top of her head. "What kept you away so long?" he asked with sudden seriousness.

Ruth was not prepared with an answer. Even though she'd asked herself that same question many times, Jacob's interest startled her.

"Was it a man who occupied your time so completely?" he pressed against her silence.

"Are you always this bold?" Ruth replied, undisturbed by his curiosity. "Or do you just want to know about all the lovers in my past?"

"We agreed, remember? I answer your questions; you answer mine." His breath brushed lightly against her hair. "Besides, there haven't been many lovers in your past. Not in the recent past, anyway."

She raised, propped her elbow against his shoulder, and looked him squarely in the eye. "And what makes you so sure?" She jabbed him with her finger, oddly delighted by the accuracy of his statement.

Jacob smiled wryly. "Because you don't make love like an experienced woman. Oh, I know you've been around"—he began to chuckle again—"but I'd say you didn't go in for much intimate research."

"I'm into social anthropological research," she reminded him, "not clinical sex research."

124

"Ah," he retorted, "but you are a very alluring woman." He touched her lips and followed their outline with a steady finger. "Why would a woman like you—obviously loving, caring, and sensitive—stay away from family and home so long, if not for the love of a man?"

To Jacob's mind only the necessities of love could bring distance to a family. And the only rational explanation for Ruth's absence was a love affair she wanted to keep a secret from everyone, including her aunt. Mamie had even shared her concerns about Ruth with Jacob. "Was he married?" Jacob finally added, when Ruth still did not answer.

His voice did not accuse her, and she felt certain his boldness stemmed only from concern.

Ruth lay back and stared up into the moonlight.

"It's not quite that simple," she began slowly, organizing her thoughts as objectively as she could. "He wasn't married to another woman; he was married to his work. And as for our love affair, I'm afraid that that was all in my mind. But you're right, Jacob." Looking over at him, Ruth smiled as she accepted her own truth. "It *was* the love of a man that kept me away so long. And, as it turned out, it was a very poor decision on my part."

"The man was Dr. Lane, wasn't it?"

Ruth simply nodded her head.

"And when you finally told him of your love, he rejected you?" offered Jacob in explanation.

Ruth sat up and kissed him. "You give me more credit and courage than I deserve, dear Jacob." The sincerity in his eyes compelled her to tell him the truth. "I was in love with what Dr. Lane was. Like so many students do, I idolized the man for his scientific ability. He was all I hoped to become as an anthropologist—brilliant, dedicated, respected for his contribution to society. But we never had what you would recognize as a love affair." Ruth chuckled at her own folly. "It was only a work affair—he knew I admired him and, in return, he gave me his work."

The original anger and hurt of Lane's dismissal had diminished to little more than a memory. The pleasures of being home, added to the wonder of Jacob's loving, had effectively erased the pain. She could stand apart from the past now and find some humor in it.

Jacob was frowning; ridges formed across his handsome brow. "Now I understand why you were so upset the night you arrived," he said. "So you finally got tired of being *used* and quit." Jacob finished the story for her.

"Wrong, again, dear Jacob. He fired me. Replaced me with a more promising grad student." Ruth could tell by his worsening frown that she'd confused, rather than clarified, her story, so she wrestled back beneath the blanket and pulled Jacob close to her. "This may take a while to explain," she told him. "Do you have a few hours?"

Cradling her head in his arm, Jacob took a deep breath and sank, relaxed, into the hay. "The night's still young," he said, wickedly toying with her breasts. "But let's not use it all up talking."

He kissed her forehead, and she told him her story.

"No wonder you're so anxious about your dissertation research," Jacob commented when she had finished. His voice was warm with sympathy.

"I'm going to earn that Ph.D. with flying colors, and then I'm going to show Phillip Lane what real independent research looks like." She rolled over. "I'm going to contribute, Jacob, not waste time with petty politics. And I'm going to teach my students to think for themselves, not worship other people's theories. I'm going to give the world something of value; I know I am." With a final confirmation, Ruth cuddled safely and silently again.

Looking at the woman in his arms, Jacob felt he knew Ruth's frustration. He'd lived through a similar fate himself. Still, he found no comfort in this new insight. Something in her story disturbed him. But he tried not to dwell on it.

There in the moonlight, holding her inviting body, Jacob found it easy to forget any misgivings. Nothing mattered but that they were together.

"I'm very talented," Ruth whispered provocatively as Jacob pressed against her. "And I have a very vivid imagination."

"Oh?" he responded. "Why don't you show me?"

"You Amish are all alike." She giggled, pulling free of his embrace. "Never convinced."

"Never satisfied," he corrected her.

Playfully, she pushed him over, face down in the soft hay, and began massaging his back and legs. With her fingers Ruth drew lazy, wide designs across his body, then walked, on fingertips, down the back of his muscled thighs.

"Nice," he murmured, head resting in his crossed arms. "But not too imaginative."

"You don't think so, huh?" she grumbled, leaning up to his ear.

Jacob chuckled and shook his head no.

In silent response, Ruth began to carefully retrace the imaginary designs with the tip of her tongue.

They woke with a start. The barn was lit, not with moonlight, but with the first real glimmer of dawn.

"What time is it?"

"I don't have my watch."

They sat up and stared at one another, wide-eyed.

127

Aunt Mamie! The thought bolted, unspoken, between them.

"Clothes!" each demanded simultaneously, scurrying out of the haymow and feeling like delinquent adolescents.

"Here! Your skirt," shouted Jacob, throwing a wad of limp cotton over his shoulder at her.

"Shhhhhhh!" Ruth warned as she caught the skirt and struggled into it. "Aunt Mamie will hear us." Lifting his pants off the window ledge, she tossed them to Jacob. "And your shirt!" She extracted his crumpled shirt from the blanket at her feet and held it out for him.

"Panties and bra!" he announced in an excited whisper, and exchanged articles with her before diving back into the haymow to sort handsful of their bedding feverishly.

"Blouse. Blouse."

"I can't find it," he muttered. Flat on his stomach, he felt through the hay with both hands. "Put on my shirt!"

And Ruth did.

Garbed in Jacob's gigantic white shirt and the wrinkled skirt, Ruth grabbed her sandals and underwear and started toward the door.

"Wait! Wait!" Jacob called hoarsely as he pulled on his pants over bare feet and little else. "I'll scout ahead. She might be up already."

They crept out of the barn commando-style, Jacob, barefoot and breathless, running nimbly across the barnlot to the back of the greenhouse. Ruth waited, holding her own breath, until he slithered along the glass-paned walls—bent and expectant—to the corner closest the house.

He turned and motioned her ahead. Watching him,

128

Ruth started to giggle, but she followed his example and ran, stooped and swiftly, to where he crouched.

"Shhhhh." It was his turn to warn her. "You can't go in giggling; she'll hear you for sure." Jacob looked at Ruth's flushed face and broke into a grin. "Don't get me started," he protested. "Or your aunt will find us both sitting here—hysterically up to our ears in poison ivy."

Ruth forced back her laughter and kissed his cheek. "Okay, okay. But where do we go from here?"

"*We* split up; *you* go in the kitchen, through the house and up the stairs to your room—q-u-i-e-t-l-y."

"Aren't you even going to walk me to the door?" She'd started laughing again. "Am I ever going to see you again, handsome stranger?"

Jacob thumped to the ground, playfully exasperated. "I'm not walking you to the door looking like you've been rolling in the hay all night," he said with a chuckle. "Here." He pulled straw from her braid and tossed it aside. "And, yes," he answered, this time more earnestly, "you'll see this handsome stranger again."

"Soon?" she asked, her voice low and provocative.

"Very soon," he said, rising. "Like about breakfast time." He glanced up at the eastern sky. "In about an hour, by the looks of it. Now, go on!" He slapped her behind. "And watch those stairs. Halfway up they creak like crazy!"

Ruth sprinted the short distance to the porch steps and stopped. Painstakingly she mounted the wooden planks one by one and tiptoed across the porch to the door. Slowly she inched the screen open and squeezed inside.

She slipped across the cold linoleum of the kitchen floor and past the closed door of Aunt Mamie's bedroom.

So far, so good, she thought.

Ruth made it down the hall without being discovered and started up the stairway, testing each step with her toes before plying all her weight.

Halfway up, a popping board nearly stopped her heart, but she recovered, skipped the next step, and made it into her room without further sound.

Ruth lay hugging her pillow as she had hugged Jacob through the night.

Atop the unmade bed she watched as the faint light of dawn penetrated the curtains at the window.

Vivid memories of an exquisite night in Jacob's arms and the excitement of stealing barefoot, minutes before daybreak, through the silent old farmhouse combined and overwhelmed her the moment she lay down on the quilted spread.

Her heart beat violently. Her limbs were heavy and charged with warm blood. Her head swam with color and sound.

Yet a part of her floated weightless above the bed, unwilling to accept the reality of dawn, the separation it imposed.

That part of her wanted the night to go on forever; that part now coaxed Ruth to relive each splendid second of the time she had spent with Jacob, over and over again, so that it could be committed to memory in vivid detail.

Ruth had never before experienced anything that could compare with these last eight hours of her life, and she wanted to hold on to their impressions forever.

CHAPTER SEVEN

Mamie brushed a tidy mound of straw fragments from her dust pan into the kitchen wastebasket. Then she shook the basket until every trace of the telltale straw sifted to the bottom and out of sight.

Upstairs, Ruth walked across her bedroom floor, stopped, and opened a bureau drawer. Mamie cocked her head and listened. The bureau drawer closed, and her niece walked out of the bedroom, across the hall, and into the bathroom.

The water pipes hummed as Ruth turned on the tap and dropped the metal drain plug into place.

Mamie grinned and picked up her broom again. It was safe to check out the hallway and stairs.

Her inspection turned up another handful of straw, which she dumped in the trash, as she had done with the others. Another shake and the last of Ruth's straw trail floated to the bottom of the wastebasket.

Chuckling to herself, Mamie returned both the dust pan and the broom to their rightful places in the pantry. She could start breakfast now.

"G-o-o-d morning!" Ruth bubbled as she bounced into the kitchen. "I'm s-t-a-r-v-i-n-g; what's for breakfast?" She gave her aunt a quick kiss and peered over her shoulder at the skillet on the stove. "Scrambled eggs and ham! I'll set the table."

Mamie gave the chunks of ham a turn with her wooden spoon and went back to mixing biscuits at the counter. "No hurry," she said while trying to look intent on the biscuit dough. "Fix yourself some coffee first."

Ruth poured a cup of coffee and eased herself up to sit on the counter between the stove and the kitchen window. From her perch, she could talk to Aunt Mamie while she watched for Jacob to come in.

"I'm surprised you're up so early," Mamie said casually.

Ruth's gaze twitched away from the window and back to her aunt.

"Where'd you end up last night?" her aunt asked, not daring to look up, because she knew she'd laugh if she saw the expression on Ruth's face. "What did Jacob do—take you all the way to Honeyville in that old buggy?"

"No, he took me out for some research." Ruth blurted, lacking a more reasonable response.

Mamie kept her head down so Ruth couldn't see her grinning as she calmly patted out the dough. "Research?"

"Courting practices," Ruth went on quickly. "Jacob wanted to show me Amish courting practices." Her unsteady hand clutched her coffee cup.

"And how did he do that?" Mamie asked, beginning to laugh.

Ruth sipped her coffee and took a deep breath. Steady now, she thought. Sound serious.

"It was fascinating. Just fascinating," she began. "We drove the back roads over to the campground. That's where a lot of the Amish teens congregate on Sunday night."

"Uh-huh." Mamie got a hold on herself while she cut out the biscuits.

"Did you know that the Amish give their teenage kids absolute freedom in dating? They believe in complete secrecy and privacy. Jacob says that when a couple is seriously courting, the girl's family lets the boy come calling *after* everyone's asleep, so the couple can be totally alone together."

"I didn't know that!" replied Mamie, honestly surprised. "They're so conservative in everything else. Why, I thought they'd believe in chaperoning young people right up to the time they got married."

Ruth glanced out the window. Still no sign of Jacob. "That's what I would have thought. But they let the kids run around unsupervised. It's called *rumspringa.* The young men get out in their buggies and cruise the countryside looking for girls. Jacob says the old Stutzman farm—the campground—is one of their meeting places. You should have seen it last night."

"I guess those Amish kids stay out awful late," Mamie remarked innocently. She gave Ruth a calculated look, complete with raised eyebrows, before pushing her biscuit pan into the oven.

"As late as they want," Ruth tossed back at her confidently. "We stayed at the campground until the group decided to head home." So much for the truth and nothing but the truth, mused Ruth to herself with a devilish smile.

Jacob's heavy footsteps bounded onto the porch, and he yanked open the screen door.

"What smells so good?" His voice resounded through the room. The screen door slammed shut, and Jacob sauntered up behind Mamie. He smiled warmly and winked at Ruth before wrapping his arms around her aunt's waist. "Mmm. You look so beautiful this morning," he cooed in Mamie's ear while gazing directly at Ruth.

Showered and dressed in fresh denim, Jacob only

vaguely resembled the tousled giant who'd slept in her arms just hours before.

Ruth lowered her head and smiled at him. Her lips sent a silent kiss to stretch the distance between them. With a loving look, Jacob acknowledged it.

"Stop, stop, *stop!*" complained Mamie. "If you ever want to get your breakfast, Jacob Yoder, you better stop all this smoochin'!"

He didn't let go of Mamie, and he didn't take his eyes from Ruth. "Can I go back to smoochin' after I get my breakfast?" he asked.

Ruth slowly nodded in reply to the question and slipped off the counter, coffee cup in hand.

"Why don't you help me set the table?" she offered, rubbing her hand down the midline of his back. His upper body arched at the firm pressure of her stroke.

"That's a good idea," Mamie agreed. "Pull him away from here so I can scramble these eggs."

Ruth grasped the back of Jacob's belt and playfully tugged him backward. "Set the table!" she commanded, and ran her index finger along the hollow of his lower back.

Glancing over his shoulder, Jacob winked at her, while one large hand reached behind him. He grabbed her inner thigh and held on.

Gasping, Ruth jumped back. A hot flash gripped her body. Astonished that he'd be so bold in front of her aunt, Ruth panicked and tried to pull his arm away. But Jacob held on. His eyes gleamed wickedly.

"No rough-house around the stove!" Mamie warned. Her back was to them as she shielded the skillet full of eggs.

Jacob eased his hold very slowly. "Too many rules around here," he muttered, grinning.

"I'll show you *rules,* Jacob Yoder," said Ruth in a low, sexy whisper.

"Show him the dishes instead," grumbled her aunt. Jacob quickly kissed the end of his finger and pressed it to Ruth's lips. His meaning was clear.

"Have you been out to the swimmin' hole yet?" Jacob asked as they set the table.

Ruth glanced up. He was smiling that smile again. "Not yet." He was referring to the farm's small spring-fed lake. "It's just now getting hot enough for swimming."

"Oh, you'll have to see what Jacob did to the lake," chimed in her aunt. She handed Ruth the iron skillet full of eggs and ham to carry to the table. "It's like a little park now. The weeds took over and the woods grew up with brambles over the years. But Jacob's cleaned it all up. He even built new picnic tables and restocked the pond with fish."

Mamie brought the biscuits to the table and sat down, shaking out her napkin. "It's lovely again, Ruth."

"I'd like to see it," she said to Jacob, spooning a helping of scrambled eggs onto her plate. "Do you give lake tours as well as you give research tours?"

"I give a *great* lake tour," he announced.

"Ruth told me about last night," Mamie suddenly announced.

Fork poised in midair, Jacob shot a stunned look at Ruth, then gave her aunt a cautious side glance. "And what did you think?" he ventured back.

"Well, I never would have believed it myself." Measuring her words, Mamie buttered her biscuit with care. "It just seems so out of character." She clucked her tongue ruefully. "I'm shocked!"

Jacob simply stared at Mamie in astonishment.

"Aunt Mamie can't get over the Amish letting their

teens run around unsupervised," Ruth rushed to tell him.

Relieved, Jacob swallowed a forkful of scrambled eggs. "You've seen them out running the roads on Sunday nights, Mamie. Didn't you ever wonder what they were up to?"

"Well, I always thought they were on their way back home from service and got a little rowdy because their elders weren't around. I never dreamed their elders condoned all that buggy racin', smokin', and cat-callin'. And to all hours of the morning too. My, my. It's a wonder they grow up to be such solemn, hardworkin' folk."

Jacob grinned over at Ruth. "Didn't hurt me any," he said proudly. "I grew up okay, wouldn't you say?"

It was the kind of opening Ruth had hoped for. "Yes, but you also left the Amish community and went out into the world." Her serious observation was designed to turn their conversation from its original course, so she could learn more about Jacob's early life. "Do a lot of the Amish kids decide they like the modern world better when they have this time to experiment with worldly things? After all, they're given a lot of time free from family influence during their teens. And that's a very impressionable time for kids."

"To begin with," he returned without hesitation, "those teenagers are all wrapped up in the opposite sex during this running-around time. They're out to meet and date other young people, and the object is finding a mate, *not* finding a way out. Besides, their free time is limited to a few hours on Saturday and Sunday evenings. And you can't go all that far in a few hours by buggy." Jacob pushed back his plate, knowing full well he hadn't really answered Ruth's question.

"With those limitations, a kid's lucky to find a date," he went on. "And I can tell you, dating's a lot more interesting to them than exploring the outside world. And not that many young people separate from the community, Ruth," he added honestly. "That's why I don't think you'll find much change in the Amish way of life. If anything, their numbers are increasing, not decreasing."

"That's right. Amish population has increased from thirty to forty-eight percent each decade since the 1890s," Ruth agreed, then blushed. "I opened a research book while you were gone," she admitted sheepishly. "But only as a last resort. Honest."

"I think it's just wonderful that you're gonna help Ruth with her research." Mamie spoke up again. "She explained your agreement to me—all this informant business—while you were in Goshen, Jacob. And I understand that we can't tell anyone. I won't breathe a word about it," she promised, smiling.

Rising, Jacob walked to the stove and returned with the coffeepot. "I only hope I can be a help," he said, pouring them all another cup.

"Well, we have to get this research off the ground," her aunt said impatiently. "Ruth didn't make much headway these two weeks you were gone. Now it's time to knuckle down to business, stir up the natives, and see what we can squeeze out of them."

"Spoken like a true professional," Ruth said with a giggle. What Aunt Mamie lacked in concrete knowledge, she made up for in enthusiasm. "But don't think I was on hold for two weeks because Jacob wasn't here to advise," she informed her aunt.

"Well, it was probably *my* fault; she didn't have time to make any contacts or . . ." Mamie went blank.

". . . research strategy," Ruth supplied.

Her aunt repeated the words and committed them

to memory. "Anyway," she continued, "I kept her pretty busy with everyday things."

"Don't think that, Aunt Mamie," Ruth insisted. "I told Jacob about our two weeks. It was fun, and I needed a break to get my head clear." Jacob caught her eye and winked.

"Well, one thing's for sure," Mamie said, standing to clear the table. "Ruth got a lot of tourist observation in. Lord, lord. I've never seen so much weekend traffic this early in the season."

"Lots of tourists around?" he asked Ruth.

"That first Saturday you were gone, we had thirty cars come in," she told him.

"And thirty sales," Mamie injected proudly.

"It was a steady traffic pattern both Fridays and Saturdays. I don't know how she stands it," Ruth added.

Midway back to the table, her aunt stopped to listen. The sound of a car coming up the drive drew her to the door.

"Local customer," she announced. "I'd better go on out." Untying her apron, Mamie left them.

"Did you get any sleep?" asked Jacob, stretching across the table to hold Ruth's hands as soon as Mamie left.

"I don't think so," she said lovingly. "Did you?"

"Not a wink." Lifting from his chair, Jacob bent to kiss her. His lips were warm and supple against her mouth. A car door slammed. Jacob glanced at the door and sat back down.

"I think people sleep too much," Ruth said, chuckling. "I feel great after a sleepless night."

"Want to go for two?" He squeezed her hand.

"Maybe." They laughed and relaxed.

"Does Mamie know?" Jacob questioned.

"No. But she almost got a confession out of me too.

138

I came into the kitchen, and she started with the 'where were you last night' quiz. But the look on *your* face, when she—"

"I didn't know what she was talking about," Jacob admitted, laughing.

Ruth got up and took more dishes to the sink; Jacob followed. As she stacked the plates on the counter, he drew close behind her, put his arms around her, and kissed the tip of her ear. "Ruth, I—I'd like to keep this a secret from your aunt," he whispered. "At least for the time being."

He pressed her between his body and the counter, and Ruth felt wonderfully weak in his embrace. She wasn't sure she understood his reasoning, but she didn't care. "Whatever you want," she told him honestly. *"Our secret, right?"*

"Uh-huh. Strictly private."

Ruth turned around and slipped her arms around his neck. "Privacy is going to be a bit of a problem," she said. "We can't go buggy riding every night till dawn."

"No. But we can go swimming in the afternoon." He winked and nuzzled her hair. "And you can help me building bookcases at night."

She punctuated his sentence with a light kiss. "Well, that accounts for a few rendezvous," she told him.

"Well, we always have your *research* to work on."

The car door slammed again. Mamie's voice sounded just beyond the kitchen window, and Jacob moved across the floor to his former spot at the table. No sooner had he sat down again than Mamie breezed in.

"Big market for oregano this summer," she informed them, and put her apron back on.

"Ruth's been telling me about her research strategy," Jacob said out of the blue.

"So, where are we starting?" Mamie shooed Ruth away from the sink.

Walking back to the table, Ruth smiled coyly at Jacob. She'd caught his curve, and she was ready to return it. "Well, I think it would be very helpful if I went to talk with this district's bishop," she proclaimed firmly.

"And ask his blessing?" Jacob asked, tipping back in his chair casually.

"In a manner of speaking. The bishop serves as the head of the local order. So, if I can talk to him, explain what I want to find out and why, maybe I can get his approval. It would be like a letter of reference when I approach other Amish in the district."

Jacob nodded. "That's a very practical approach."

"Do you think it will work? I mean, if he'll talk with me, won't the others follow suit?"

"If he doesn't disapprove, it might help. Yes."

"So, when do you start?" pushed Mamie, her hands in the soapy dishwater.

"Today, I guess. No better time than the present. That is, unless you need help with the laundry."

"No, no. You've been helping too much with the chores. Can't work a farm and do research at the same time. Jacob will help me!"

"I always do, don't I?" He chuckled back at Ruth. "She lets me carry the wash baskets out to the line."

"Not skilled enough to help her hang clothes?" jabbed Ruth.

"I like to mix everything." He laughed, glancing at Mamie. "I don't make a neat laundry display."

"He won't put like things together," her aunt complained. "Hangs dresses with shirts and sheets with jeans. Clothesline's a mess when he hangs things out."

Ruth grinned. "And everyone knows a good housekeeper hangs a neat laundry."

Jacob clutched his chest. "And what would the neighbors say if everything wasn't hung by category and size?"

"You laugh, Jacob Yoder. Go ahead. Laugh. But it's no different from those tools of yours in the barn. Everything in its place, in nice straight rows along the wall." She pulled the sink stopper and dried her hands. "I like a pretty wash."

"Okay," he submitted. "I'll carry it out; you hang it. So, that's settled. What are you and the bishop going to talk about?" he asked Ruth.

"I'm still going over that in my mind," she answered. "What do you suggest?"

Jacob stretched his arms over his head and looked up at the ceiling. "I wouldn't suggest you tell him that I sent you."

"Why don't you just go over and get reacquainted?" suggested her aunt. "That ought to break the ice for you."

Ruth frowned. "Reacquainted?"

"You remember the bishop, don't you, Ruth?" asked her aunt.

"I know the Amish bishop?"

"Don't you know who he is?" queried Jacob.

"I was going to ask *you.*"

Mamie sat down at the table, laughing. "It's Amos Stoltzfus. You remember him. The beekeeper."

"You mean the man we always buy our honey from? *He's* the district's bishop?"

"While you're over at Amos's farm, pick up a couple of pounds of . . ."

"Clover honey," Ruth finished Jacob's thought.

"That's a good idea, Jacob. Ruth can go over like she's there to buy honey, and it'll give her a good reason to talk with Amos. Won't that make it easier for you, Ruth?"

Her aunt's idea wasn't a bad one at that. Having a reason to approach the bishop would make it much easier for Ruth to start a conversation with him. And she liked that much better than starting off cold.

Nearly a century separated Mamie's farm from the Stoltzfus place. The distance, measured not in miles, but in decades, was like a time tunnel that stretched from the present, back to the turn of the century. And though she'd been over the miles many times, today Ruth sensed the time shift more than she ever had before. Her present mission was like none before.

The road, like every other, was trimmed with miles of electrical lines and telephone cable. Power transmission towers transversed a section of the land like silent steel sentinels, and orange meter boxes indicated the presence of the county's underground water lines.

At a glance, it all looked very ordinary, very modern. But a closer inspection proved the area was not so usual.

Not one of the farmsteads was tied to the electrical service, and not a house was connected to the phone. The utility lines simply followed the road, on their way to somewhere else. And the water lines lay untapped.

Instead, tall, fragile-looking windmills turned with lazy regularity at every farm, providing what little power and all the water needed from the predictable winds.

Ruth stopped at a crossroads and saw a pay telephone booth on the opposite corner. The simple convenience looked ridiculous sitting there surrounded by cornfields. The only emergency connection to the outside world, it had probably been erected there by some inventive English telephone executive, bent on reaching out to the Amish, she thought.

The seeming inconsistency of Amish thought fascinated her. They wouldn't own cars or have any modern utility or convenience. Yet they would pay to ride in an automobile and would use a pay phone without reservation. Shaking her head, Ruth made a mental note to ask Jacob to explain and continued on.

For miles and miles, only Amish farms dominated the landscape—small squares of land set side by side, each with its assembly of barns and coops. Each with its wooden two-story double-houses, stark white against the blue summer sky.

No clouds of pale dust hung above these fields, stirred by massive tractors straining to conquer vast quantities of land. There were no engines to disrupt the natural tranquility.

Passing, Ruth saw an Amish farmer, strapped to his horse-drawn plow, out turning new earth laboriously and silently behind a giant draft horse. Even their normal farm work made little sound, it seemed, to disturb the land. The countryside, pristine and serene, was reverently quiet.

Except for well-tended beds of bright, mixed flowers, the Amish world was varigated green. Colored mainly by the trees, the fields of ripening corn, and rough grass lawns, their unassuming farms were tinted with the verdant shades of life.

Even the clotheslines, taut with Monday's wash, did not distract from the scene's earthy hue. Steel-gray cotton dresses and denim shirts of muted blue—hung by category and according to size—flapped in the breeze.

Ruth thought of Aunt Mamie's wash, just as neat and organized, but alive in bright gingham checks and calico florals that danced on the line like proud, colorful flags.

As she drove on she tried to concentrate on her

research work, but her thoughts kept returning to Jacob. In a matter of hours, her life had turned full around. A life dedicated to impersonal observation had finally blossomed into something very tangible and highly personal.

Ruth realized she had never missed the physical expression of love, because she'd never known it. And though she had often wondered why much of the emotional satisfaction of loving had eluded her as well, she now realized that everything once missing from her life had finally appeared.

The beautiful physical desire, deep emotional need and fulfillment, even laughter and a sense of belonging, they had all been waiting here, at home. Everything had been waiting for her in the form of Jacob Yoder.

Parking the car near the front of the house, Ruth got out, tugged the wrinkles from her navy-blue skirt, and looked around. The farmhouse was really two houses joined by an open breezeway; both were large, two-story clapboards with roofed porches across the front. The slightly smaller of the two was Bishop Stoltzfus's residence.

The smaller house must be the *Grossdaadi Haus,* thought Ruth: a retirement home for the bishop and his late wife. The larger house was now occupied by the bishop's son and his family. They operated the farm, since old Stoltzfus had retired.

Hearing voices coming from the kitchen of the larger house, Ruth walked up to the back door and knocked. Through the screen, she saw six women, about her own age, canning peas.

"*Ja,* can I help?" asked one of the women, coming to the screen. She was barefoot, dressed in light blue. A white bibbed apron was safety-pinned to the front of her work dress; her long sleeves were rolled up to her elbows, and her face was flushed from the heat of four kerosene stoves that lined one wall of the kitchen.

"I'm Mamie Detweiler's niece," she began with the only introduction she could think of.

The young woman gave her a genuine smile. *"Ja.* I know your aunt. Can I help?" she repeated and opened the door.

Now that Ruth could see the woman's face, she recognized her. "Is your name Naomi?" she heard herself ask.

The Amish woman looked puzzled; she took a very close look at Ruth. "I am. Do I know you?"

"I'm Ruth. Ruth Mueller. We went to grade school together. Remember? Your last name was Keim. Right?"

"Ja. Ja. Naomi Keim. I *do* remember you." She stepped out onto the cooler porch and closed the door behind her. "And Frau Detweiler is your aunt?" Pulling up the hem of her apron, Naomi daubed at her moist forehead.

"Yes, she is." Ruth said, happy that at last one Amish person was talking. "I remember you had a pony and cart. You drove it to school when we were in fifth grade."

"Ja. I had a cart. It was a long way to the school." She stopped, thought again, and then grinned. "Are you still in the jelly business?"

Ruth cringed and Naomi laughed. The easy, full laughter surprised Ruth as much as it delighted her. There was nothing intimidating about this young Amish woman.

"I bet you got a real *bletching* over that jelly," Naomi said, chuckling.

Bletching? "Oh, oh, yes," replied Ruth. "I couldn't sit down for a week after my aunt found out."

Naomi rubbed her palms against her apron but

didn't offer another response. Ruth knew she'd have to keep the exchange going.

"Do you live here now?" she started over.

"I help with the canning." Nothing more.

"Well, I don't want to keep you from your work. I've come to see Bishop Stoltzfus. Is he home today?"

Naomi shook her head. "I can get you honey," she offered, assuming Ruth had come to see the old man on business.

"Thank you. I did want to buy a couple of pounds of clover."

Naomi started toward the porch steps. "It's in the barn."

"Well, you needn't get it yet. I really came to talk to the bishop. Is he here?" Ruth did not move from her spot on the porch. Though pleasant, she was determined to see Stoltzfus.

"Wait here a minute," Naomi told her, and went back into the kitchen. A moment later another woman came out to where Ruth stood.

"My father is in town," she informed her.

"Can I wait for him?" Ruth asked doggedly. "It's very important that I talk to him today."

Hesitantly, the woman conceded. "You can wait in here," she said, opening the door for Ruth to enter.

She led Ruth through the kitchen and into a sitting room. "Please sit. It may be awhile." She smiled as Ruth said thank you, then went back to her work in the kitchen.

Alone and unobserved, Ruth sat down hard on one of the straight-back wooden chairs and quietly sighed in relief. One barrier—no, two, she thought—met and circumvented. But the accomplishments of sustaining a conversation and gaining admittance were only mild hurdles compared with meeting the bishop. The real test was yet to come.

She sat up on her chair and tried to concentrate on what she would say and how she would say it, but it wasn't long before she found herself staring out the window and daydreaming once again about the man who had held her so gently in his arms the night before.

"I'm Amos Stoltzfus. You wanted to see me?"

A mild voice pierced the quiet. Startled, Ruth stood up. She hadn't heard the bishop walk in; her mind had been miles away.

"Yes, Bishop Stoltzfus," she replied, holding out her hand. "I'm Ruth Mueller . . ."

He shook her extended hand politely. "You're Mamie Detweiler's niece. Please, sit down. My daughter said you wanted to talk to me." Ruth did as the old man said and he pulled a rocking chair up in front of her.

Amos Stoltzfus was a small man with a face carved by the seasons and a heavy chest that taxed the hook-and-eye closure of his rough denim jacket. His cheeks and upper lip were shaved smooth, but his beard—whitened by age—reached midway to his waist.

"I apologize for dropping in like this," Ruth told him. "But I've come back to live this next year with my aunt so that I can work on a research paper. I'm a teacher."

The bishop offered no response except a slight nod of his head.

"This research paper I'm writing is a requirement for a degree, so I can get a permanent university teaching position." Ruth didn't want to oversimplify the situation, but she wasn't at all sure old Stoltzfus would understand a more sophisticated explanation.

"You make a living as a teacher?"

"Yes. But I'm primarily a researcher," she ventured. Stoltzfus took a pipe from his shirt pocket and a tobacco pouch from his overalls. "What is a *researcher?*" he asked casually, stuffing the pipe with his fingers.

"As a researcher, I study people and how they live. In the last few years I've been all over the world, studying all kinds of different people and their cultures and then writing about what I find out." She prayed he wouldn't think she was talking down to him.

Bishop Stoltzfus struck a wooden match on the heating stove and lit his pipe. "And you make a living also by this research. This writing about people?" he asked skeptically.

"That's right. My career is in anthropology."

"A very big word," he mused. "Why are you talking to me about this anthropology?"

Ruth steadied herself and hoped her words came out the way she meant them to. "I want to write about the Amish in Elkhart County, Bishop Stoltzfus. That's why I've come back. I plan to work here for the next year, learning about the Amish and how they live."

His bushy eyebrows raised slowly, and he looked at her with piercing blue eyes. And then he rocked. Tobacco smoke curling around his head, he thought. "And you will write about us?"

"Yes. But my research won't be very widely read. I mean, what I write will be read mostly by other professors and scholars." She searched his eyes for a clue to his thoughts and found none.

"We are plain people. Simple people. We have nothing you would want to write about. Our days," he said, gesturing around the room, "are lived in work. You can see what we are; there is nothing complicated or interesting about Amish ways."

He was trying to close the conversation; Ruth could feel it starting, but she refused to let it happen yet.

"Your lives are simple," she agreed. "And I'm fasci-

148

nated with that simplicity. That's what I want to know about—how you maintain simple lives in a very complex world. To the outside world, your simplicity is remarkable."

The bishop's placid expression never changed, but the tone of his voice became more determined.

"We hold on to simple ways because we do not become involved with worldly things," he said, as if reminding her. "We do not need to explain our lives to others."

"Bishop Stoltzfus, I have no intention of explaining your ways to the world, or exposing your people to worldly things," Ruth said honestly. "Ever since I was a little girl I've admired the Amish, and I've wanted to know more about them. For myself, not for others. For my own knowledge and understanding, I'd like to be able to talk to the Amish here. Ask them questions. Just find out what they think and how they live. Just for my own knowledge."

"We seek no one's admiration," he stated in a softer tone.

"I realize that. Seeking the admiration of others is prideful. And I realize that pride and personal glorification are not acceptable traits. Excuse my poor choice of words. I meant that the Amish way of living is interesting to me."

He drew on his pipe and was silent. Ruth was afraid she'd made a grave error and that he'd never reopen their dialogue. Silence followed, and just when Ruth had decided she should give up and leave, Bishop Stoltzfus stopped rocking and leaned toward her.

"So, why have you come to me?" he asked.

"I came because you are the elected leader of this district, and I wanted to explain my objective and ask your opinion."

The bishop nodded slightly.

"I was hoping that you would see that my intentions are honorable," she went on when he did not speak. "And I was hoping for your approval."

"I see nothing worthy in all of this research—nothing of any importance," he finally said. "But if you wish to waste your time talking to people and writing down what they say, I cannot stop you."

Ruth smiled politely; the bishop was giving his approval by not disapproving—just as Jacob had predicted.

"Thank you for your time, Bishop Stoltzfus." Ruth offered him her hand, and he took it.

"Your clover honey is on the back porch," he said. Rising from his rocker, the bishop escorted her to the door.

CHAPTER EIGHT

Jacob was assigned the task of gathering up an assortment of lawn chairs, coolers, and folding tables, not because he had real expertise in assembling Aunt Mamie's picnic paraphernalia, but because he was such a nuisance when it came to picnic preparations.

"That's it!" Aunt Mamie informed him after he'd opened the oven door for the fourth time in fifteen minutes. "I want you out! Out of the kitchen. Here, you take this list and go find everything on it." Stuffing a scrap of paper in his shirt pocket, she planted both hands in the middle of his back and started shoving Jacob toward the back door.

"I can load that stuff in the morning," he complained, while trying to stick his finger in the potato salad on his way out.

Ruth slapped his hand away and gave him a playful shove as well.

"I don't just want it *loaded,* I want it all scrubbed up nice and clean. Now, go on." Mamie maneuvered him through the screen door and locked it behind him for good measure.

Grumbling, Jacob bounded off the porch; he really preferred being at the center of the action in the kitchen. But he accepted his fate cheerfully and headed to the barn to carry out Mamie's orders.

Jacob was looking forward to tomorrow as much as the women were. He'd never really celebrated the Fourth of July before coming to live with Mamie, and even at that, this was the first year he'd actually caught the spirit of the holiday.

But then, Ruth hadn't been around to share it before now. Even Mamie, who was always ready for a picnic or a party, seemed more excited than usual.

Jacob climbed up into the storage loft, turned on the light, and started rummaging for the items on Mamie's list.

The sun had set an hour before, but still the oppressive heat of early July hung thick and damp in the twilight.

Jacob hurriedly collected everything and carried it all out to the open barnlot. It was cooler outside, but only barely. He advanced on the chairs, tables, and coolers with a rag and a bucket of soapy water. Alternating swipes of his cloth with cold wellwater from the garden hose, he finished quickly. Not able to resist

151

temptation, Jacob doused himself with the hose before retiring to air-dry in the porch swing.

Lazily he listened to Mamie and Ruth chatter over their cooking. The sound of their voices lulled him comfortingly.

Everything was better, more real, since Ruth had come. The farm work went more easily; his days were more interesting—they passed almost effortlessly. And the nights . . .

Jacob grinned to himself in the darkness. The nights were magical.

His energy was inexhaustible now. Ruth had somehow transferred a measure of her own boundless vigor to him. After the day's thought and toil were finished, he discovered a new reservoir of energy that carried them both through much of the night.

He chuckled, thinking how cleverly they managed to keep their lovemaking a secret, but then his expression darkened. Ruth had wanted to tell Mamie of their relationship, but he had steadfastly refused to let her divulge the information. He remembered the look of confusion in her eyes when he told her he wanted to keep their secret. How could he tell her that he couldn't admit his love for an English woman, especially now when he was back home, so close to the world of his childhood?

There was no need to creep around now. They had given Mamie enough plausible excuses to cover up their meetings. They told her that Jacob had to help Ruth in her research and, in return, Ruth was acting as his helper in the cabinet shop. Mamie even voiced concern about them working together such long hours. Still he felt guilty. Perhaps in time he would tell her. Given enough time he would be able to tell Mamie and perhaps the world.

He kicked out his leg; the swing creaked and rolled.

Jacob closed his eyes and envisioned that first morning as he helped Ruth creep back into the house at dawn.

Jacob's mouth turned to a straight line, as he felt a strange pang of uncertainty in the otherwise delightful memory.

Their lovemaking was always marked by Ruth's departure. She left him early each morning, just when he longed to wrap her in his arms and settle into sleep. Her leaving marred their nights and always left him unfulfilled.

But, he thought, separation was the price he must pay for secrecy, for privacy. And Ruth seemed unaffected by it. The English were more accepting of easy love affairs. He'd experienced their attitudes before.

But the night was too enticing and the excitement of tomorrow's festivities too compelling for Jacob to waste thoughts in brooding over his misgivings. He kicked out at the porch floor and set the swing in motion once more.

The scene of that first morning, when he led Ruth back to the house from the barn, pushed aside his anxiety and brought a smile back to his mouth.

It had taken him an hour to find Ruth's blouse in the haymow, he recalled.

And the memory of his search made Jacob laugh out loud.

"Are you through with that list?" Mamie demanded from the kitchen.

"Yes, ma'am," Jacob replied. The porch swing creaked under his weight.

"Want some iced tea?" called Ruth.

"Got anything to go with it?" he wisecracked back in the code that they'd perfected in the last few weeks.

Ruth appeared at the door, a tall glass of iced tea in her hand. "Aunt Mamie says you'll get something to go with this tomorrow." She handed him the amber glass but kept her distance. "If you're good tonight," she added.

"Do I have to wait until tomorrow?" he asked, pretending to sulk.

"Yep!" shouted Mamie. "You've got all you're gonna get today. Miss Ruth!"

"I didn't get anything today," whispered Jacob.

"Miss Ruth!" commanded her aunt again. "Better check those pound cakes."

Ruth winked and retreated as ordered. "Tomorrow's another day," she said, blowing him a kiss.

Jacob rocked in the swing, pacified with the thought. Tomorrow had had little meaning to him before Ruth. Now every *tomorrow* was better than the one before.

In just a few weeks Jacob Yoder's life had taken on new perspective. The handsome woman he'd envied and even argued with at first was now his lover and the mirror in which he'd begun to see himself more clearly. But more important, Ruth had unknowingly helped him to take a new look at life. She had pulled his will back into focus and had stimulated him to start living again.

How could he have ever seen her as English? he wondered. Her determination, energy, and caring were beyond any simple classification, let alone that of *English.* Ruth knew who and what she was, and she accepted Jacob as he was. She had an inner light of excitement about her; around her even the commonplace took on exotic tone.

Yet, if for no other reason, it was that acceptance in her that had gained Jacob's respect—both for their mutual desire and for Ruth's research work. And it was through her work that Jacob unexpectedly found a window into himself.

Innocently enough, Ruth had asked him to accompany her to the historical research library at the college in Goshen. The idea of a long day with her, alone, was enough to ensure his company. But that first day, spent silently among the stacks of books and diaries, gave him a new view of his Amish self.

Jacob realized he'd never been exposed to Amish history or heritage. Believing that their lives have meaning only in their immediate work, the Amish had never chronicled their own past. Such a waste of time was intolerable, and a sure sign of vanity. To the Amish, history was man's vanity and assumption, permanently recorded for other men to waste time recounting?

As Jacob spent the afternoons reading his own history, he couldn't believe he'd grown to manhood knowing so little about his own culture. Beyond the skeletal geneologies sealed in aged family Bibles, he never realized anything else existed.

He remembered asking questions of his grandfather, who gave him quick, shallow answers that extended less than two generations back. Those placating answers bothered him now, and often he would sit reading, wondering why the Amish had refused to record their own history.

If it hadn't been for the Mennonites, who adopted the burden of writing Amish history along with their own, Jacob knew he'd never have known his people's past.

Eventually it occurred to him that his heart *was* Amish; since his people had never thought their history was important, neither had he.

During the long years of his shunning, Jacob had tried to shut out all that was before, including any reference to his or his people's past. Since he never told anyone he was Amish, no one ever pressed him for information, so he had never realized his own lack of knowledge.

Yes, he knew how the Amish thought, how they would react, but he didn't know the whys involved. Through those trips to Goshen, Ruth had given Jacob Yoder the greatest gift he'd ever possess—a sense of *who* he really was and *why* his people were as they were.

Jacob smiled to himself and stretched. Now he saw life not only as a *present* but as a *past* replete with two hundred years of tradition and purpose.

As for his *future?* Jacob refused to consider it. He focused on the marvelous present and his newfound past.

But even as Ruth had opened new doors to him, her presence somehow undermined Jacob's having a total sense of peace and well-being.

He watched her closely as she worked at the library and talked with the other professors. And what he saw alarmed him. She fit so well within the English walls of Goshen College that he was forced to see how different their worlds really were.

In his arms, Ruth was a natural extension of himself —a country girl with gentle, tempting ways who could have blended into his life with little effort.

But away from him—away from the farm—she was a sophisticated social scientist who spoke a foreign, academic language with the others of her kind.

"We'll never finish all *this,* " he heard Mamie say. She'd been on her feet all day in the hot kitchen, and the weariness in her voice brought Jacob out of his reverie.

"Can I help?" he called, getting up from the porch swing to walk to the door.

Mamie stood in the middle of the kitchen, surrounded by vast quantities of potato salad in various

156

stages of preparation, trays of baked beans waiting their turn in the oven, and two pecks of unstemmed strawberries still to be prepared. She looked like a general evaluating battle strategy.

"Can I trust you to help Ruth stem strawberries?" she finally asked, one eyebrow raised.

"Yeah. Sure," he returned with a smug grin. "I love strawberries." He entered the hot kitchen, stepped over a basket of strawberries, and slid in across from Ruth at the table.

"Yeah. Sure," repeated Mamie, mimicking him. "I *know* you like 'em. What I want to see is you *stemmin'* 'em." She handed him a pail of washed berries and an extra mixing bowl. "You pull the stem off, then you put the berry in the bowl. The *whole* berry. Every berry."

Jacob looked at Ruth. Her head was lowered, but she was grinning, while her fingers nimbly continued to twist stems and toss the berries into her bowl.

"See how Ruth's doin' it?" asked Mamie before leaving him on his own. "She puts all the berries in the bowl. Nothing goes into her mouth."

"You don't have any faith in me, Mamie Detweiler," grumbled Jacob.

"Nope. Not where food's concerned." She watched him stem half a dozen strawberries and put every one of them in his bowl whole. Convinced he was going to follow directions, she went back to check on the cakes in the oven.

Ruth had been assigned to making pound cakes that would serve as the base for strawberry shortcakes at tomorrow's picnic. Mamie had provided her famous Butter Pound Cake recipe, the ingredients, and even some unsolicited supervision. She'd watched Ruth through each stage of the recipe. But now, as Mamie pulled the oven rack out and looked over the dozen loaf pans that had already baked twenty minutes longer than usual, she wondered if she hadn't missed something while Ruth was preparing the batter.

Mamie checked the temperature again. Everything seemed to be right—except the pound cakes. They were pale, not golden brown, and they were rather flat, not fluffy and high in the pans. Mamie shook her head. It was probably a good thing Ruth had chosen anthropology as her life's work, Mamie thought. She'd never have made it as the next Betty Crocker.

"Ah, I'm gonna tell," chimed Ruth from behind her.

"Don't you dare eat another strawberry, Jacob," replied Mamie without looking up. "And don't be a tattle tale, Ruth Marie," she added automatically.

Mamie rinsed out a clean dish towel and laid the moist cotton across her neck and shoulders. It was just too hot for this early in the season, she thought as she splashed cool tap water on her face and patted it with another towel. But even the heat couldn't curb her enthusiasm.

She stopped for a moment to watch Ruth and Jacob working diligently at the table. They were talking about Ruth's research. But Mamie wasn't listening to what they were saying; she was hearing what they were meaning. A smile crossed her lips. Nothing in the world could have made her happier than to have them here with her like this. Happy and playful, loving and learning, she knew they were made for one another. It was more than she'd ever hoped for.

The telephone rang, and Mamie reached for the receiver. "Is the Mueller taxi lady here?" Mamie asked Ruth, her hand over the phone's mouthpiece.

On her way to the phone, Ruth grabbed a pen and note pad from the counter. "Thank you," she said, taking the phone from her aunt. "Good evening, this is Miss Mueller."

Ruth could hardly keep from trembling as she listened to the Amishman ask about her taxi service. It was a venture she had just begun, and she was hoping this would be her first job. But she knew better than to let her excitement show. Calmly and politely she answered the man's questions.

"I charge a flat rate." She quoted him a figure, based on the information she'd been given.

Jacob grinned. "Ruth won't make any profit at that rate," he whispered to Mamie.

Mamie clapped one hand over her mouth to signal Jacob to be quiet.

"No, on any trips requiring overnight stays, you provide for my sleeping accommodations. What? No, no. I pay for all my own meals." Nervously she began to make notes on the pad. "Kalona, Iowa? How many? Hmmm." Ruth looked over at Jacob. "Just a moment, please." She put her hand over the mouthpiece and smiled sweetly at Jacob.

"Too many for your minivan?" he asked her, knowing what that smile was asking.

"Five adults and an infant. They'll be packed like sardines in my minivan. And luggage . . ."

"When?"

"Ah, just a sec." She put the phone back to her ear. "And when did you want to leave? Uh-huh. And how long will your visit last?"

Mamie and Jacob watched Ruth's face stiffen as she tried to hold back a giggle.

"Yes, I see. Four days, including a return trip to the Museum of Natural History in Chicago. Yes." She glanced over at Jacob, and he nodded yes. "Well, that will be fine, but *when* do you want to leave?"

Ruth held the phone away from her ear and looked

at the picnic fare stacked around the kitchen. Then she took a deep breath, straightened her shoulders, and replied, "Well, I would like the job, but I can't leave until day *after* tomorrow—the fifth. Tomorrow is the Fourth of July, and I must spend that with my family."

Mamie smiled approvingly and slapped the counter with her hand, while Jacob waited silently to hear the results of Ruth's declaration.

"Well, that will be fine, Mr. Hostetler. I'll pick you and the group up at your farm at six A.M., the fifth. And thank you for calling."

Everyone waited until the phone was safely disconnected before whooping their congratulations.

"Just takes one," Mamie announced. "After one successful trip, you'll have more business than you know what to do with."

"At those prices"—Jacob chuckled—"all the Amish in Elkhart County can afford to visit the field museum annually."

"It's not a real business, Jacob," Ruth reminded him as she sat back down at the table and started back on the strawberry mountain at her feet. "It's for research. I'm not looking to make any profit. I just want the opportunity to be closer to the Amish for extended periods of time."

As she poured three glasses of iced tea, Mamie remembered Ruth's returning from her initial visit with Bishop Stoltzfus and Mamie's original skepticism over the plan.

"Well, I'll say one thing, Ruth Marie," she said, handing them each a cold glass, "I didn't understand how you were goin' to make this taxi idea fly. Why, Bud Hamilton's practically made a livin' from runnin' taxi for the Amish. I really thought he had all the business tied down."

160

"A little competition never hurts, Aunt Mamie," Ruth reminded her with a wink.

"A little competition is one thing," said Jacob. "Cutting the going rate by twenty-five percent makes it a sure thing."

No matter how Jacob teased her, Ruth knew that he was proud of her. She'd come a long way—farther, perhaps, than anyone realized—since that visit with the bishop.

And as with Jacob, Ruth had experienced a radical change in both her perception of the Amish and her perception of life.

"We're going to spend two nights in Kalona," Ruth continued explaining the trip to her aunt and Jacob as her fingers flew over the berries again. "I'll be staying both nights in an Amish home. Isn't that great?"

Jacob gave Mamie a quick glance. She was taking cakes out of the oven. "They'll feed you real good," he assured Ruth before popping a big strawberry in his mouth. "There will be mush and sausage gravy for breakfast. And with the strawberries in, you'll probably get rivvel soup for lunch—"

"What's that?"

"Strawberries and bread cubes covered with fresh milk. You'll *love* it. And for dinner . . ."

"All you think about is food," Ruth accused him, pointing a strawberry in his direction.

Jacob glanced at Mamie, now loading the oven with trays of baked beans. "That's not *all* I think about," he reminded her quietly with a foxy grin.

Blushing, Ruth turned her attention back to the strawberries. If she let her mind wander along with Jacob's, the picnic work would never be finished.

The berry juice had stained her nails a sticky vermilion, and her fingers were slick with pulp. The hot kitchen smelled of baking and berries; the scent of love and security hung in the air. Ruth could feel it as distinctly as the ripe fruit in her palm.

What had once been familiar to her had taken on new depth and meaning. After years in an academic ivory tower, living life as a trained observer, Ruth Mueller was relishing every moment of every day. Here, at home—in the real world—she was a participant, not an observer. What she had once revered as an opportunity to see the world had been nothing more than unemotional tunnel vision. This was the real world; she was a part of it. A living, breathing, loving participant.

Jacob got up and wandered to the oven. Her gaze followed him lazily across the room. It was Jacob—a gentle, genial giant—who had made the transition possible. Their relationship had built the bridge from observer to participant.

She watched him steal a pinch of cake, then lean innocently over her aunt's shoulder and try to sample more potato salad. He was impossible and incorrigible.

Ruth sighed to herself. He was also wonderful. She wondered what he would say if he knew she'd already inquired about a teaching position at Goshen College. But she couldn't tell him yet. Nothing was definite, at least nothing about having a job for next year was definite. Only her decision to stay, permanently, on the family farm was definite.

Still, she was hesitant to tell either Aunt Mamie or Jacob about her decision. What if she couldn't get a job at Goshen and she was forced to return to Boston? The buildup and then the disappointment would be unfair to her old aunt, she thought. But in her heart Ruth knew that that was only part of her reluctance.

How would Jacob react? He might feel pressured, thinking Ruth expected more of their relationship.

Such a radical change in Ruth's plans might force too much too soon. No, until she was sure of Jacob's feelings, she couldn't reveal her plans.

Time was her ally now. There was plenty of time for them. She believed their love would grow, unhampered by limitations of time, decisions, and changes.

She knew it as distinctly as she knew that her life was meant to be lived here in Elkhart County, near the earth and all the people who loved it. Amish and English, commercial farms and family plots—it made no difference. Each in his own way believed in the simple life, and each lived close to the earth he worked.

It's the small things in life that make a difference, she thought, plucking another stem from her strawberry pile. Like the Fourth of July with its picnics and parades.

Gathering up a bowl of finished berries, she walked to the sink to run cold water over them. As she watched the water, Ruth wondered where she'd be today had she stayed with Dr. Lane.

July fourth. She knew the schedule by heart—she'd prepared it. There she would be somewhere in Central America applying calomine lotion to Phillip Lane's bug-bitten legs, wrapping cassette tapes in plastic to protect them from mildew, and preparing to observe some secret jungle fertility ceremony.

No, she thought. I'd much rather be here, stemming strawberries and participating in a traditional midwestern Independence Day celebration.

"All done," she announced, turning to hand her aunt the last bowl of strawberries. "How did the pound cakes turn out?"

"They'll be just fine for shortcakes," Mamie assured her.

But Jacob picked up one of the loaf pans. "How did

you make a *pound* cake that weighs five pounds?" he teased, hoisting the pan over his head like a barbell.

"You put that down, Jacob. They're just fine, Ruthie. They didn't quite rise like usual, but they'll be just fine for soakin' up all that strawberry juice."

Ruth took the cake pan from Jacob and groaned. "I followed the recipe to the letter, Aunt Mamie," she apologized. "How did I get a dozen pound cakes with the same specific density as uranium?"

"Never you mind, Ruth. These will be just fine. Jacob," Mamie commanded with a solemn look. "Cut these into one-inch slices. Now, you cover all the potato salad and put it in the fridge, while I crush up the berries." She opened the oven door and peeked inside. "These baked beans will be done in a few minutes, and then we'll be done."

Jacob sawed the cakes down to serving size, Ruth finished her assignment, and soon the kitchen work was done.

"Whew. I'm glad that's out of the way," Mamie murmured approvingly over another round of iced tea. "It's almost ten o'clock. We're all gonna need a good night's sleep." The announcement was made not to signal Ruth and Jacob that their *private* time had arrived, but rather to ensure Mamie one good night's rest.

Though she'd purposefully and happily scheduled earlier-than-usual bedtimes these last few weeks, Mamie never really got to sleep until she heard Ruth creak back through the house.

She'd gone along with their secret game because Mamie was glad they'd found each other.

The world's changed, she told herself. Young people are more liberal than in my day. And because she realized they probably thought she wouldn't approve of such things, Mamie gave them unquestioned privacy.

164

Love, even in her day, was always given a priority.

Tonight, however, she planned on *everyone* being well rested for the festivities in town tomorrow.

"I think I'll cool off on the porch before going to bed," Jacob replied. "Why don't you come out for a while, Mamie?"

"That's a good idea," added Ruth, somehow knowing her aunt would decline but wanting to include her just the same.

Mamie pulled her apron off and patted her face. "I'm goin' to cool down with a shower."

"I'll take a bath when you're through," Ruth assured her as she and Jacob withdrew to the seclusion of the back porch.

Hand in hand, they walked to the swing.

"Here, sit on my lap," offered Jacob. Not waiting for a reply, he pulled her down onto his legs. His arms went around the bare skin of her midriff. "Halter tops are my favorite type of clothing on you." He chuckled, running a warm hand beneath the fabric. "That is, if you have to wear something."

Ruth put her arms around his neck and kissed him —the first kiss of their day. Full and tender, his lips met hers with a longing drawn from hours of forced abstinence, from hours of being close but not touching. Hours of waiting for their special time.

Jacob smelled of hay and earth. The sweet, arousing smell clung to him like an expensive cologne that mixed with his body heat to create a uniquely personal scent. It was so distinct that Ruth could close her eyes and recall it even when they were apart.

"You smell like vanilla," Jacob said, as if reading her thoughts. His lips were dangerously close to her ear, his breath brushing sparks against the lobe. "Did you get any vanilla in the pound cakes?"

"Maybe that's what I left out," she said with a laugh.

"Oh, well. There's more than one way to a man's heart."

Caught in a spell of their own design, they rocked in the cool night air. The intense damp heat of the day had drained all but a fraction of their energies. It felt wonderful just holding one another in the darkness.

"How 'bout a midnight swim?" Jacob finally asked, knowing a trip to the swimming hole would revive them.

"No swimmin'!" Mamie injected unexpectedly from somewhere within the kitchen. "It's time you two turned in. Big day tomorrow."

Though Jacob tried to hold her, Ruth, giggling, squirmed free of his embrace.

"Well, I guess I'll turn in," she said in a clear voice. "See you bright and early, Jacob."

He followed her to the door for a final kiss.

"Turn out the kitchen lights, Ruth!" her aunt ordered.

"Tomorrow. After the picnic, at the pond," whispered Jacob, as he let Ruth slip around the screen door.

Ruth kissed a fingertip and touched his lips in reply.

CHAPTER NINE

"I saw that murderous look in his eye," Aunt Mamie cackled from the backseat. "He pitched that ball right at ya, Jacob. Saw that clear as day. That boy was out for blood!"

"Yeah, thought he'd scare me off! Well, now Bib Towers knows I don't scare so easy."

Ruth reached into the small cooler between her feet and pulled another pop top. "A big orange for the softball king of Goshen City Park," she said with great ceremony, handing Jacob another soft drink. "Cola or an uncola, Aunt Mamie?"

"Whatever's the coldest." Mamie adjusted her pillow and leaned back against the window. Her small feet were swollen from the heat, her back hurt, and her head still buzzed from the day's noise, but she wouldn't have missed the action for anything.

"Want another pillow for under your legs?" Ruth asked turning to hand her a drink. "Want to get your feet a little higher?"

"Don't fuss so much. Ruth Marie. Fussin' makes old people nervous. Turn around there; I'm fine. Just a touch of the heat. I feel lots better now."

The air whipping through the open car windows was hot, but at least it was moving. And the steady gust of heat was better than the thick, stagnant atmosphere of the city park. They were more comfortable, if not much cooler.

It had been oppressively hot all day. "Regular Fourth of July weather" was what Mamie called it, but Ruth could hardly remember it ever being *this* hot so early in the summer.

When they finished breakfast, the thermometer already stood at 70. By the time they packed up and headed for Goshen City Park, a spunky radio voice confirmed that the day was going to be a record-breaker; "Hot as a firecracker," the announcer appraised happily, as if he'd coined the phrase. And sure enough, it hit 94 before noon.

But no one seemed to care about the heat at first. The loose gathering of locals that always piled into the city park used the lazy holiday like an annual family reunion. People arrived from every corner of the county to relax between planting and harvest with the people they seldom had time to really socialize with the rest of the year.

Everyone brought the year's new babies and grand-babies to display; newlyweds and the recently engaged showed off their photo albums and rings before the appreciative crowd. And, of course, Ruth—*local girl turned super-anthropologist*—patiently endured a lengthy exhibition herself.

"Are you runnin' for election?" teased Jacob as they filed through the pitch-in lunch line. "Mamie sounds like she's stumpin' a campaign."

"Or for a sideshow," Ruth mused. Ahead of them, her aunt stood on the opposite side of the long line of serving tables, spooning mounds of her potato salad and baked beans on the plates that passed before her.

Jacob attacked a platter of Mrs. Hancock's famous baked ham. "What office you out for, honey?" He winked at Ruth and stabbed some ham for her plate too.

"What kind of office you got, sailor?" Everyone's attention was on the food, so no one noticed Ruth pinch a substantial handful of Jacob's behind through his thin athletic shorts.

Appropriately, Jacob responded by losing control of the two ears of corn he was trying to lift from a hot pot. The corn rolled off the serving table and hit the dirt, but Jacob refused to bend over to retrieve them.

"Can't discuss it now," he whispered back to her. "I need all my energy for the big softball game later."

"That's a myth," she whispered back. "Sex does *not* affect an athlete's performance."

He handed her a thick square of cornbread. "Oh, yeah? Well, tell that to the guys. They think I'm out of shape."

"What's that got to do with me?" she asked innocently, picking up an extra set of silverware for Jacob as they left the line.

"They took one look at you coming in with me and said Jacob, old boy, you've been holdin' out on us. Then they started lookin' me over." They found a picnic table apart from the crowd and sat down. "Muscles look a little flabby, Jacob," he went on, smiling. "Dropped training, have you? It was disgusting, just disgusting." He gave her a quick kiss on the cheek and started his meal. His friends' admiration only added to the pride he had in Ruth's company.

Ruth watched Jacob as he ate. He didn't seem to mind his teammates' teasing. Far from it, he seemed quite pleased with himself and their reaction. But best of all, Jacob was more relaxed and talkative than Ruth had ever seen him.

Hurrying through his lunch, Jacob quickly gave her

a peck on the cheek and went off with two men his own age.

She'd not seen Jacob interact much with any of the other farmers—English or Amish. He stayed close to the farm, and when they went into town or to the library at Goshen, he kept inconspicuously in the background. Speaking when spoken to; friendly but reserved. Ruth wondered if he felt uncomfortable, out of place in the rest of the non-Amish world beyond their farm.

But observing him now, talking with other members of his ball team, accepting their teasing and obviously enjoying it, Ruth forgot her concerns. After all, she reminded herself, they'd only known each other for five weeks, and most of that time had been spent in blissful, self-imposed seclusion.

Jacob was well liked and appeared completely at ease. He played catch with some of the children, talked with the elderly men, and teased the old women just like he always teased Mamie. This new side of Jacob was one that pleased her very much. He seemed to be an accepted member of the community, not the loner she had always thought him to be.

The day's festivities took on a new dimension for her. The laughter, food, and hospitality became secondary; Ruth kept her attention on Jacob. This was a perfect setting to observe this other side of him.

The day followed an unspoken tribal tradition that Ruth remembered distinctly. Immediately after lunch, without a verbal signal of any kind, people organized into specific groups.

There were the volleyball enthusiasts, who strung up three nets on imaginary grass courts and promptly went into a round-robin tournament, the rules of which were known only to those dedicated souls who participated annually in the volleyball ceremony.

There were the softballists. Two teams of robust, shirtless farmer-warriors who squared off once a year to savagely compete for territorial supremacy: the winners gaining undisputed recognition as *The Champs* for an entire year.

And, of course, there was the ceremonial gathering of the clan matriarchs, a smaller clustering of ancient women who sat and talked among themselves. They knew everything about everyone who had ever lived in the county.

One of the old women motioned to Ruth to join them. Surprised and pleased, Ruth ambled over to the little group of matriarchs and greeted them warmly. Before long she was deeply involved with their chatter.

"I tell you, Ruth, I knew you the minute I laid eyes on you. Did I say that, Cora? Didn't I say, well, there's that sweet Ruthie Mueller?" Emma Denton was eighty-eight and the oldest member of the group, which gave her chief interrogator status, Rugh realized.

Cora Mayper, perhaps a year her junior, barely endured her second-in-command position. "I wasn't so sure," she said softly, taking her crocheting out of her handbag. "I remembered her being taller, I think."

"That's statuesque, Cora. All the magazines say tall is in. Isn't that the word, Ruth? In? Anyway, you've always been a tall girl, hasn't she, Mamie?"

"Took after her father," injected her aunt. As the youngest member of the tribunal, Mamie left the main interrogation to her elders.

"And that *handsome* man you came in with," Lora Brown began to Ruth. "He'd be quite a catch for some lucky girl."

171

"Oh, that nice Jake Yoder," Emma said.

Jake? thought Ruth, trying to keep a solemn face. "You mean Jacob?"

"Jacob reminds me of my grandson," commented Ellie Bradshaw. "A big strappin' boy, with a sweet disposition."

"Are you married yet, Ruth?" Emma asked.

"No, Ruth's an anthropologist," Mamie said, as if that explained her marital status.

"Anthropologists don't get married?" Emma wondered aloud.

"I never knew any that did," Cora said flatly, not looking up from her crocheting.

Emma peered over her glasses and stared at Cora's snowy head, indicating minor irritation. "Is Jacob still living with you, Mamie?" she went on.

"He's still livin' in the barn. That is, in that apartment over his cabinet shop." Mamie gave Ruth a look that said "Didn't I tell you?"

"Must be nice having a good man like that one around," bubbled Ellie. "Eligible bachelor, good farmer . . ."

Emma looked at Ellie approvingly. "Ready-made match, I'd say. Maybe you two have been doin' a little pen-pal courtin'?" she said as she peered at Ruth with a little grin. "And now's the time to come home and check it out in person?"

"Oh, no, no. Nothing like *that,*" protested Mamie. "Ruth's just home for a year. She and Jacob never corresponded."

"Keepin' him all to yourself, Mamie?" accused Ellie.

Mamie's face, already flushed from the heat, reddened another shade of crimson, and Ruth almost laughed.

"Ruth is doing research for her Ph.D.," Mamie announced, ignoring Ellie completely. "She'll be here for a year, studying the Amish."

"Amish, huh?" muttered Cora. "More stuff about the Amish. Don't see what all the fuss is about."

"Why, they're positively archaic," Emma replied. "Aren't they, Ruth? Isn't that why you're researchin' them? To show how backward they are?"

"I—" was all that Ruth could get out.

"Archaic, my foot," Cora replied firmly. She dropped her crocheting in her lap and looked Emma straight in the eye. "We were all just as *archaic* once, Miss Emma Denton. Why, your family didn't hook on to the electric power until the thirties. Half the county didn't have indoor plumbin' till after the war. Humpf. Not so long ago we all lived pretty much alike. Weren't no big archaic difference then. Why, every one of us here was courted in a buggy."

"But things change, Cora," Emma tried to counter.

"Humpf. Change. Maybe. But there was nothing wrong with the way things was. Amish might have been smarter than the rest of us. They set no store by all these newfangled gadgets like credit cards and cable television. Don't depend on nothing, 'cept theirselves. Don't take nothing neither. The rest of us went soft—got all caught up in this modern business. Humpf. Now the moderns think there's somethin' strange about the Amish. Phooey." She picked up her handwork and started in again. "Well, the Amish think we're strange, and they just might be right too."

"You're behind the times, Cora," Emma shot back the moment Cora stopped to take a breath.

The debate was on, and Ruth, her marital status, her research, and her ceremonial questioning were forgotten. Politely Ruth excused herself, saying the slow-pitch softball game was starting, and she didn't want to miss it.

The shade of the picnic area at least gave some shelter from the burning sun. Out in the open softball field, the heat was almost unbearable. Still, that didn't keep Jacob's Farm Stars team from giving their adoring fans a real show. Even the matriarchs left their shady shelter to see what all the commotion was about.

The game was totally one-sided, and the action ran fast and furious for five innings. By that time, the Stars were ten runs ahead—four of which were attributed to Jacob, affectionately named the "Amish Slugger" by his teammates. The opposing Elkhart Bombers conceded to a loss and everyone headed for the shade and a cold drink.

"You were terrific!" Ruth told Jacob as he joined them at home plate when the game broke up.

"He ought to be," said Mamie. "With all that muscle he's got to put behind a bat."

Jacob chuckled, put his glove under his arm, and drank the cola Ruth brought out for him.

"I think we ought to call it a day," Ruth said to him. "I think the heat's too much for Aunt Mamie."

After only a few minutes' standing in the open playing field, Mamie's face had begun to lose color. Jacob took a good look at her.

"Think it's time we got you home, Miss Mamie. You don't look so good." Jacob and Ruth each took one of Mamie's arms and started back to the picnic area.

"We'll miss the fireworks," she protested. But her voice was shaky and the protest wasn't convincing.

"I'll tell you what," suggested Jacob. "Let's go home, cool down, and I'll set off a bundle of firecrackers for you after dark."

Mamie nodded quietly.

Through a barrage of farewells, they got Mamie to

the car and had her stretch out on the backseat for the return trip.

By the time they reached the farm, her color was much better.

"All I needed was a little air," Mamie told them. "We should have just taken a drive around town, cooled off, and gone back for the fireworks."

Jacob looked at Ruth and shook his head. "Well, I'm not big on fireworks. After Ruth and I take a swim, I'll do a firecracker display off the porch for you." He gave Ruth's hand a final squeeze as he stopped the van.

"Looks like we're gonna get a break in the weather," Mamie commented as she got out of the van. "A storm's moving in." She pointed to the horizon; the western sky was a sulfur yellow. "It's got some wind behind it too. Look at the dust in the air."

"Let's hope it's got a good rain in it," remarked Jacob as he and Ruth carried the picnic gear onto the porch. "We can use it. Been way too dry this season."

"I'd better check the radio. That sky looks ripe for a tornado," Mamie grumbled. "Weather's been awful calm this season. We might be in for a big one." She trudged up the steps and into the house.

"Maybe we shouldn't go out to the pond," Ruth murmured anxiously looking to the angry sky. Tornados had always terrified her. Even the possibility of one made her queasy.

"Would I let anything happen to you?" Jacob whispered. "We'll keep a watch out. Don't worry." He kissed her quickly and Ruth's anxiety faded.

"Jacob and I are going swimming at the pond," Ruth told her aunt as she ran through the kitchen on her way upstairs.

Mamie frowned, turned on the weather scanner, and sat down to wait for Ruth's return.

Five minutes later Ruth reappeared in her two-piece swimsuit, a bath sheet slung over her shoulders.

"Are you sure you're feeling okay?" She gave her aunt a quick kiss and paused to hear her reply.

"Oh, I'm fine," Mamie confirmed. "Just tuckered from the heat."

"Well, we'll be back before dark."

"You two keep an eye out. Hear me?" Her aunt's tone of voice drew Ruth's attention. "Don't get caught out in that open field or in the water if there's lightning. Hear?"

"We'll keep a watch out," she assured her.

"I'll keep the radio on, and if they put out a storm alert, I'll ring the dinner bell. You can hear it out by the pond, and if you two hear that bell, I want you to high-tail it back home."

"Yes, ma'am!" Ruth saluted and ran out.

Between the cornfields, down the dirt truck trail, Jacob and Ruth sprinted the quarter mile to the swimmin' hole. The spring-fed pond, nestled in a stand of trees, had become their favorite haunt.

"Last man . . ." Jacob shouted to her as they rounded the last turn in the trail. The pond lay straight ahead—twenty yards across a grassy knoll.

"That's right!" screamed Ruth, springing ahead of Jacob at a dead run. "Last *man!*"

The bathsheet flew out of her hand and a second later she dove into the cool, clear pond, with Jacob right behind her.

"Beat ya that time." She muttered as he surfaced next to her.

"Oh? Think you're fast, huh?"

She knew what he was thinking, and before he had the words out, Ruth dove down into the water and started their race back to the shore.

But before she could struggle up on the bank, Jacob grabbed her by the waist and pulled her back into the shallows.

"Trying to get away from me, lady?" Buoyed by the water, he held her to his chest. Suspended in his arms, she floated, weightless, in his embrace.

"Never." She sighed, positioning her palms on his shoulders.

His body glowed warm and wet against her, and his hair—damp bronze ringlets—brushed her chin.

The cold water surged about her legs, but it could not cool the flame kindled by Jacob's desire.

Ruth lowered her head to accept his devouring kiss. His lips were damp and tasted deliciously foreign; his tongue—so soft and large—sought her mouth and its sensitive interior. In slow, deliberate strokes his tongue invited her to even greater desire.

She tried to hold him to her mouth, ablaze with the passion she now thrived upon, but Jacob began kissing her neck and shoulders. Weaker yet with each tiny, hot kiss, Ruth tried to steady herself against his shoulders.

Jacob's lips kissed the border of her suit top. His tongued flickered beneath the fabric while his hands unclasped it.

Ruth's body arched to offer him the tender flesh of her breasts. As his mouth opened on her, she felt his breath on the wet nipple. And then his tongue danced around the hardening surface, burning into her body like a torch.

Moaning with delight, she closed her eyes against the blazing sun and concentrated on the delicious fire that Jacob had once again kindled in her.

His mouth moved slowly into the valley between her breasts, marking her with tiny kisses that sent her blood pounding into her ears. One hand kneaded the firm muscle of her bottom, while with the other he slipped away the rest of her swimsuit.

Nothing existed at the moment. Nothing save the two of them. His every move, each gentle caress brought them closer. Her heart seemed to beat with the rhythm of his; their bodies fit together like pieces of a puzzle.

He was her love. That part of her life puzzle that had been missing. The piece that gave life meaning— the heart piece. And now found, Ruth never wanted to let him go.

Ruth felt herself being lowered; her toes touched the sandy floor of the pond. She pulled her arms down around Jacob's waist. Their lips met.

He was hard against her, making her weak with desire.

Her long fingers grasped the band of his swim trunks and pulled the light fabric down as far on his thighs as she could reach. And then she let her legs float up around him.

Their bodies met, then separated, and met again.

The water flowed between them in cooling ripples that spun around their limbs, forming small eddies on the surface. But when they joined, the soothing water was pushed back, and Ruth felt the red heat of Jacob seize her again.

"Hold on to me," she heard him whisper breathlessly. Holding himself deep within her, Jacob carried her out of the water.

"And then, do you know what Ellie Bradshaw said to Mike's wife?" Ruth lay on her side next to Jacob in the soft grass of the pond bank. "She's due in November, you know."

Jacob, his arm shielding his eyes from sun, was

stretched out on his back, enjoying Ruth's recap of the day's gossip. "What'd Ellie say?"

" 'Well, Linda Miller,' " Ruth quoted, trying to reproduce the old lady's expression, " 'it's about time.' " Ruth couldn't help but grin before continuing. " 'I thought you never were gonna foal.' "

"You're *kidding!*" Jacob laughed.

"Nope. Made it sound like Linda was a stock animal everybody'd been waiting on to reproduce!"

"That Ellie Bradshaw's somethin' else," remarked Jacob.

"Linda took it fine," Ruth told him. "Have you known Mike and Linda Miller long?" She had noticed that Jacob seemed especially friendly with Mike and his twin brother, James.

"I was best man at Mike's wedding," Jacob said to her, smiling. "And I'm to be best man for James, if he ever settles down and gets hitched." He ran his hand down her smooth back. Ruth was the softest thing Jacob had ever touched. "How come you're so soft?" he asked.

"Women are naturally soft," she replied, weaving her fingers through the hair on his chest. "Why are you being evasive again?"

Jacob frowned. "Evasive about what?"

"Mike and James. How long have you known them?" There was something special in the way the three men interacted. More like brothers than friends. She was curious, and now that she and Jacob had grown intimate, Ruth wanted to know more about his past. She questioned him as gently as possible.

"I went to school with them," he told her, realizing he had no reason to withhold the English part of his life. "And later they helped me through high school."

Jacob chuckled to himself, remembering. He realized how little Ruth had asked about him, and he

179

knew she deserved more than his habitual sidestepping. "Did you see that Amish family at the picnic?" he went on, propping himself up on one elbow.

Ruth had thought it very odd that one Amish family would attend. "I was going to ask you about that too," she answered.

"Well, they're *not* Amish anymore. They left the order a month ago, and Mike and James brought them to the picnic. They're trying to help them adjust to the outside world—meet people, get to know the town, experience things they've never been exposed to." Ruth nodded but said nothing to interrupt. "Mike and James did the same thing for me years ago. You know, one day you're Amish with a certain set of rules to live by, with a close community of family and friends— and then one day you make the decision. The next day, like magic, you aren't Amish any more. But you aren't English either. You suddenly discover you aren't anything." He shifted restlessly, his face now somber.

Jacob, not used to talking about himself, didn't really know how to explain that part of his life he'd never disclosed to anyone before.

"And Mike? James?" Ruth asked.

"They're Mennonites; they come from a family that has always extended a helping hand to Amish who decide to leave the order. They help resettle them, find them work, meet new friends."

"Millers' halfway house?"

"Right. Exactly. They help ease them into a new life." Suddenly Jacob felt vulnerable again. He couldn't break away from this line of conversation, but he really didn't want to go into things he'd buried long ago in his heart. Yet he felt obligated to be honest with her now that he'd allowed Ruth to broach the subject.

"Why did you leave the order, Jacob?"

180

"I never *joined* the order," he corrected her. Where to start? It was a complicated story. "Are you sure you want to hear all this?" Smiling, he tugged at her wet braid.

Ruth pulled her knees up under her chin. "Very sure."

How could she do this to him? he wondered. No one—nothing else in his life—had ever made him feel so secure yet so totally vulnerable at the same time.

Something about Ruth made him want to tell her everything about himself, while something else in her made him withdraw. Perhaps it was knowing that she was only a temporary part of his life, that in a year she would be gone. Perhaps, he thought, it was better that way.

Maybe he could tell her enough to satisfy her interest while not unburdening all his painful memories. He took a deep breath.

Perhaps it didn't really matter as much as he thought.

"Okay. Remember when everyone attended regular public school? Well, I was classmates with Mike and James. Oh, I knew that I wasn't supposed to be friendly to English, but when you're a kid you don't understand all the whys. Anyway, besides having two English for pals, I made the grave mistake of liking school. Yep, there I was, a ten-year-old already bitten by the worldly bug. My parents found out about my friendship with Mike and James and took care of that real fast. Nothin' was ever said. But except for seeing them on regular school days, I was given enough work on the farm to keep me productive, close to home, and too tired to sneak off and play."

He lay back on the grass and put his hand over hers on his chest. "It wasn't so bad during school. We saw each other five out of seven days. But man, those sum-

181

mer vacations were tough. I couldn't find any Amish boys who were as much fun as Mike and James." He looked wistful, but smiled.

"Well, when I figured out what happens when you go against the rules, I got smart fast. I wasn't going to let my folks know how much I liked school. No telling how they'd put a stop to that. So, by sixth grade I'd mastered the art of deception. Never mentioned school around the house and kept my library books hidden in the chicken coop."

"A closet reader," Ruth said automatically, feeling a twinge of pity for the lonely child Jacob had once been.

"An addict, really. Do you know I read *Moby Dick* four times in three months?" Remembering, Jacob laughed. "I used to take books out of the library, sneak 'em home, and read out behind the barn. Well, this one librarian must have guessed what I was up to, because I was the only Amish kid who used the library. No matter how late I was returning a book, she never made me pay a fine. Mrs. Williams was her name. She'd just say, 'Now, Jacob, you take good care of that book and bring it back when you're done.' That is, until the *Moby Dick* incident.

"I borrowed *Moby Dick* two weeks before summer break. It was planting time, so I was too busy working with my father to get to read it, and I forgot to take it back the last day of school. It was all I had to read, so I read it over and over until my father found it stuck between two bales of straw in the storage shed."

His brow creased at the thought.

"What did your father say?"

"Didn't say a thing at first. He just took me out to the shed and had me watch as he tore that book apart page by page. He made me burn it. Then he said, 'Jacob, we are Amish. We have no need of these worldly things. You will see when you are older. You will be a good Amishman.' "

"And that turned you against your father?" Ruth was puzzled that Jacob's voice showed not a trace of anger.

"No. I never turned against my father. He thought he was doing the right thing. But from that day on I knew I'd never be the good Amishman he expected me to be. There were just too many things I wanted to know about. I loved the farm, and I loved my family, but I *had* to see what the outside world was like."

"And Mike and James?"

"I told them how much I wanted to go to high school, but when the time came, by father refused to let me go. I left school after the eighth grade and went to work with my father on the farm. But I didn't end my friendship with the Miller boys. Every Saturday night, after I got my own buggy, we'd meet somewhere, leave the buggy, and take their car to a movie or a burger place. We even triple dated together. Finally, the summer I turned eighteen, I told them I wanted to leave home. I didn't want to hurt my family, but I was tired of trying to appear to be something I wasn't. And, then too, the time was coming for me to become a member of the order."

Ruth understood his reasoning. The Amish believed in giving their children a choice. If they chose to become a member of the order, they were expected to remain in the order. Separating from tradition after making a free choice to join was considered much worse than never making the commitment in the first place.

"The Millers let me live with them until I finished high school. I graduated just before my twenty-first birthday."

"And your family?"

183

"I was shunned," he said unemotionally. "And I expected it. But I honestly thought that having done the *right* thing—not joining the order," he clarified, "I'd be able to reestablish ties after I graduated. But it didn't turn out that way."

"Shunning is a terrible thing."

Jacob looked up at her and smiled. "That didn't sound like an objective anthropologist speaking," he said.

At the moment, she didn't feel objective. They were talking about Jacob, the man she loved. Ruth empathized with the awesome pain of total separation Jacob must have endured in his many years of being shunned, totally ostracized from the group.

"You must have felt very much alone," Ruth said quietly. "It must have been very hard for you."

"Mike and James helped me through," he admitted as unemotionally as he could. "They've done it for others since." He reached out and touched her cheek, wanting to tell her how much it meant to have her listen and try to understand.

Instead, he pulled Ruth down to him and kissed her full lips. He wanted to tell her more, but he couldn't bring himself to go on. The past had converged on him with such intense power that Jacob found himself swallowed by the long-suppressed memories—and the emotion they still carried.

The hot, humid air that had hung over the earth like a heavy, motionless bubble for days suddenly shifted around them. The dry, brittle leaves overhead rustled in the unexpected gust of dusty wind.

Ruth and Jacob instinctively looked up.

The western sky was black. A monstrous thunderhead—dense storm clouds piled a mile high—stretched for as far as the eye could see. Like a great blue-black dragon, it churned toward them.

184

"We're going to get that rain you wanted," Ruth told Jacob as they struggled into their damp swimsuits.

"And smething I *didn't* ask for, by the looks of it," he replied.

Jacob grabbed their towels just as they heard Mamie's dinner-bell signal.

"Oh, no." Ruth froze.

"Come on, hurry!" Jacob urged, thrusting her swimsuit into her hands. "We've got to get home. Get dressed!"

She struggled into her suit, never looking away from the sky.

"Come on!" Jacob shouted over the growing wind.

Seeing her terrified expression, he threw one hand around her arm and pulled her away.

As they raced back up the truck trail, the wind picked up. In punishing, gritty gusts it pushed them toward the house. Just before they reached the small barn, a blanket of rain engulfed them, turning the dry ground beneath their feet to instant mud.

"Almost there!" Jacob panted as he took a tighter grip on Ruth's arm.

"Hurry up now," they heard Mamie shout. Through eyes blurred with rain, they saw her stooped beside the porch, holding the storm cellar door open for them against the ferocious wind.

Jacob grabbed the heavy door as soon as they met her, and Ruth helped her aunt down the steep cement steps into the dark underground shelter. Climbing in behind them, Jacob fought the wind for the heavy door and finally pulled it down into place.

"I've got candles right over here," Aunt Mamie muttered in the dark. "Everybody stand still, I'll have a light in a minute."

Ruth shivered and coiled her arms around her body.

The cellar was cold and dank. "Are all the windows open in the house?" Ruth asked, trying to remain calm and subdue her fear.

She'd learned from experience to open the windows. Mamie believed it allowed the air pressure to equalize to that of the tornado and kept the house from blowing apart.

"I got as many as I could," Mamie replied as she struck a match and lit several emergency candles. "They've spotted two funnels over the west part of the county. Looks like we're really in for it."

Ruth closed her eyes. Her hands formed tight fists, as if she could actually fight off the fear that clawed at her.

Wind and rain battered the cellar door and howled above them. Then something hit the door with a dull thud. Another thud. And another. Large hail, thought Ruth, feeling her control slipping away as the storm intensified.

"There goes the greenhouse," her aunt cried angrily as they heard the sound of glass shattering.

"Don't worry," Jacob shouted back as he sat down on a crate next to Ruth. "We'll have it fixed in no time."

Aunt Mamie nodded and pulled up her own crate. Ruth rubbed her arms, but her shivering had turned to uncontrollable spasms that revealed her terror.

She couldn't speak, so great was the terror in her mind. Eyes wild and pleading, she looked at Jacob. "Here, sit down by me," he said, pulling her unsteady body to him.

He slid over, and she sat down beside him. The racket outside was almost deafening.

"Here," offered Jacob, wrapping one of the muddied towels around Ruth's shoulders. The towel was wet and slimy, and she shook even harder.

"I'm here, Ruth," Jacob said. Putting his arms around her, he held Ruth tightly to him and kissed her forehead. "Don't be afraid. We'll be all right."

Mamie watched as Jacob tenderly reassured her niece. He looked up once and saw the old woman's face smiling at him. Then she looked away, and Jacob knew their secret was no more.

Suddenly the hail stopped. A second later the rain quit and the wind died. Not a sound.

"Th-this is it," Ruth stammered, bracing herself against Jacob. She'd been through this twice before, as a child. That absolute silence always came just before a twister hit.

"There goes my rhubarb," Mamie said with a moan.

Jacob tightened his hold on Ruth and squeezed her. "Didn't I promise you girls some fireworks tonight?" he said, trying to break through her fear.

But before either one of them could respond, the silence was split by a low, distant rumble.

Steadily the hollow rumble advanced, pounding at the earth like a giant machine. It came closer. The rumble became a deafening roar that reverberated through the cellar.

Ruth clung to Jacob in terror as the storm moved above them. He held her as tightly as he could, trying to comfort her and praying that the tornado would not cause too much damage. Finally, just when it seemed it would never stop, the wind began to die down until soon the only sound was the rain drizzling against the cellar door.

Mamie pulled herself up off the crate. "Let's see what's left," she said wearily.

CHAPTER TEN

The first thing that struck them after they'd left the cellar was the damage to Mamie's greenhouse. Hail the size of golf balls covered the ground, mixed with chunks of glass from the greenhouse roof.

"Doesn't look bad," Jacob told Mamie. "No structural damage. We'll get new glass in."

But the damage to the greenhouse was forgotten as they walked out into the barnlot. Automatically they all turned to appraise the house. Aside from a few shingles curled up from the wind, it appeared untouched. But much to their amazement, the barns and outbuildings were also standing.

"I would have sworn that twister came right down on top of us," Mamie declared as they slogged their way through the pouring rain. Instinctively they all moved toward the back fields. "Those funnels do some strange things. I remember once when a twister skipped over a mile, hit a couple barns—nothing else, mind you—then skipped another mile and took down four miles of fence. Never know what they're gonna hit and what they're gonna skip." Steadying herself between Jacob and Ruth, Mamie trudged bravely along with them.

"There's what you heard," Jacob said abruptly. They had reached the open expanse of fields behind the house and stood in the middle of the truck path, agape at the sight before them.

The tornado had cut a path a hundred yards wide across their cornfields. For as far as they could see— from southwest to the northeast—the fields were scarred with a black mud gash, inflicted by the fierce tail of the tornado.

The thick stand of hardwood trees where Jacob and Ruth had made love next to the pond had been thrown like kindling on the soggy earth. Torn out of the ground, the tall trees lay prone—their roots exposed and their heavy green limbs thrust into the sky at grotesque angles.

Aunt Mamie, suddenly silent, shook her head and leaned against a fence post, as Ruth and Jacob plodded on to take in the full impact of the scene.

Jacob's picnic tables were gone; the lush grass was littered with splinters of their whitewashed wood. And the pond was no more than a mud puddle—a sinkhole with brackish water standing an inch deep in the bottom. Their lovely pond—water, fish, and all—had been sucked up and carried away by the incredible power of the funnel.

"Oh, Jacob," Ruth cried. "Our place—our special place—it's . . ." She couldn't finish.

She felt an odd premonition, as if the devastation of their lovely hideaway was but a symbol of something worse to come. Ruth's eyes filled with tears.

They had been so happy there. Where could they go now? What other place could ever mean so much to them, or draw them as close?

"It will take some time," Jacob promised her, putting his arm around her shoulder as they started back to where Mamie waited, "but we'll have our special place back—someday."

"We really were lucky," Ruth repeated her aunt's

words to Jacob. She knew it could have been much worse; she wondered if the other farms had fared as well.

In the light of a kerosene lamp, Ruth sat huddled at the kitchen table. Wrapped against the damp night air in an old blanket, she warmed her hands over her teacup and waited for Jacob to return.

It was after midnight, and Aunt Mamie was asleep. A cold, steady rain persisted. The intense heat of the last week had been displaced by a northern cold front; the two weather giants' clashing had spawned the half-dozen tornados that had ripped across four Indiana counties that Fourth of July.

Tornados were as much a part of life on the flat farmlands as the four seasons; they were a frequent summer reminder of nature's power.

Ruth had survived many storms, and she could vividly recall other summer afternoons spent in the cellar, with her aunt and uncle, sheltered from the furious wind. So many other times they had sat in the musty darkness, listening and waiting and wondering—wondering what would be left when the storm passed.

Ruth began to shiver; she pulled the blanket tight about her shoulders. It didn't matter that she'd experienced the twisting winds before. Ruth knew she would always feel the same stark terror that gripped her now.

The transistor radio on the table was tuned to a local station. She half listened to the slow country music; it would be followed by another report on the damage. For the past three hours the station had alternated its music format with countywide news updates.

Ruth got up from the table, holding the blanket about her, and walked slowly across the wet floor to the kitchen window. Jacob should have been back by now. She wished he'd never left. In the big silent house, with only the rain and the radio for company, the black night intimidated her even more.

Her eyes turned from the lane to the dark distance beyond the greenhouse. All was black. Even the mercury vapor security lights of the barns had been knocked out by the storm. But even so, she still imagined the vivid details of the damage, now hidden by the dark.

"Lucky," Mamie had said. "Damn lucky," she kept muttering as they all sloshed ankle-deep through the mud in the drizzling rain that trailed behind the storm.

As they had assessed the scene, Ruth had been thankful that the terror within her had turned to a numbing silence. Her greatest fear never materialized immediately; it always waited to seize her until what had to be done was done. When she was a child, it always waited until she was alone in her bed long after everyone else had fallen into an exhausted sleep.

Now, as an adult, total fear gripped her in the stillness of the kitchen, alone—with time to think, as she waited for Jacob.

New thunder rattled the windows; a thin streak of gray-blue lightning darted from the sky to illuminate the horizon for a split second. Heavy thunderstorms were to continue through the night. The radio announcements verified they were not expected to produce more severe weather. But Ruth wondered.

She forced herself to listen to the radio's positive forecast, and turned to look down the lane once more. This time headlights flickered through the rain. It was Jacob's truck.

Quickly she relit the stove and put the kettle on to boil.

The van stopped by the porch; she heard Jacob

climb the steps, but when the door didn't open, Ruth hurried to pull open the solid wood door for him.

There on the porch she saw Jacob wrestling to remove his waterlogged jacket.

"Don't bother taking it off," she told him, holding the screen door wide. "Come on in where it's warmer."

"Let me get these work boots off," he insisted. "They're caked with mud." Sitting down on the swing, he tugged at the swollen leather laces and left the boots where they landed.

"Do you want coffee or tea?" Ruth asked as he came into the kitchen and sat down at the table.

"Coffee. Real hot coffee," he told her wearily.

She handed him another old blanket. "Strip off those wet clothes and wrap up. I have the furnace on; you'll warm up in no time."

"We're lucky to have heat," he told her, rolling the soaked blue jeans down over his hips. "All the English on total electric are knocked out. Smiths and Davieses —they can't even cook. All electric."

Ruth smiled and patted the old propane stove, thankful that her aunt had insisted on staying with propane, even when natural gas and electricity became available.

"I guess Aunt Mamie's right," she replied, testing the kettle with a quick stab of her finger. "She always said bottled gas was better." Ruth chuckled nervously, relieved Jacob was back safe and sound.

"Well, nothing's perfect," Jacob went on, peeling off his socks and shirt. "Twister took O'Connor's propane tank. I think I found it, though. Big tank landed in the middle of Levi Byler's front yard. When I drove in to check on 'em, I said to Levi, 'Say, old Amishman, when did you go English?'" Jacob wound the blanket around himself and sat back down. "Of course, old

192

Levi just looks at me. Then he looks at the propane tank and says, 'Oh, I thought I'd give it a try, seein' how they're sending out free samples.' "

"You're kidding." Ruth laughed, stirring the instant coffee in Jacob's mug. "Don't forget to tell Aunt Mamie that in the morning." Walking over to the table, she put his cup down and leaned to kiss his forehead. "I was worried," she told him. "I thought you'd be back sooner."

Jacob reached up and rubbed her arm. "Don't ever worry about me, Ruth. Only the good die young." Smiling, he smacked her behind.

"And you're so rotten, you expect to live forever?"

"Sure," he said, taking a drink of coffee. "I intend to be the oldest dirty old man in history."

His teasing helped relax her. If Jacob was joking, things must not be all that bad.

"I also think I found our pond," he told her. "Well, not the water, of course, but the campground road was covered with blue gills and crappies."

"I've heard of it raining cats and dogs," Ruth exclaimed, "but never . . ." Then she laughed. A full, hearty laugh that forced all the fear of the aftershock from her body.

"I didn't mind losing a little of the corn crop so much," Jacob continued, laughing himself. "But when we found the pond missing, *that* perturbed me a mite."

Ruth smiled at Jacob. He was there with her and that was all that mattered. "I'm all right, Jacob," she said as if to convince herself. "How could you tell those were our fish out on the campground road?" she tried to tease, pouring him another cup of coffee.

Jacob winked. "I recognized a couple of the big ones. I've been trying to catch them since last year." He reached over to pat Ruth's hand again. "Don't worry about the pond," he said with sudden seriousness. "It's spring-fed. Water will come back clear as a bell. We'll restock, clear the timber, plant some more trees, and that place will be prettier than ever in a few years."

The minor damage they'd sustained was nothing compared to that of others. "I've been listening to the radio," Ruth said. "No one was killed, but the damage is bad. What did you find?"

Jacob took a deep breath and balanced back on his chair. "Well, it's not good, but it could have been worse. I got over to Bishop Stoltzfus's place just behind Tom Sanders. I guess Rudy, Amos's son, had some of his kids out cuttin' alfalfa when the storm hit. Amos was trying to saddle a horse when we got there to go out and look for 'em." Jacob rubbed his tired eyes. "Everybody else was okay, so Tom and I took his four-wheel drive out through the fields looking for 'em." He shook his head. "Talk about lucky. Rudy threw his three boys down in a ditch and lay down on top of 'em. The boys were okay—shaken up—and Rudy came out of it with only a broken leg. Luckiest son-of-a-gun I've ever seen."

"Did you get him to the hospital?" Ruth said, shocked.

"Tom took him into Goshen; I went back to the house with the kids." Jacob smiled wistfully. "Sure was some family reunion, when everybody saw the kids were okay and heard that Rudy wasn't hurt too bad. Maybe you could take his wife into town tomorrow to visit him. Saw Tom Sanders later. Rudy's gonna be in hospital for a few days. Had to do surgery."

"I'll go over and offer her a ride in tomorrow. I should stop over at Hostetlers' and cancel their trip to Kalona, I guess."

"Right. They aren't going anyplace for a while. Lost both their barns and most of their livestock."

Ruth nodded. "Nobody hurt, I hope."

Jacob shook his head and yawned.

"How was your mother's farm?" Though Jacob hadn't said so, Ruth knew that he had gone specifically to check on his family.

Jacob looked at Ruth with narrowed eyes. "They faired pretty well," he replied at last, his manner slightly distant.

"Did they have much damage to the house? The barns?" she went on, wanting him to know her genuine concern. "There wasn't anyone hurt, was there?" she added, thinking of his aging mother.

Jacob put down his cup. "No one hurt," he reported stiffly. "Tornado picked up the brooder house—chickens and all. Didn't see a sign of it anywhere. Lost a barn roof too."

But Ruth knew that the chickens represented a large portion of their farm income. Perhaps that accounted for Jacob's sudden shift in mood. Without pushing further, she said, "I'm sorry. Will they manage?"

He shook his head, choosing not to discuss it. "Long day tomorrow. Best get to bed." Standing, he pulled the blanket up around him and tucked it in like a long sarrong. "How's Mamie?"

"She's fine. We mopped the floors and took down the curtains. There wasn't much we could do tonight, so I made her a sandwich and then she went on to bed. Why don't you sleep in here tonight?" Ruth offered quickly. "It's warm and the beds are comfy, Jacob."

Ruth kissed his mouth. His eyes were rimmed with red. Jacob was near exhaustion. "I promise not to bother you," she said softly. "I'll leave you all alone in the other guest room."

Jacob frowned and let her go. "Okay," he said. "But let's not make it a habit, okay?"

Ruth was the first one up the next morning. The rain had stopped, and the bright early rays of morning sun were a welcome sight that lifted her spirits.

Quietly she tiptoed across the upstairs hall to where Jacob slept in the second guest room. His door was ajar, so she peeked in. There, curled in the middle of the big bed, covered up to his ears in one of Mamie's bright quilts, Jacob lay sound asleep.

Returning to her room, Ruth dressed in long jeans and a college sweatshirt before creeping down the stairs. She hadn't heard a sound downstairs and assumed her aunt, like Jacob, was still sleeping.

Ruth put the kettle on to boil and started breakfast. It was going to be a long day. Everyone could use a good meal with which to get started.

At first, she considered trying to make biscuits, but decided against it, knowing failure was inevitable. Instead, Ruth beat up a half-dozen eggs, sliced some fresh vegetables, and grated together three kinds of cheese for her omelet specialty.

"What's this?" asked her aunt as she emerged from her bedroom. "Breakfast is ready?"

"Sure, sleepyhead. Here, have a fresh cup of coffee."

Her aunt took the cup and sat down at the table.

"I thought Jacob and you were going to sleep the day away," Ruth teased.

"Hmmmm. Do you want me to go up and wake him?" asked Mamie.

Ruth turned. "How did you know he slept in the house?"

"I heard somebody upstairs this morning."

"That was me."

"No, I heard somebody upstairs after I heard you out here."

"And you *knew* it was Jacob?" Ruth asked, wondering what else her aunt had heard.

"Of course. Don't know anybody else that sounds *that* big."

"Oh." But before Ruth could question her further Jacob could be heard descending the stairs. Yes, Ruth thought, he does sound big. Still, Ruth wondered just how much her aunt really knew about their other comings and goings in the big house.

Then, wrapped tightly in a blanket, Jacob cruised into the kitchen.

"What happened to you?" asked Mamie, wide-eyed.

"Ruth took my clothes last night," Jacob answered. Walking to the stove, he picked up the kettle.

"I put them out on the line," Ruth explained. "He was soaked to the skin. And you should have seen his boots."

Mamie immediately looked at the floor. "You better not have tracked mud through the house, Jacob."

"Left 'em on the porch," he told her. "What's for breakfast?"

"Nothin' till you put some clothes on," Mamie grumbled. "Can't eat with no naked man around. Enough to give decent folk indigestion."

Jacob took a sip of coffee and headed for the door. "Better have breakfast ready when I get back," he warned, closing the door behind him.

Ruth and Mamie laughed. "That boy knows how to make decisions," Mamie observed.

"I thought I'd stop by Hostetlers' and see if they need anything from the hardware or lumberyard, and go over to Stoltzfus's and ask Rudy's wife if I can take her to the hospital," Ruth told Jacob as they sat finishing breakfast.

"You'd better take my truck. It's big enough to haul quite a bit of material." Jacob sat, pad of paper in his hand, making a list of repair supplies he needed. "This glass ought to be in stock at the lumberyard. If not, tell 'em to deliver it when it comes in."

"If the lumberyard didn't blow away too," mused Mamie.

"The radio said Goshen had wind damage mostly," Ruth told her. She turned to Jacob. "Want me to go out and see if I can get anything in town for your family?"

Jacob didn't look up, but Ruth saw his fingers tighten on the pencil. "No," he replied slowly. "My brother will have everything under control."

"It's not that far out of the way, is it?" Ruth asked, realizing she didn't even know the farm's location.

"No. But thanks. I'll check with my brother later to see if he needs a hand," Jacob said quickly.

His weekly visits home had become very important to him in the past month. Ever since discovering the wealth of Amish history and tradition at Goshen College, Jacob had experienced a strange shift in perspective. Conversations and simple routines took on new reason; the visits had greater significance; Jacob was finally beginning to understand that part of him that was Amish.

And he wanted to protect his new discovery—that emerging understanding of himself and his own family —from Ruth. Somehow he felt as if she was prying whenever she asked about his family.

As Jacob watched Ruth drive away down the lane, he suddenly felt a stabbing resentment. Frowning, he turned and walked toward the barn, trying to drive the sensation from his mind. He shouldn't resent someone who had presented him with insight and pride in his own culture. He didn't *want* to resent her—the lovely, energetic woman who had captured his heart.

He stopped inside the barn door and leaned against the wall. Jacob Yoder didn't want to think about his love for Ruth. It was a painful thought that he'd kept locked out of his mind until now.

One heavy fist pounded the wall behind him angrily. Why had he let himself fall in love with her? All along Jacob had known Ruth would leave when her research was done; all along he should have remembered that she was English. Soon she would be back in her world of books and learning and he would still be here, tending the farm and helping Mamie. Ruth was from a universe that was foreign to him, one he could never fully become a part of, anymore than she could become a part of his.

His fist hit the wall again. What did she really think of their relationship? he wondered. She seemed to care for him as much as he cared for her, but how could he tell? She had never mentioned staying with him after her year of research was over. Perhaps that in itself was her answer.

Stop, he commanded his mind. *Stop thinking all this nonsense.* His fingers relaxed slowly as he forced himself to be rational. *I have no reason to suspect Ruth of anything.*

Jacob tried to forget his worries but found he could not. It was the reality that she would not be staying that had triggered it all. The reality that there might be nothing more between them when she left. Perhaps she would one day remember him as only a romantic interlude in her sabbatical year.

Face the truth, Jacob said to himself as he gathered up the tools he would need to repair Mamie's greenhouse. You finally know who *you* are; you know where *you* belong. Things Ruth has always known about herself. You live in two different worlds. Accept it. Make the most of it. And, when its over, you must forget her.

By the time Ruth reached the Stoltzfus place, she'd gathered a tidy bundle of hardware lists from the surrounding farms. Her little taxi service was quickly becoming a light hauling operation.

"Here is fifty dollars," Mr. Hostetler had told her. "I think it will cover my order." The Amishman carefully counted the money into her hand. "Just tell them to have the big order of lumber delivered as soon as they can."

"I have some of my own money," Ruth offered. "If it comes to more, I can probably cover it."

Mrs. Hostetler shook her head. "You tell us how much. We have money to pay you back," she insisted.

From English farm to Amish, Ruth drove her hardware route. Everyone needed something. Many needed major lumber supplies. For those, she would place orders and have them delivered.

And everyone asked about the damage to her aunt's farm.

"I have children to clear the downed trees," an Amish farmer told Ruth after she described the damage. "I go over right now to help Jacob Yoder with the glass repair."

"Thank you," Ruth replied. It was a generous offer, considering the extent of clean-up he had to face on his own place.

"No thank you," he answered stiffly. "It is the way we are supposed to live—helping when we can, who we can."

And as Ruth drove into Bishop Stoltzfus's farm, she remembered reading that the Amish believed they were obligated to come to the aid of *anyone* in need—whether Amish or non-Amish—and that they never expected or sought gratitude, let alone repayment.

But it wasn't just the Amish way, she thought. As she braked the van to a stop near the Stoltzfus barn, Ruth saw that George Huff had arrived before her. His dump truck was already half full of debris. The English of Elkhart County believed in the same philosophy.

"Morning!" Ruth announced, approaching George and several of the Stoltzfus children as they loaded tree limbs into the truck. "Is the bishop here?"

"Barn!" shouted George, jerking his thumb toward one of the barns behind him.

Ruth found the bishop taking inventory of some stored lumber.

"I'm going into Goshen," she said, approaching him. "Can I take your daughter-in-law in to the hospital to visit Rudy?"

Stoltzfus turned from the woodpile, took his handkerchief, and mopped at his forehead. "She can't go," he said. "Too much to do here." He walked over and sat down on a stack of hay bales. "We asked Emma Yoder to go in and sit with Rudy. Could you take her?"

Ruth didn't know *which* Emma Yoder he meant. One of the things that still confused her about the Amish was that so many of them had the same name.

There were only about twelve Amish family names common to the county, and they only used a total of twenty-four first names: a dozen names for girls, a like number for the boys. And middle names, which could have distinguished individuals better, were never used at all. The Amish just rotated a small number of first names from generation to generation.

Ruth knew of at least four Emma Yoders in their area alone.

"I'll be glad to take her," Ruth told him. "But which Emma Yoder? Where does she live?" Ruth asked, wondering if the woman was a relative of Jacob's.

Surprisingly, the bishop gave her a big smile. "Not far from here," he said. "And you know her son. Jacob Yoder."

"Oh. Okay," she went on, suddenly very intrigued to meet this woman. "How do I get to her farm?"

The bishop gave her the directions and explained that Mrs. Yoder would stay with Rudy until someone else went in to town who could relieve her.

Before Ruth left, she asked if she could pick up anything for the bishop's repair work, and he gave her a list he'd already made out.

"Too much for your vehicle," he said flatly. "I go in and pick up the order with a wagon. Later. Tell the lumberyard I pay then."

Ruth recognized Emma Yoder the moment she stepped from the van and saw the elderly woman bent over the ragged remains of a flower bed.

She was tall and thin, and her profile had been perfectly duplicated in Jacob. The finely shaped nose, the broad sharp jaw line, and the pronounced chin were unmistakable. But when she straightened and glanced up at Ruth, her striking blue eyes—exactly the shade and shape of Jacob's—were cold and piercing. It was as if she were looking right through Ruth, and the uncomfortable gaze sent a chill down her spine.

"Ja?" she asked as Ruth came closer. "Can I help?"

"I'm Ruth Mueller," she explained, feeling a lump forming in her throat. "Bishop Stoltzfus asked me to take you into the hospital." The woman stood motionless, her eyes moving from detail to detail down

Ruth's body. "To sit with Rudy," Ruth added in the strained silence.

"I'll get my hat" was all she said before walking toward the house.

With great effort she hobbled up the porch steps of the smaller house, her bones obviously stiff and painful with arthritis. Respectfully, Ruth went back to the van and waited for her.

Somehow Ruth felt a strange pang of guilt. She had known for a long time that Jacob preferred her to have no contact with his family. It bothered her that he seemed to want to keep his Amish past completely separate from his present life with her and Aunt Mamie, but she had always respected his wishes. Now she felt as if she were prying even though her visit to his mother was perfectly innocent.

Unwittingly, Ruth had been placed in a very uncomfortable position. Could Jacob possibly misinterpret her intentions if he found out she'd gone out to his family's farm? she wondered.

As Ruth waited for Jacob's mother she silently hoped that Jacob wouldn't find out. Some vague fear gripped her; Ruth tried not to think about the consequences—though just *what* the consequences might be she didn't know.

A few minutes later Emma Yoder reappeared on the porch, her black bonnet in hand. Ruth got out, opened the passenger door, and helped her up into the high seat.

Silently, they started to town, and Ruth concentrated on turning her fears into positive action.

Suddenly it seemed very important that Jacob's mother like her—or, at the very least, accept her. Perhaps, she thought, if they could find a common ground and become acquainted, Jacob's own uncertainty might be eased. And then, when he eventually did find out that they had met, he wouldn't be angry with Ruth. At least, that was what Ruth fervently hoped.

Recently Ruth had been finding it easier to talk with the Amish. She really thought their intimidating affect on her had been conquered. But sitting next to Emma Yoder, Ruth sensed that old feeling of stony indifference, and it made her very uncomfortable.

As the miles passed without even a passing look of interest from the old woman, Ruth began to see that Emma's silence was more than just stoic indifference. A sensation of icy dislike enveloped Ruth, and try as she might she couldn't suppress it.

She had to find something appropriate with which to start a conversation between them, something to test the validity of her feelings. Ruth had to find out what was happening between herself and this woman she'd waited for so long to meet.

This was the mother of the man she loved. This was Jacob's mother. She desperately wanted to establish some kind of rapport with her. Jacob was a part of this woman, and Jacob was a part of Ruth now. There was so much Ruth wanted to understand about them both for her own sake, as much as for Jacob's.

Just then she saw Mrs. Yoder rubbing her gnarled hands together, trying to warm them in the sunshine.

"My aunt has arthritis," Ruth offered, grasping at the opening.

"Your aunt is Mrs. Detweiler." Her reply was a simple statement of fact. Nothing more.

But Ruth was determined now. "My aunt's doctor has her on a new medicine for her arthritis," Ruth continued. "It has helped her a lot. The swelling isn't so bad, and she says the pain is much better."

Emma Yoder still stared out the windshield. "What is this medicine?" Her voice gave no clue to her interest. "My doctor has not mentioned this medicine," commented Mrs. Yoder after Ruth had given her the drug's name. "Is it new?"

Now, thought Ruth, if I can only keep her talking. She'd hit on something Mrs. Yoder would talk about. "Very new. And it isn't very expensive either."

Emma Yoder looked over at her. "My doctor's office is at the hospital. Maybe I will ask him about this new drug today."

"The hospital pharmacy probably has it," Ruth continued as they turned out onto the main highway. "You might be able to get a prescription filled while you're staying with Rudy."

"Ja, ja. Good idea."

The traffic slowed to a crawl as they approached the scene of an overturned semitractor and trailer.

"Must have been blown over last night," Ruth said.

Mrs. Yoder shook her head. "It was a bad storm. Not the worst I have seen, but a big one."

"Jacob told me that you lost your entire batch of brooders."

"We start over. More chickens." She turned and looked directly at Ruth. "You are living with your aunt again?" Ruth nodded. She was glad that traffic was tied up. It gave their conversation more time to develop. "You are not married," Mrs. Yoder stated. Ruth had to smile at the old woman's tactic. Rather than appear curious about an English, Mrs. Yoder made her question a statement.

"No, I'm not married. I teach at a university in Boston."

"University teachers do not marry" came another comment-question.

"Most of them do," Ruth answered honestly. "I've been too busy with my work until now to think of marriage."

"You waste your life on unimportant things," she told Ruth. "A proper match is not hard to find. We should concentrate on only the important things in life." She turned away from Ruth and stared out the window. There would be no more conversation.

Three small sentences had given Ruth the key to Emma Yoder's attitude toward her and her work. Ruth decided it best not to question her any further.

Ruth swallowed hard. Mrs. Yoder was Old Order Amish. A woman's place was in the home, raising children and preserving tradition. Ruth had done none of these things. She was *English.*

Emma Yoder's thoughts came through to Ruth as clearly as if she'd spoken them. Ruth wondered what Mrs. Yoder would say if she knew that Ruth was in love with her son.

The answer would probably be silence. Stony silence and indifference.

Perhaps Jacob had meant to protect her from such total rejection. Maybe he'd been trying to keep Ruth from his family because he knew how unyielding and closed they would be.

Perhaps, Ruth thought as that vague fear clutched at her again, perhaps he was trying to protect himself as well.

CHAPTER ELEVEN

It seemed as if nature was making amends for all the damage it had wrought. The fields of corn, washed clean by torrential rain, were a brighter, deeper green, and the crops appeared to grow by inches every day.

As if providing a second spring, nature renewed the land; the air was filled with the clean scent of fertile earth once again.

But, as nature tended the fields, man was forced to double his efforts. With less than six weeks left before the harvest was to begin, everyone was pressed into service. The normally slow midsummer routine of painting, repairing, and visiting was forgotten.

Barns and silos had to be built, if there was to be storage for next month's crops. Equipment necessary for the harvest had to be replaced or pieced back together.

Timing was essential; nothing save the most important work could be done. Tons of debris were left untouched; only essential areas such as barnlots, roads, and fields were cleared. Homes with roofs torn away by the wind were given only temporary cover. The recovery plan focused on survival, not comfort. Everyone's livelihood depended on the harvest. By comparison, simple creature comforts were luxuries.

"We're real lucky to get back in business so quick," Aunt Mamie said to Ruth as they worked in the greenhouse early one morning. "Not many folks as lucky as us." She sat down on a crate.

"I'll go on and see if Jacob's finished with the other tables," Ruth offered.

"When you get back, we'll start repotting these." Mamie looked around at the long rows of shallow tubs and tables that had once been filled to capacity with potted herbs. "I'm surprised we didn't lose more than we did," she went on as Ruth walked out.

In the two weeks since the storm, Ruth, like everyone else, had been caught up in a frenzy of work. The activity around the farm increased dramatically. From sun-up to sunset, buggies and trucks drove down the lane. Neighbors came to help with the greenhouse repairs, while others came to enlist Jacob's carpentry skills for repairs of their own.

The hot, humid days were long and tiring, but there was a wonderful atmosphere of friendly, excited camaraderie that made the hard work and tedious hours genuinely pleasant.

Mueller's Taxi Service became a full-fledged light hauling operation, as word of it became known. Ruth picked up and delivered everything from lemonade to sledgehammers and even towed a damaged buggy into the Honeyville Buggy Shop for repair.

The countywide emergency proved to have positive results. Not only had the storm brought the community together in mutual aid, but it allowed Ruth to slip into a comfortable, useful niche; she quickly became a recognized part of the whole community again. She worked for anyone who asked—English and Amish alike—and she began to sense a feeling of purpose and personal identity again.

Without a doubt, Ruth Mueller had come home, back to where she was meant to be. She knew it, and she liked the way it made her feel. She hadn't felt a sense of belonging in all the years she'd been away, but now, after years of self-imposed exile, she felt as if she really *fit* into the scheme of life again—not just at her aunt's farm, but within the whole of Elkhart County.

Ruth walked across the barnlot to where Jacob and two Amish boys were constructing gigantic barn trusses.

"Aunt Mamie wants to know if her plant tables are ready," she shouted above their hammering. "How's the truss business going?" Ruth asked of one of the boys.

"Fine," he replied with a smile. "We'll be ready to raise the barn when these are done."

They all stopped pounding at once. Jacob put down his hammer and stretched his arms over his head. "What did you say?" he asked her, wincing as he exercised the tight muscles.

"Tables for the greenhouse," she repeated, walking over to him. She was about to touch his arm, when Jacob gave her a quick warning look. Ruth drew her hand back instantly. Embarrassed by his silent rebuke, she tried to cover up for her near-indiscretion. "Could you all take a break for some iced tea?" she asked, feeling her face flush hot.

"I think so," answered Jacob. "The sun's fierce."

Followed by Jacob and his crew, Ruth walked toward the house. The younger men took off their straw hats and sat down in the shade of the porch, while Jacob went with Ruth into the house.

"I'll make Aunt Mamie a glass," Ruth declared, her voice reflecting irritation at Jacob's unspoken reprimand.

"I thought you understood," he whispered to her as he filled three glasses with ice.

"I was just going to touch your arm," she snapped.

"You can't be so open when there are people around." Taking the iced tea jug from the refrigerator, he filled the glasses.

Not when people are around, she thought. *Not when Amish people are around, that's what he means.*

Silently Ruth took the jug from him, and Jacob started toward the door with the drinks.

"Later," he whispered again and winked, as if *that* alone was all that was needed to erase the embarassment and confusion she felt.

The door slammed behind him, and Ruth sat down at the table. Through the screen she watched Jacob and the boys sitting on the porch steps, talking and drinking their tea.

While she'd begun to feel more a part of the community's life in the past two weeks, Ruth had begun to feel less a part of Jacob's life. Something was happening to him. He refused all but minimal contact with her when there were Amish around.

Since the storm, Amish neighbors came daily to his shop for carpentry work. Others, like the young men working with Jacob today, had volunteered to assist with various jobs and were at the farm every day working in the shop.

And when the Amish began to frequent the place in substantial numbers, Jacob immediately established new rules for his relationship with Ruth. He acted as if they hardly knew each other.

Ruth tried to understand his feelings. She knew that around other Amish he would feel a need to be more formal, less overtly friendly, to adopt once more some of the Amish customs he had grown up with, but his obsession with secrecy bothered her nonetheless. It seemed to permeate their relationship.

At first, it had added a delightful element of mystery and romance to their encounters, and Ruth had willingly participated in his design.

But now it was more than just a devilish pattern of hide-and-seek with Aunt Mamie whom, Ruth suspected, had known about their game almost from the beginning. No, now the secrecy Jacob imposed had lost its glitter.

Ruth watched as he worked and talked with the other Amish, and when they were together, Jacob was much different. She saw a kind of secret personality come forth.

His mannerisms changed and his voice was less commanding. Even his walk was different. The long, aggressive strides were shorter, more controlled. And when he spoke to her in their presence, it was in the clipped, stoic tones of the other Amish. What was happening to him? she wondered. He was becoming a different person, one she didn't know and one she wasn't sure she liked.

As Jacob and his helpers returned to their work, Ruth stood and finished pouring her aunt's iced tea. Give it time, she reminded herself patiently. Time gives us all answers. Perhaps, with time, I'll understand him.

She really wanted to understand, because she loved him. And because she loved him, Ruth struggled to be patient.

"Fannie Hostetler says their barn-raisin's gonna be this Saturday," Mamie announced as they sat down to dinner that night.

Jacob salted a pile of fresh tomato slices on his plate. "Yep, I'm going over and give them a hand."

"Mrs. Hostetler wants me to take her in to pick up her buggy in Honeyville next week," added Ruth, handing her aunt the bowl of fresh green beans. "Says she can't stand driving her boy's buggy much longer."

"Those red fuzzy dice he's got hanging from the roof make her feel a might conspicuous, I imagine," Mamie said with a chuckle.

"And I'll bet she's not too happy with the yellow shag carpeting he laid down on the floorboards," Ruth went on.

"No. Fannie's real conservative," Jacob said absently.

"You're gonna have quite a research experience Saturday," Mamie told Ruth. "Amish barn-raisin's about as much fun as there is. I told Fannie we'd make up a big batch of cole slaw for lunch that day and some sweets for the kids."

Jacob's fork stopped short of his mouth. "No need for you two to go," he said. "Putting up a barn is just hot, sweaty work."

"Hot, sweaty work for the men," Mamie informed him. "But the women get to visit. You're gonna like this, Ruthie. Ought to be . . . how many families you think'll show up, Jacob?"

"I don't know. Probably not many families. Just the men, I suspect."

Ruth noticed Jacob tense under her aunt's insistence.

"Too much other work to be done," Jacob went on. "Most of the woman and children will probably stay home and work on their own places."

"Surely not," retorted her aunt. "Some more barbeque, Ruth?" Ruth took the platter but watched Jacob's reaction more closely. "Most of the clean-up work's gonna have to wait till after the crops are in," she insisted. "And I can't imagine any Amish missin' a big barn-raisin'. You know, I'd bet half the Amish in Elkhart County show up. It'll be a lot of fun, and

Ruthie will get to see them in action. Bet she'll get to talk to a lot of new Amish she hasn't met yet."

"You're sure it's okay for us to go?" Ruth asked her aunt. "I mean, did Mrs. Hostetler invite us?"

"Invite us? Why, I told her we wouldn't miss helpin' out for anything. You know, it's the very least we can do after her husband came over and helped repair the greenhouse. No, no, Ruthie. You ought to know better. When there's work to be done, no invitation's necessary. Isn't that right, Jacob? Shouldn't we lend the Hostetlers' a hand?"

Jacob pushed his unfinished plate away and stood up. "I can handle repaying the debt by myself," he replied sullenly. "I don't think you two need to spend a whole day outside, getting sunburned, just to show your gratitude."

"Nonsense," replied Mamie, unaffected. "Some of the best fun I ever had was at barn-raisin's. And it'll be good for Ruth's research. She's never been to one."

Ruth shook her head. "I can't remember any," she replied, keeping an eye on Jacob. His face showed no sign of emotion, but his hands ran erratically up and down his work jeans.

"Think it over before you go spending twelve hours out in this ninety-degree heat," he said. And then, looking directly at Ruth, he added, "It's been a long day. I'm going on to bed."

His message was all too clear, and his words hurt her deeply. Jacob had never before missed an opportunity to be alone with her. Yet his terse declaration left no room for misunderstanding. He did not want to be with her tonight.

Long after her aunt went to sleep, Ruth lay beneath her quilted coverlet and thought of Jacob. She longed to hold him close to her, to feel his body against the full length of her and to hear his quiet breathing as he

213

lay in her arms. She wanted him to confide in her again, to explain his troubled thoughts and help her understand.

More than once she looked out her bedroom window to his apartment above the cabinet shop. Had a single light been on, Ruth knew she would have made the trek across the lot to talk with him. But no light invited her, and Ruth was left to spend the night alone.

Jacob paced the dark lane for hours, his mind a bog of conflict.

He didn't want to exclude Ruth from his life. He didn't want to hide the love he felt for her.

But something had taken command of his thinking and dictated callous thoughts to him. He hated what it was doing to him, but he was powerless against it. It made him listen. It warned him to pull away from Ruth.

Like a man drowning, Jacob was caught in the undertow of his own uncertainty.

He knew he could never love Ruth and then let her go, so he felt it would only cause him pain to give her more of himself than he already had. Why not face the truth and be done with it?

Ruth would leave him someday, and he would have to go on—here, in this place, alone except for his family and Mamie.

It had taken him too long to mend the breach between himself, his family, and the Amish community. He could not risk losing all he'd regained for a love affair that was sure to end.

If he could not love Ruth for a lifetime, then he would hold on to what love he had. No one would ever know he had loved her or that he had helped her in anyway. There could be not a single gesture, a casual word, or any sign of familiarity between them, nothing to hint of his treason. The smallest clue to his betrayal might destroy what little he had.

It was one thing to keep Ruth at arm's length on Mamie's farm when other Amish were around and then love her when they were alone once more. But what about the barn-raising? There would be so many people watching him, watching her. She would ask questions of them; they would ask questions of her. Something might give him away.

As Jacob turned to walk back to his apartment, he ran both hands through his thick hair.

Why must his life always be a series of choices? Why could he have only this *or* that, never a measure of both? Why did he have to choose again now, when he thought his life had finally stabilized?

Early that next Friday morning, Mamie climbed the stairs to Ruth's bedroom, only to find her lying wide awake.

"We need to get going by six," she told Ruth. "They'll want to get the framing done in the cool of the morning."

"I'll be right down," Ruth assured her and wearily got out of bed.

She hadn't slept well for nights. The feeling of estrangement between her and Jacob had kept churning through her mind, refusing to let her rest.

Jacob repeatedly discouraged them from attending the barn-raising. Aunt Mamie stubbornly ignored his deterrents, and Ruth was caught in the middle.

There were no more evenings in Jacob's small apartment, and no more gentle words seemed to pass between them. She remembered the one evening she'd ventured to follow Jacob out after dinner.

"Maybe if you explained to Aunt Mamie that you'd

prefer she didn't go to the barn-raising she'd understand," Ruth offered as they walked toward the cabinet shop.

"It's not that," Jacob protested. "I just think it's ridiculous that she's making such a big deal out of a construction job."

They'd reached the barn, and Jacob slowly paced back toward the stairs to his apartment.

"Why don't you tell the truth?" Ruth finally said. "You don't want *me* there."

He looked at her and then away.

"Are you afraid I'll do something to embarrass you? Is that what all these new conduct rules are all about?" Jacob didn't answer. "I know the Amish don't show affection much but I don't see what that has to do with your wanting me to stay home."

"I'm really tired, Ruth. Let's not keep rehashing this thing. You're making a mountain out of a mole hill." He gave her a quick, dispassionate kiss and turned to climb the stairs alone.

With each passing day, Jacob grew more edgy. He'd argue over the smallest things, and Ruth, unable to get him to talk seriously about what was bothering him, gave up in frustration.

"I thought we'd better eat something light this morning," her aunt commented as she came into the kitchen. "Gonna be a scorcher today." She placed three cantaloupe halves at their places on the table. "I've got toast too, and some cold boiled eggs."

Ruth poured herself a cup of coffee and walked to the window. Jacob was crossing the barnlot, tucking his denim shirt into his jeans.

"Aunt Mamie," she said quickly. "Maybe it isn't a good idea for us to go today." Her aunt turned to her and frowned. "Jacob really doesn't want us to go."

216

"Listen, Ruthie," Mamie replied calmly. "Jacob's just cranky from the heat. He's been puttin' in some long hours since the storm; he's just overtired. Don't pay him no mind." She looked through the door and saw him approaching. "Mark my words, he'll get a world o' good out o' this barn-raisin'. Give him some relaxation and socializing. You'll see, he'll be a different person tonight."

Jacob stepped on to the porch. Mamie put one finger to her lips and nodded wisely at Ruth.

"Mornin', Jacob Yoder," Mamie said cheerfully as he came in. "It's a fine mornin' for a barn-raisin'. Coffee?"

"Sure," he replied, giving her a quick kiss on the cheek. He looked at Ruth and produced a smile—the first one she'd seen in days. "You ladies are lookin' lovely this A.M. All fancied up for the fun."

His words did not come out as naturally as he'd hoped, but at least *he* was back in control.

Wagons loaded with families, picnic baskets, and tool boxes, topless buggies filled to overflowing with frisky teenagers, and seniors in their black box carriages jammed the road to the Hostetler farm.

It was just after six A.M., but the sun had climbed above the treetops to reheat the dewy landscape. Clouds of fine white mist hung over the fields; the thick, early-morning air echoed with excited voices and the constant pounding of horseshoes on pavement.

Ruth joined the procession behind Jacob. Her minivan, packed with Mamie and her assortment of delicacies, followed slowly behind the trailer loaded with barn trusses pulled by Jacob's larger truck.

"See? Didn't I tell you?" Her aunt chortled in delight. "Nobody's gonna miss a barn-raisin'."

"I wish we weren't driving a car," Ruth replied. She

felt rather conspicuous surrounded by the horse traffic and she wished she could be riding to the festivities aboard one of the hay wagons up front.

"I'll drive, if you like," offered her aunt. "You can hop right out and hitch a ride." Ruth gave her a grin but shook her head. "Nobody'd mind," Mamie insisted.

The idea was tempting, but Ruth just chuckled. "Have to remember my professional image," she declined, grinning. "Hitching a ride wouldn't be very dignified."

"Dignified, phooey." Her aunt laughed. "If I was ten years younger, *I'd* be up on that wagon."

The boisterous convoy thundered into the Hostetlers' barnlot and came to an orderly halt just behind the house. Beyond, where the barns had once been, the ground was barren, except for a new cement block foundation.

Without any formal direction, the mixed workforce was an immediate swarm of activity. There must have been at least a hundred fifty souls, all talking, laughing, and moving at once—in every direction.

Men and older boys began unloading and organizing toolchests, while the women and girls chattered excitedly and carried baskets and boxes full of food into the house. Children, from toddlers to six-year-olds, tussled about in mobs, screaming and shouting, already choosing up sides for a full day of uninterrupted play.

Amid the organized pandemonium, Ruth watched Jacob, assisted by several other men, start unloading the trusses. He glanced up and saw her too, but his eyes were unresponsive, empty. He looked right through her.

Ruth looked away. For another day, it seemed they would pretend to be strangers.

"Hello, Mrs. Detweiler!" called one of the Amish women as they entered the kitchen. Her wide cotton skirt swished around her bare ankles as she pushed her way across the room to where they stood. "Let me take that from you," she said, taking the picnic basket from Mamie.

"How have you been, Miss Stutzman?" asked her aunt.

"Fine, fine," the woman replied. "And is this your niece?"

Her arms wrapped around a box of canned pickles and jams, Ruth was unable to extend her hand. "Ruth Mueller," she answered. "Nice to meet you."

"What do we have here?" Mrs. Stutzman examined the box. "Pickles in that corner." She pointed behind Ruth. "Jams go there." She pointed to one of the large tables, and Ruth made her way through the crowd to deliver her cargo.

"Bring my apron on your next trip in," Mamie shouted to Ruth above the noise.

Her aunt's original contribution of "some" cole slaw had mushroomed into a wide assortment of canned delicacies, cookies, in addition to untold pounds of creamed slaw. It took three trips from the car to get it all into the kitchen.

Not knowing the organizational plan, Ruth cautiously followed her aunt's lead. She helped prepare trays of sweet rolls, bread and jellies, and carried vats of coffee, tea, and lemonade out to long plank tables that had been set up under the trees in back.

Yet, as the Amish brunch was set out, preparations for lunch began. Ruth was assigned to slicing bread.

219

Shortly after ten she was finished and excused from kitchen duty.

She hadn't seen Jacob since their arrival and was eager to find a spot where she could watch him unobserved. Several women sat in the shade on rows of boards balanced between sawhorses near the tables. Joining them, Ruth sat down on the end of the make-shift bench, certain her curiosity would be camouflaged within the attentive audience.

Nearly sixty Amishmen moved about the job site with smooth, unhurried precision, each at his own particular task predetermined by past experience and skill. They joined together often to build new homes and barns, and over the years their communal labor, rehearsed to perfection, required absolutely no supervision. Their work plan was flawless; their effort orchestrated almost intuitively.

Ruth finally located Jacob; he and eight other men were nailing wall studs into the fourth wall section. In just over four hours the crew had constructed all four wall sections. Others were preparing to hoist the first wall section into place.

"Watch the ropes and pulleys," the woman beside Ruth said unexpectedly. "They're secured to the horses. See?" She gestured to a team of four huge draft horses being lined up parallel to the framed wall section that lay flat on the ground.

"And the horses pull the wall up into place?" asked Ruth, glad the other woman had offered to explain.

"*Ja.* But the men have to guide it up. Each section's very heavy," she went on, shaking her head. "And not easy to handle. Watch. There they go now."

One man coaxed the team of horses slowly forward. The skeletal wall began to tip up on end, while fifteen men wrestled the total weight of the section into position atop one edge of the barn's foundation.

"That's my husband," added Ruth's new confidante. "He works the horses."

"He has a very difficult job there," Ruth commented.

"Yes, but others can do it just as well."

"They are all very skilled," said Ruth. "I don't believe we've met." She turned to the young woman. "My name is Ruth Mueller."

"You have a taxi. I know of you," the woman said warmly. "I am Barbara Troyer. My husband is John Troyer."

Unlike so many of the Amish Ruth had met, Barbara Troyer was a pleasant extrovert. Her voice had a soft, excited lilt, and her genuinely friendly manner let Ruth know that she did not find English people offensive or threatening.

Tall, with glossy chestnut hair and deep-brown eyes, Barbara was a natural beauty with an enchanting smile and flawless charm.

As the third wall was pulled into place, Barbara and the other spectators got up and started back to the house.

"The men will want to eat soon," she told Ruth. "When the walls are up, half of them will eat while the rest set the trusses. Men eat first," she explained. "Then the children. As soon as the little ones are fed, we will eat."

"I see," Ruth replied.

"Don't worry." Barbara chuckled as they began to carry the food out to the tables. "There's plenty for everyone."

Ruth picked up a tray of summer sausage and laughed. "Do I look that hungry?"

Clutching a big ceramic bowl of sweet pickles against her aproned body, Barbara stopped for a moment and surveyed Ruth from head to toe. "Yes, you do," she finally answered with a laugh.

The feeding, as Barbara called it, began promptly at noon. The only signal needed appeared to be the tables themselves. Stacked with fresh breads, salads, pickles, and plates of homemade meats and cheeses, twelve long tables piled with food attracted both workers and children.

"Here, you take a cookie and wait," Barbara told some of the younger children when they tried to join the men eating. "Not now, Lizzie." She picked up the toddler patiently. "Poppas eat first; they are working."

"How many children do you have?" Ruth asked her.

"Four. This is our daughter." She held the cherub-faced toddler out to Ruth, who took the little girl into her arms. "And this is Dannie. Here is Eli." As she spoke, Barbara gathered in her brood from the surrounding mob of youngsters. *"Wo ist* John?" she asked of Dannie who was not much more than six.

"Ich wisse niche." He shrugged.

"Eli?" She questioned the next eldest boy.

Eli simply pointed over to one of the lunch tables. There, beneath the rough plank table, Ruth and Barbara found three-year-old John sound asleep, oblivious to the noisy conversation of the men sitting all around him.

"Four? That's a nice family," Ruth murmured as Barbara pulled the sleeping child out from under the table.

"There will soon be five," Barbara answered. Cradling her son in her arms, she patted her slightly swollen abdomen. "Maybe six, if we have twins like my sister. You are not married, Ruth?" she asked as they settled on the ground with the children to wait their turn at lunch.

"No," Ruth replied, surprised at the wistful tone of her voice.

"But you like children?"

Lizzie offered Ruth a bite of her sticky cookie and Ruth obliged with a smile. "I love children," she answered through a mouthful of the oatmeal and raisins.

"You will have a big family, like me," announced Barbara smiling. "John and I want many children. As many as we can."

"But can so many children all have their own farms?"

Barbara shifted her sleeping son onto the ground. "That is not for us to know," she answered thoughtfully. "When the time comes we will do what must be done."

With the children fed and the men all back to work, the women finally settled down at the tables.

"Aunt Mamie, I'd like you to meet Barbara Troyer," said Ruth as they joined her aunt for lunch.

"Yes, yes. You were a Raber, weren't you?"

Barbara nodded. "I married John Troyer."

The large crowd had been in constant motion all morning, and it wasn't until Ruth sat down beside her aunt that she first saw Emma Yoder.

"Ruthie," Mamie began, "you haven't met Jacob's mother. Emma, this is my niece."

"Miss Mueller." Mrs. Yoder nodded politely without giving any indication that they had ever met before.

"Mrs. Yoder," responded Ruth. The wall between them was still intact, but Emma Yoder's silence did little to relieve Ruth's sudden anxiety.

In the weeks since their unplanned meeting, Ruth had tucked her earlier fears away in a vacant corner of her mind. So much had happened: the repair work, the

223

hauling, and Jacob's bewildering change in attitude had completely occupied her every thought. Now, faced with an unexpected reunion, Ruth felt her fears rekindled.

Was this why he'd been so adamant about them not coming? Was Jacob *that* concerned about her meeting his mother?

Well, she thought with a flash of courage, *I've already made contact with Emma Yoder, and neither one of us was injured* or *enlightened by the experience.*

As Ruth expected, Jacob's mother did not speak to her again through out the luncheon.

When the food was cleared away, Ruth wandered back to her seat near the worksite. Barbara, occupied with Lizzie, promised to join her later.

The men had already set several trusses across the top of the open walls. And to Ruth's surprise, Jacob was perched on the peak of one wooden truss hammering a ridge board into place.

"You are interested in carpentry too, I see."

The deep male voice drew her attention momentarily away from Jacob. Looking up, Ruth discovered that Bishop Stoltzfus had joined her on the makeshift bench.

"I've never seen anything quite like it," she admitted, trying not to show how nervous Jacob's balancing act was making her.

"I don't suppose the people in the city ever build buildings?" He took his pipe from his pants pocket and filled it with tobacco.

"They are constantly building something in Boston," she answered, watching Jacob creep his two-hundred-pound body along the fragile ridge board to the next rafter. "But not like this. Isn't that dangerous?" she asked as the ridge board sagged beneath Jacob's weight.

"He knows what he's doing," the bishop said. "Everyone has a job to do. His job is tying the trusses together. No more important or dangerous than another job. The work is equally hard for all." He lit the tobacco and crossed his legs. "So, are you still doing this research you talked to me about?"

"Yes and no," she replied flatly. "I've had more important things to do since the storm."

The bishop's eyebrows arched slowly. "So I have noticed," he replied, pipe between his teeth.

"I don't understand everything about the Amish," Ruth began, not looking directly at him. "I'm sure there are things that I will never understand. Yet I'm fascinated by your people, Bishop. I wish all peoples were as dedicated to the land and their community as the Amish. It would make the world a better place to live for everyone."

To her amazement, he nodded in agreement. "This is the way all men are meant to live," he told her quietly. "We are examples of what should be. We take care of one another and dedicate our labor to the earth. These are the only things that are important."

"But how long can you go on like this, untouched by worldly ways?"

"Forever," he answered firmly. "The Amish will always be different. Our plainness will remain a sign of our decision to live a simple life. We will not be enticed to change. What more could we want? What more can the world offer us than this?"

Ruth looked him squarely in the eye but could not find the words to answer. She understood what he meant.

"We are a people who know the value of discipline and sacrifice. No one goes hungry; no one need be

225

lonely or unsheltered. Because we live the right life, we do not want. Belonging is a precious thing, Ruth Mueller. These people know they belong. Can the world offer us that?"

CHAPTER TWELVE

"You've got it all wrong, Mamie," said T. Monroe. "Them Amish didn't come over here and help you out to be neighborly. They're only interested in protectin' their investment."

His voice sliced through the night air, carrying the razor-sharp words out to where Ruth sat on the porch.

"They only come to give that Jacob a hand, 'cause this place is gonna be half his when you're gone. Amish don't give a damn 'bout your problems; they only help their own."

"Your talkin' through your hat, Monroe," Mamie grumbled in reply.

"Oh, yeah. That's easy for you to say. You won't be 'round to see them Amish take over this farm. When you're gone they'll carve this place up into a dozen homesteads. Quick as that!" His fingers snapped a rude accent.

"Ruth won't let that happen," replied Mamie, her voice clearly exasperated.

"Is that so? What's Ruth know 'bout farmin'? How's she gonna keep tabs on what's happening here? Huh? Travelin' all over the world like she does.

What's she gonna be able to do? Naw, she can't hold them Amish off. That Jacob'll make her an offer, and that'll be the end of it."

Even at a distance, Ruth could hear T. Monroe's wheezing in more breath.

"You made a bad decision, Mamie Detweiler. You should've never made that Amishman a partner. Bad decision."

Rising from the porch swing, Ruth tuned out Sullivan's words. She'd put up with his nasty disposition all day, and enough was enough. Ruth didn't care if Monroe ever came back for Sunday dinner, and from the tone of her response, it sounded as if Aunt Mamie didn't care either.

Another sleepless night and a long day of Monroe Sullivan's endless harping had nearly drained Ruth of her patience. Her head throbbed from tension, heat, and exhaustion. She rubbed at her temples and anxiously scanned the distance for a sign of Jacob's return.

She had to talk to him and put an end to all this.

The stress of their emotional estrangement had become unbearable.

Tonight they must talk it out. Tonight, before Ruth had to face another lonely night tied in a web of dismal half dreams and tortured by vague suspicions, she must escape that invisible prison Jacob's hard silence had condemned her to.

"I waited up for you last night," she'd said to Jacob that morning, following him from the house out to the barn.

"Most of the men stayed late," he answered. "We wanted to finish the barn."

"Jacob," she said, taking hold of his arm. "We have to talk."

His flesh was warm and tight beneath the long-sleeved shirt; he smelled deliciously of soap and shaving cream.

Just being this close to him again—unobserved, alone in the bright morning sunshine—made her weak with longing. It seemed like light-years since they'd been alone like this.

"We'll talk tonight, when I get home," he answered. His wide blue eyes, framed in deep tanned creases, were dull with fatigue.

"Why are you putting me off again?"

"I'm not putting you off," he insisted. Gently, but firmly, he took her hand from his arm. "I haven't been to visit my family in over two weeks. Don't you think I deserve a day of rest?"

Of course she did. But something in his voice told her that Jacob meant a day of rest away from her.

"If you want a rest," she told him sharply, "stay home. I won't bother you." She stepped back, glaring. "I just want to talk."

"Can't it wait until I get back?" He saw her stiffen again. "I won't be late."

Jacob looked so tired and drawn that Ruth put aside her frustration. "Okay," she replied softly, and reached up to touch his smooth, tanned cheek. "But only if we can have the whole evening to ourselves."

Unable to resist, she stepped nearer and kissed him. The hand that had caressed his cheek slid into his soft hair, and her fingers tangled through the curls of his head. She held his mouth to hers and brushed his lips with her tongue. But Jacob did not yield to her persuasion. The embrace she longed for did not appear. He did not reach out to her. He did not offer to hold her.

"I won't be late." His breath, broken and shallow, sailed along her cheek as he pulled away.

Girls in organdy caps and crisp gray dresses walked along the dusty road. Shiny black buggies with drivers decked in Sunday best appeared from every farm lane.

Summer twilight. Bullfrogs. A hint of rain in the air, carried on a cool evening breeze.

Yet Jacob Yoder saw only the narrow road before him. He heard only his own heart beating against his chest.

Jacob could no longer control that callous voice within. Anger swept over him.

Ruth was not to be trusted. She was drawing too much attention to herself—and to him.

The buggy rolled down the lane and across the barnlot. Ruth waved, but Jacob did not look up. Quickly she descended the porch steps and followed him to the barn.

"I saved you some strawberry shortcake from lunch," she told him as he climbed from the carriage. Trying with all her might, Ruth wanted to appear as neutral and unthreatening as possible.

She held out her arms to greet him with a simple kiss and a hug.

"Watch the horse," he grumbled. "He's been spooky all day."

Immediately Ruth backed away, and Jacob walked around her to unhitch the horse.

"Would you like me to bring your shortcake out here?" she asked, shaken by his stiff rebuff, but managing to remain calm.

"I'll get it later."

The tension between them was even worse than it had been that morning. The air was charged with emotional static. Even Rainbow sensed it and danced nervously as Jacob took hold of the bridle to lead him into the barn.

"I see you got the latest *Budget.*" Ruth picked up the Amish newspaper off the buggy seat, took it in with her, and sat down in the haymow next to the horse stall. Scanning the paper, she held her frustration in check.

They had to talk this out rationally. Anger would only muddle the situation more. She must hold on to her equilibrium, remain objective.

"Here's an account of the Rabers' trip to the Grand Canyon," she said, holding out the paper to show him. "Would you mind if I borrowed this issue for a day or two? I'd like to make some notes for my research file —maybe get a copy of Mrs. Raber's article."

"Haven't you done enough research already this weekend?"

"I haven't done any work on my paper for weeks— not since the storm."

"That's not what I hear," he countered. "I hear your little missions of mercy have been panning out in plenty of research data—just like that fake taxi service of yours."

"What are you talking about, Jacob?"

He whipped the brush along Rainbow's flanks. "I'm talking about going out to my family's farm and trying to cozy up to my mother. You didn't need to be out there. I told you, you weren't needed. Can't you take a hint, Ruth? *I didn't want you out there.*"

"I knew that, Jacob. And I never intended to go against your wishes. I didn't do it behind your back— purposefully. I wanted to tell you what happened . . ."

"Then why didn't you?" he demanded.

"Because I was afraid you'd misunderstand—that you'd react just like you *are.* You've barely been civil to me lately," Ruth retorted in confusion. "You won't explain what's bothering you—"

"What's bothering me? *You*, that's what's bothering me. And this damned research of yours," he snapped, cutting her off. "Great social scientist—out studying Amish. Not *people*—oh, no. You're studying Amish—some archaic little relics of American life. They're no more than fossils to you. It's like you have this invisible microscope with you all the time, and you use it to *examine* a sample of Amish you can find in the county. Well, these are people, Ruth. *Real live people*. They have feelings; they have rights. *I* have rights. Or don't you care? I have a right to privacy. My family has a right to its privacy. But that isn't important to you, is it? You're a social scientist—and you think you can do anything you please—as long as it's done in the name of science. Right? What do I have to do to get you to *back off?*" Suddenly, everything about him was foreign. His voice—raspy and sharp—was someone else's voice, and his face was an alien mask of baffling resentment that stunned her. "You'll use any excuse to pry and probe—even a phony, good-neighbor approach."

"You're blowing this all out of proportion. Surely your mother told you that I went out there because Bishop Stoltzfus asked me to. I took her in to sit with Rudy at the hospital."

"But it was a great excuse for another research interview, wasn't it? And you just couldn't resist. That's why you didn't tell me. You knew I'd see right through your ploy. Angel of mercy, my foot. Worked out pretty good for you, didn't it? Get an old woman trapped in a car and roust her with a lot of questions." He was nearly shouting now.

"Is that what she told you?" shot back Ruth. "Did she say I rousted her?"

"She didn't have to; I've seen how you work. I could fill in the blanks on my own."

231

"Tell me what she *said,* Jacob," Ruth insisted, barely holding on to her anger as she stood to face him.

"*You* are not privy to my private conversations. My private life—my family—is *not* open to your research. Or can't you understand that? There's no way to get away from you and that research, is there? You just won't give me—or anyone else—any breathing room."

He went on brushing the horse with angry strokes. "I can't even go to a barn-raisin' without you tagging along. Bet you got some real juicy research done yesterday, didn't you? Don't you ever give it a rest, Ruth?"

"What are you talking about? I only went to the Holstetlers' yesterday because Aunt Mamie wanted me to. I didn't do any research; I didn't interview anybody."

"You didn't? Then why were you glued to Barbara Troyer all day? Everybody saw it; you didn't get ten feet from her all day."

"Barbara Troyer started talking to *me;* I didn't initiate the conversation. She's very friendly, that's all. She's more open than most Old Order Amish."

"Don't you ever stop with that research lingo?" Jacob volleyed. "Old Order Amish! That's just how you see people—by scientific categories. How do I fit into your research? What category have you slipped me into?"

"I don't categorize people. You know that I don't think that way."

"I fell for that pure and noble routine of yours once," he lashed out indignantly. "But I'm savvy to it now." Slapping the horse on the rump, Jacob threw down the grooming brush.

Ruth approached him warily. "Why are you judging me like this? I don't understand."

"You don't understand," he mimicked. "Well, see if you can understand this: I'm tired of being used. I'm sick and tired of being your patsy. I've known plenty of English women like you, Ruth. They were only interested in what they wanted and couldn't care less *how* they got it. With you, it's this Ph.D. crap. And what's in it for me?" His eyes flamed with emotion. "Was I supposed to be satisfied with all the sex I could handle in a year? Is that how you reward your informants—roll 'em in the hay twice a day?"

Her hand split the air and cracked against his solid jaw. Jacob's words plunged deep into Ruth's heart, wounding her very soul.

"Me? *Using* you?" she spat. "That's insane. You've never been my informant; you've done next to nothing in that department. Oh, no, Jacob Yoder. You won't throw this off on me. Your little game of turning the blame won't work with me."

Neither of them moved, locked together by the searing voltage of each other's eyes.

"You're *tired* of me," she seethed. "And you aren't man enough to say it. Apparently I've lost my usefulness to you. What was I, Jacob? Just some English who was good enough to bed, until something better came along to wed?"

Her voice smoldered with contempt. "You worked awfully hard at keeping our relationship hidden. Afraid, were you, that your fine Amish family would find out about us? Have you found someone more acceptable now, and so it's time to break it off between us?"

Jacob looked away. His fear and confusion had been spent in a single burst of mindless retribution. Shamed by his own words, Jacob could not look into Ruth's anguished eyes.

"So it's true then, Jacob." Ruth appraised his reaction. "I'm right. There is someone else more acceptable. Well, let me tell you this, Jacob Yoder. Listen carefully. You knew—that first night we made love—that I wasn't experienced with men. Maybe if I *had* been more experienced, I would have recognized you for what you really are. But I didn't, and now I have to live with the results."

Tears began to form in her eyes; her throat tightened with the pain of what she was about to say.

"Fine. Now I'll have to live with that mistake. But I will never barter my body for anything—or anybody. I do not use people. What I felt for you was genuine, and don't you ever forget it."

Without another word, Ruth walked past him and out the door.

Ruth was seized with pain she'd never known before. A hostage, held and tortured against her will, she lived out those next few weeks in constant agony.

The heart-pain clutched at her chest and made her breath come in ragged, uneven gasps whenever she saw Jacob—and *always* when she thought about him. Her heart actually ached.

At night, alone and crying, Ruth would put the palm of her hand on her breast to try to soothe the awful, dull throbbing deep inside. But the pain refused to leave her. It haunted her, growing stronger every day as she worked to come to terms with the reality of Jacob's rejection.

Jacob had seemed to be all she'd ever wanted in a man. Powerful, yet gentle; independent, but committed. Caring, hardworking, fun-loving. The thoughts were endless, and they drummed in her mind day and night.

Finally she admitted to herself why she had fallen so desperately in love with Jacob. Because he seemed whole—utterly, totally real. But now it seemed Jacob had never been what she believed him to be. And that realization hurt Ruth more than anything else.

Jacob had deceived her, just as Dr. Phillip Lane had. They were mirror images, emotional twins separated only by place and circumstance, but motivated by a single, common thing: self-interest.

Phillip Lane had used her to further his career, and when someone else came along who could benefit him even more, he had dismissed her.

Once again Ruth had let herself be duped by her own illusions. She wanted Phillip Lane to be more than he was, so she made him fit her mental image of what he could be.

But Lane had given Ruth much less to work with than Jacob Yoder had. Phillip Lane never hid his hasty, unpleasant disposition, and, to his credit, Lane never encouraged Ruth's delusions. Certainly he had not encouraged her affections.

There had been a measure of civility to Phillip Lane's manipulation. Yet, in Jacob's deception, there was no such corresponding element of redemption.

Jacob had falsified himself to procure her love until he had no further need of her. Then he fabricated an ugly excuse to dissolve their relationship.

Cold, numbing anger replaced her agony.

For days, silent rage festered inside her, infecting every thought, every memory of him with vile suspicion.

If Jacob had used her, then surely he must be using Aunt Mamie as well. Perhaps he was trying to gain complete control of the old woman's land, she thought. Ruth tried to dismiss these thoughts, but found she could not. They haunted her for hours.

"Ruthie's awful sick," Mamie told Jacob the next morning. "I knew somethin' was wrong when she came in last night. All pale and trembling. Why, she's been up half the night. Probably couldn't sleep. Must be one of those stomach viruses," she diagnosed, watching Jacob closely. He looked drawn, tired. His eyes, like Ruth's, were rimmed in red, and his hand was unsteady as he lifted his coffee mug.

Jacob couldn't comment, and he just went on picking at his breakfast.

"You not feelin' good too?" Mamie finally asked, touching his forehead. "Any fever?"

"I'm okay," he managed to assure her. "Tired. That's all. Just tired."

Mamie's sweet, smiling eyes and tender concern only made him feel worse. The guilt was compounded by realizing that he'd hurt Mamie when he hurt Ruth. The old woman's niece was her world—her pride—the cherished daughter of her heart.

How could he have done anything so vile to them?

Within the week, Ruth began a slow reentry into the farm's daily routine.

Jacob knew that he must face her again, but their first meal together was more difficult than even he had anticipated.

It was breakfast and Ruth looked oddly fragile— thinner than the week before. She wore her faded cut-offs and a school T shirt; her lovely hair, the color of grain, was double-braided in pigtails.

"Good morning," she said quietly to him as she came in and sat down. Her eyes, sullen and gray, forced him to reply.

"Are you feeling better?" His words came out hollow and flat, not as he meant them at all.

Ruth's eyes darted to Mamie standing by the stove, her back to them, and then back to Jacob.

"Better," she answered, then frowned.

"I—"

Ruth shook her head no and looked over at her aunt again. She was telling him that she didn't want Mamie to know what had happened.

Slowly, Jacob nodded in compliance. How did he ever doubt Ruth? he wondered. Even now, after what had happened, her thoughtfulness prevailed.

Their work increased in proportion to the heat. The sticky heat of July became an unyielding blanket of torrid humidity in the early weeks of August. The air was thick and damp; it hung over the earth like an incandescent cloud.

With the necessary repair work completed, everyone went to work on the harvest.

Jacob spent the days far from the house, withdrawn in thought. The twelve-hour work days at hard labor gave him little peace of mind; his seclusion only brought more time to reflect on his transgressions.

But distance, heat, and work could not remove the memory of Ruth's face that last night in the barn from his mind. He would never forget how her sad green eyes searched his—confused and anguished. Jacob saw those eyes each time he tried to sleep.

Preoccupied with her daily work, Mamie seemed unaware of any problems, and that was how Ruth wanted it to be.

Ruth returned to her own work routine, while making a pointed effort to reopen normal communications with Jacob. They would have to remain friends, she told herself, even if they would never be lovers again. That much was necessary if they were to live in such close proximity.

Her plan worked. Jacob slowly began to respond to her openness, and their kitchen conversations became much as they had been. They talked about crops, her aunt's blackberry preserves, and Ruth's research. The only missing elements were the late-night retreats to Jacob's apartment and the easy, playful twists of coded conversation that had become their second language.

Yet, as the weeks passed, Ruth found it more and more difficult to concentrate on revenge. She couldn't look at Jacob without remembering what had once been. Even though she went upstairs early each night on the pretense of working, she couldn't avoid the thoughts of him as easily as she could avoid being alone with him.

Jacob's charisma was astonishing, she reasoned. No wonder Aunt Mamie had been bewitched by him. Even Ruth, shattered by his rejection, still dreamed of loving him.

On a Friday afternoon late in August, as Mamie tended to the tourist customers at the greenhouse, Ruth received a call from Goshen College. There would be an opening in their anthropology department after the next school year. Ruth was offered the job, based on her pending Ph.D. She gratefully accepted.

The job secured, certain she could remain on the farmstead and still have her career, Ruth deemed that steamy Friday night in August the appropriate time to bring up the farm's future management with her aunt.

They ate later than usual that night. Weekend sightseers had streamed into the farm until evening. The last few weeks of summer break, before school began, had brought them out in droves.

Jacob, hastily trying to beat the rain forecasted for

the weekend, stayed out in the fields until dark, picking corn.

It was nine o'clock before they finished dinner and Jacob said good night. Carrying dishes to the sink, Ruth watched him stroll across the barnlot.

"I sure will be glad for Labor Day to get here," Mamie told her niece. "Weekend traffic slows down after school starts. People are too busy to travel, what with shopping for kids' clothes and gettin' organized for school."

"Your business has grown so," Ruth told her. "You could use a hand 'round this place. I don't see how you keep up with the canning, the greenhouse, the laundry and all."

"Careful, Miss Ruth. If I didn't know better, I'd think *you* were volunteerin'."

Ruth put down her dish towel and leaned against the cabinet. "That's funny," she answered. "Because that's exactly what I'm doing."

Mamie's hands, covered in soapy froth, stopped moving, and she looked at her niece.

"I'm staying, Aunt Mamie. Permanently," Ruth said with a broad smile.

"Oh! Ruth!" Her aunt screamed. Her arms, wet and foamy, flew around Ruth's neck. "Oh, my. That's wonderful, honey. Oh, my. How? I mean, what made you decide?" Tears glistened on her flushed cheeks, and her body trembled as she held Ruth in a bear hug.

"Let's sit down," Ruth said with a grin. She handed Mamie the towel and guided her to the table. "Want a cup of tea to settle your nerves?" she teased.

"Tea? Heavens, no. An occasion like this deserves my elderberry wine." Crying and chuckling, Mamie beat the soap bubbles from her arms and hands with the towel. "Get the *big* glasses," she instructed Ruth with a giggle.

"Want that wine on ice?"

"Nope," replied her aunt. "I'll take mine straight, thanks."

Ruth filled two water glasses with her aunt's home-made wine and returned to the table.

"Now, tell me," Mamie began. "What brought this all about?" It's Jacob, of course, she thought. I knew it! In the excitement of the moment, Mamie Detweiler forgot how she'd been worrying over both of them this last month. They've patched things up. A little lover's quarrel, that's all it was. "Tell me *everything*," her aunt insisted. "Don't leave out a thing."

"Well, you know I've been doing a lot of research over at the college . . ."

"Yes, yes?"

"And in June, I was talking with the head of their anthropology department, and asked him if he would accept my application. He said he didn't expect an opening, but he'd keep me in mind."

"Way back in June, huh? Why didn't you say something about it?"

"I didn't want to get your hopes up," Ruth admitted. "I mean, without a job at Goshen, I would have been forced to go back to Boston."

"But you don't need a job to stay," her aunt came back cautiously. "This is your home."

"I know *that*," Ruth answered, patting her aunt's hand. "But this way, everything works out perfectly."

"Oh?" Mamie put down her glass, preparing for the big news.

"You see, I can teach in the fall and winter, when the farm work is minimal, and help you manage in the summer. And," she added seriously, "my teaching salary can give us a financial cushion in case we hit a bad crop year."

Mamie nodded slowly. "That's a wonderful idea,

Ruth. But what exactly are you trying to tell me? Are you gonna quit travelin' and doin' research?"

"I've made some important decisions, Aunt Mamie," Ruth continued gravely. "I'm honestly tired of all the expeditions and university politics. I know I'll be happy in a smaller setting, like Goshen College. Happier there, and happy here. I love this farm, but I didn't realize how much I missed the whole Elkhart County until I came back this time. This is where my heart is." Tears misted in her eyes as she thought of how really perfect it would have been if only Jacob . . . "I sound like a Pollyanna again, don't I?" she said to disguise the meaning of her tears.

"Not at all," replied her aunt.

Ruth smiled and wiped a tear from her cheek with the back of her hand.

"We must tell Jacob," said her aunt. Ruth gave her no other choice. If she wouldn't introduce him into the conversation, Mamie would have to. *Where did Jacob fit into all of this? And why was Ruth still crying?*

"I don't think we should do that right now," Ruth replied stiffly. "I won't start my teaching assignment at Goshen for another year. And in that time, while I'm finishing my Ph.D., I want to learn all I can about managing the farm from you *and,* especially, from Jacob. When I have my feet on the ground and have a better understanding of how it all works then we can tell him I'm staying."

Mamie frowned. "But, Ruthie, Jacob and I—and now you—we're all partners. And partners don't keep secrets from one another."

"I know we're partners with Jacob, Aunt Mamie," Ruth began slowly. "But perhaps it's not the best thing for the farm or for any of us."

"What do you mean, Ruth? Jacob Yoder's been a

godsend to this farm." Her aunt's weathered face twisted with disbelief.

"I know he's done a lot for the farm." Ruth tried to start over. Her ideas were suddenly elusive, as if she'd not thought them through at all. "But the reasons may not be what he's made you believe they were." The sentence was stiff and jumbled. Ruth's breath became shallow. "Remember what Monroe Sullivan said that last time he was here for Sunday dinner?"

Mamie gasped. "My Lord, Ruth, you haven't been taking T. Monroe Sullivan seriously. Good heavens!"

"No, I didn't—not at first—but there may be a grain of truth in what he says." Ruth was panicking. Nothing was coming out as she'd planned it; her mouth refused to form the sentences that she'd rehearsed for so many weeks in her mind.

Her aunt gulped down a healthy swallow of elderberry wine and steadied herself with one hand against the table. "If there's a grain of truth to T. Monroe's reasoning," her aunt muttered, "you'll need a microscope to find it."

"But he might be right," Ruth persisted with growing disorientation. "He said I might have to sell my share of this farm someday. I don't know anything about farming techniques or management, and if I hadn't gotten this position at Goshen, I'd have been halfway round the world most of the time. Jacob Yoder knew he'd eventually be in complete control of the farm, and maybe that's what he always had in mind."

Ruth suddenly stopped talking, her eyes filled with tears, and she looked away.

"Cry it out, Ruth. Go on, sweetie. Let it all come out." Mamie stood next to the chair, cradling Ruth's head against the folds of her soft cotton apron. "You'll feel better if you let it out. You'll see," she cooed softly, stroking Ruth's hair. "Okay?" she asked, kissing her head.

"Tell me about it," her aunt offered. "You can talk it out with me."

Ruth looked up weakly. "He said I *used* him, Aunt Mamie. He said that all I cared about was *using* people. But he's been *using* me." She blushed at the meaning of her words. "And I believe he's using you too."

"I see," her aunt replied. So little had told her so much. "Will you listen to what I have to say?" she asked. Ruth nodded silently. "I'm no anthropologist, mind you. I never even graduated high school, so I'm no great intellect, I guess. But I've lived a long time, Ruth Marie. And in seventy-odd years, I've come to know people."

Mamie stopped and handed Ruth a rumpled tissue from her pocket. "I won't ask all the details of what happened between you two. That's none of my business. But you must believe me when I say that I know Jacob Yoder like the back of my hand. As well as I know you, Ruth. And there's not a treacherous bone in his body."

"He said some terrible things, Aunt Mamie." Ruth sniffled.

"Sometimes even good people say terrible things, Ruth. You have no way of knowing what's going on in his mind. We don't even know what's going on between him and the other Amish. Think of what Jacob must have gone through to get back in good with his people. He's a man walking a tightrope, Ruth, and his relationship with you may have thrown him off balance."

"He didn't want me at the barn-raising—or meeting his immediate family."

"That makes sense," her aunt reasoned. "His mother is a tough old Amish bird who'd like nothing better than to have Jacob safely back in the fold. Can't you see how he must have felt?"

Ruth did see. Now. She had needed her aunt's uncluttered perspective weeks ago.

"Give him time, Ruth. He'll work it out. Forgive his anger. Why, already you two are speakin' again."

Ruth gave her aunt a wary look. "You knew?"

Mamie laughed and picked up her wine glass. "Didn't have to be no Einstein to see you and Jacob were on the spritz." She chuckled, pleased with herself. "You used to pull that same stomach flu routine when you were little and didn't want to go to school. Remember? Just put two and two together, that's all."

Ruth laughed too. "I guess you're right. We are talking again," she mused, feeling more optimistic.

"Things will work out," her aunt responded positively. "You two are gonna be terrific partners one day."

CHAPTER THIRTEEN

"I want you to just stay in bed today. Rest, take your medicine and stay warm." Ruth fluffed Aunt Mamie's pillow. "Keep that heating pad on your shoulder. Don't turn it up, now. Not too hot."

Mamie smiled valiently and pulled the quilt up under her arms. "Don't fret, Ruthie," she said in a tiny voice. "I'll be fine. Now, you go on. There'll be a big crowd in town today. I'll be good as new tomorrow."

Ruth frowned. "We'll talk about *that* tomorrow." She kissed Mamie's forehead and started to the bedroom door. "If you need anything . . ."

"I know, I know. Now, go on. You and Jacob have got a lot of work to do before the market opens."

"Okay. Bye bye." Ruth smiled, walked out, and closed the door behind her.

The weekend tourist trade had kept Ruth and her old aunt on the run for two solid days. As forecasted, it had rained steadily both days, but the dreary weather hadn't slowed their greenhouse business in the least. As a matter of fact, it seemed like the rain pulled *more* people than usual into the greenhouse.

Ruth had wanted to find a way to talk with Jacob all weekend, but she never found the right timing for it. If she wasn't busy, he was with customers of his own in the cabinet shop. On Sunday, they had company for dinner and Jacob stayed late visiting his family.

Then, after an exhausting weekend, her aunt had insisted on taking advantage of Monday's milder, sunny weather, and Ruth helped her all day doing the laundry. And, as if that were not enough for one day, Mamie cajoled her into preparing a huge load of herbs and spices for Tuesday's market at Shipshewana.

"Last big market day of the season," her aunt explained. "Got to get everything cleared out, so we can start a new crop."

Ruth tried to get her to slow down, but Mamie wouldn't hear of it. No wonder her arthritis had flared up, and she couldn't get out of bed this morning.

"Aunt Mamie must be feeling terrible," Ruth told Jacob as she walked out to the van moments later. Pulling on her jacket, Ruth inspected their inventory of dried and potted herbs. It looked as if her chance to talk with Jacob had finally materialized. Ruth tried to appear calm in spite of her rising anticipation.

"Some rest and that medicine will have her back on her feet in no time," he assured her, placing the last flat of small potted plants in the van and closing the door. "She just can't keep pushing herself like she does."

Mamie listened intently at the bedroom door. There was muffled conversation outside the house. The van's cargo door swished shut. One car door slammed, and then the other. The engine started with a powerful roar, and they pulled away.

Mamie giggled, stretched, and glanced at the clock. "Good heavens," she exclaimed. "It's five-thirty already." She plucked a fresh gingham dress from the closet and started to dress.

Jacob was honestly concerned over Mamie's debilitating arthritis attack, but he wasn't really prepared to be drafted into market service.

"I hate to admit it," Mamie had said the night before, "but I just know I can't make it to market in the morning." For effect, she rubbed one arm with tender fingers and winced appropriately. "Could you two handle it? Just this once?"

Jacob remembered looking over at Ruth, wondering if she'd chance spending a whole day alone with him. But to his surprise, Ruth agreed without hesitation.

"Do you think we can handle it, Jacob?" Ruth asked pleasantly. "It's a pretty tough job."

"Well, it's too wet to work the fields," he said, wishing there was a logical excuse to avoid the situation. "But I guess I can give it a go."

In all the time since their terrible argument, Jacob

had not been able to gather the courage to get Ruth alone and apologize. He'd sorted out his anger and imaginary fears weeks ago, accepting full responsibility for his acts. Now all he wanted was for their relationship to hold at a reasonable distance.

A mile from the farm, Jacob pulled the van to a stop and turned off the ignition. He turned to Ruth.

"The market's no place to talk," he began softly, looking her squarely in the eyes. "Don't be afraid," he added quickly, "I'm not going to shout at you or anything. I just want to tell you how sorry I am about what happened. About what I said. I owe you an apology. I hope that you can accept it."

Ruth reached out and touched his arm. The fine texture of his skin and the fresh scent of his body were overwhelming. His eyes—the loving blue eyes she adored—reflected his sincerity. Emotion washed over her. Ruth had longed for just such a moment. But now the impact was more than she could handle. Voiceless, she could only nod in mute understanding.

"There's no excuse for what I did," Jacob went on, moving his arm away from her hand. He spoke without a trace of the emotion he held inside. "I know that. And there isn't any way that I can erase what I said from your memory. All I can say is that I'm sorry." Jacob looked away and leaned a heavy shoulder against the seat.

"I'm sorry too," Ruth said evenly. She had hoped he would kiss her—hold her once more, and finally reunite them. But the wounds were still open, and she didn't force more from him than Jacob seemed able to give just then.

"I'd like us to be . . ." Jacob looked out the window, forcing the words he wanted to say back down. "Can't we be civilized with each other? I know we don't agree on much of anything, but that doesn't mean we have to keep clawing at each other's throats."

"No. It doesn't." Ruth had expected a much different reconciliation. Disappointed that he maintained such emotional distance, she could feel tears mounting. She swallowed hard, reassuring herself that time would bring them back to where they'd once been. "We can't forget all that happened," she said, "but let's try to put it aside."

Jacob looked over at her. "I think that's a good idea," he replied, and then he started the van again.

Every Tuesday of the season, from dawn to dusk, great hordes of discount hunters invaded Shipshewana's farm market to duel the gypsy merchants for bargains.

Acres of open ground, right in the center of town, had been set aside for the weekly competition, with each registered merchant allotted a specific plot from which to hawk his wares.

Local farmers sold their produce surrounded by flea market pros with their tables of trinkets and boisterous nomads with their mobile food trailers.

Mamie's booth was in the very center of the market. A choice location, she was always quick to point out, that she had attained through hard work and market seniority.

By the time they unloaded the van and organized the booth, the first surge of buyers had arrived.

"Do you need me?" Jacob asked Ruth.

"No. I guess not." There was really only room for one person at a time in the tight space, what with all the plant flats and boxes stacked around.

"I want to see what's available, before it gets picked over," he answered.

Jacob gave her a reassuring smile and turned, disappearing in the crowd. Nothing in the world meant more to Ruth just then than seeing Jacob really smile again. She'd missed the bold, spirited curve of his full mouth and the deep, hearty sound of his laugh as much as she'd missed his loving.

The day passed quickly, and Ruth was busy with many enthusiastic customers. She found that when she was working she was very happy, but every time she thought of Jacob or caught sight of him in the crowd, a feeling of sadness would overwhelm her. Ostensibly they had apologized and resolved their differences, but Ruth doubted that she'd ever know the touch of his lips on hers again.

The bargaining hordes retreated that evening in a crush of wagons, concession trailers, buggies, and cars that snaked slowly out of town, clogging the narrow, two-lane road with outbound traffic. Everyone—merchants and bargaineers alike—had abandoned the market simultaneously.

"Looks like Shipshewana's being evacuated," Ruth commented. "Or it could be Boston at rush hour, if there were more buildings and less horse traffic."

Jacob leaned back, smiling slightly in response to her words. Their progress became slower until finally the string of traffic ground to a complete stop.

Just then a car whipped around them in the other lane, and Jacob craned to watch as it moved parallel to the traffic lined up, speeding ahead in the oncoming lane.

Ruth cringed. "Did he make it?"

"I guess," Jacob replied, annoyed. "Out-of-state plates. What a jerk. Doesn't he know what could happen, driving that way around horses? Geez."

Ruth shuddered at the thought of what could happen if a reckless driver like that came upon a slow-moving buggy.

"Want to stop off for a cup of coffee or something?" he asked her. "There's a place just up ahead where we can wait out this mess."

The restaurant was packed with other people who'd had the same idea. It was noisy and smoky, but better than sitting for thirty minutes in a traffic jam.

Silently they drank coffee and listened to the conversations around them. Once Ruth tried to start a conversation of their own, but Jacob shook his head. "Too noisy. Can't hear you," he answered.

Ruth smiled and looked down at her cup. *Don't push,* she thought, and tried not to feel too discouraged.

Finally they left the restaurant and started for home.

The last of the traffic thinned at the state highway, and they cruised effortlessly toward home.

An orange and crimson sunset flamed in the western sky, setting the trees and fields ablaze with color. By the time they turned onto the gravel county road, the sun's last light had joined the gray evening shadows that crept across the flat rural landscape. Crickets chorused all about them. The night air was cool and hinted of an early fall.

They came upon an open buggy, driven by two young women in starchy black bonnets, and Jacob slowed down to follow them at a reasonable distance.

The carriage, its large, metal wheels stirring the gravel dust into gritty clouds, rocked and swayed in time to the horse's unvarying cadence.

"Bet they've spent the day at the market," Jacob commented quietly.

"I'd like to do that someday," replied Ruth. "Could we drive the buggy into Shipshewana sometime?"

Jacob didn't answer. He gripped the steering wheel tightly and hit the brakes.

The buggy in front of them lurched off the road. The horse reared frantically, and they could see the driver struggling to keep the carriage upright behind the animal's immense power.

Ruth and Jacob jumped out of the van.

Rushing up to calm the frightened horse, Jacob grabbed the reins and held on. Pitting his own weight against that of the horse, he worked his way along the leather reins to the animal's bit and literally wrestled the horse down to the ground, holding on to the bridle's mouthpiece.

Running up to the buggy, Ruth was startled to find the girls frozen, staring trancelike at something beyond Jacob and their horse.

Ruth's eyes followed theirs.

Ahead, in the road, was another Amish buggy—a crushed, dismembered pile of burnished metal and splintered wood. Twisted debris was scattered across the roadbed.

Like the girls, Ruth was paralyzed by the horror.

"Ruth! Go get help!" Jacob shouted, running up to the wreckage. "Somebody's in there."

His voice jolted her. On legs numb with shock, Ruth started back to the van, then stopped. Another van pulled up behind theirs. It was Bud Hamilton.

"Get an ambulance," she yelled to him.

Running back toward the wreckage, Ruth found Jacob on his knees beside the lifeless form of a man.

Jacob, his hands covered with blood, knelt motionless in the gravel. His face was ashen, his eyes vacant.

Ruth dropped down beside him and took one stained hand in hers. "Jacob? Who is he?" she asked, looking up at his pallid face.

A single tear traced down Jacob's face. "We were

251

like brothers," he murmured, never looking away from the body. "Always like brothers."

John Troyer died before the paramedics could get to him.

Bud Hamilton returned with the ambulance and took the sobbing young girls home in his taxi.

"I'll take care of your buggy," Jacob assured them solemnly. "You take the van home, Ruth. I have to go to tell Barbara."

"Jacob did every thing he could, Aunt Mamie."

"I'm sure he did."

"Hit and run. That's what the sheriff said. Hit and run."

"They'll find the driver," Mamie said, wiping her own eyes with a corner of her robe. "He couldn't have gotten very far after an accident like that. Damned fool. Crazy damned fool," she muttered angrily. "Ya think people'd drive proper 'round them slow-movin' buggies. After all, that's what they come to gawk at. Some people got no common sense at all."

As they sat together in the kitchen, a buggy pulled into the barnlot. It was Jacob.

"Go to him, Ruth," her aunt urged. "Don't let Jacob be alone tonight."

The barn light was a pale glow against the moonless night. Silently, Ruth stood in the doorway and watched Jacob lead the horse into a vacant stall and offer it a bucket of feed.

He moved like a tired old man, his shoulders drawn beneath the weight of sorrow, his eyes vacant with grief.

"Jacob?" she said softly, walking to his side. "Are

252

you all right?" When he turned to her, Ruth put her arms around him.

Jacob pulled her tight against his body. "I've known John Troyer all my life," he whispered. "I can't believe he's gone. Not like this."

Ruth kissed his cheek, unable to offer him any consolation.

"Barbara's torn to pieces." His chest expanded, then trembled against her breast. "It's all so senseless."

All she could do was hold him and hope that the reality of her very presence—the touch of living flesh and bone—would help him cope with the tragedy.

"I have to do something," he finally said to her. "I've got to move around, do *something.*"

"Let's walk, then."

Hand in hand, Jacob and Ruth walked the farm lane together that night.

"I've known John Troyer all my life," Jacob began slowly. "And Barbara. I remember when they were courtin'. John never ran with any other girl. It was always Barbara. He was like that."

Ruth squeezed Jacob's hand. I'm listening, Jacob, she thought. Go on, you can talk it out with me.

"Barbara's the same kind of person he was. I'm glad they found each other. They're different, for Amish. Neither one of them could have been happy with anyone else. Oh"—he sighed—"they believed in the Amish way of life, but they make up their own minds on a lot of things. Like me, for instance. They didn't like my being shunned, and they told me so, right from the start. John said he wished I wouldn't leave, but he understood when I did. And Barbara—she'd write me once in a while, let me know how my family was and all."

Jacob's pace slowed slightly as he thought. "When

253

my father died, John called to tell me. That's when I decided to come back." His voice faded into silence.

Please, tell me more, Jacob. Please. I want to know you so badly. I love you so much.

They'd reached the end of the lane and paused, looking out into the black nothingness of the night.

"Why John? Why did *he* have to die? There was every reason for him to live—a good wife, children, a piece of land that was his very own. Why a man like John, who was contributing something to life in his own simple, direct way?"

Jacob reached out and took Ruth's other hand now. His fingers pulsed heavily against her wrists.

"Why him, not *me?* I haven't done anything worthwhile in *my* life."

Ruth took a deep breath before answering. "You mustn't think that, Jacob," she pleaded quietly. "Your life has a different purpose, that's all. Everyone's life has its own special purpose."

"I'm not sure that's true," he nearly whispered in reply. He let go of one hand and, turning, they started to walk again, back up the lane.

"You've done a lot with your life, Jacob," Ruth told him softly. Her mind whirled, trying to find just the right words to help him through grief's consuming guilt. "You just can't see it right now. But I *see* all that you've accomplished."

He tightened his hand on hers. "My *accomplishments,*" he told her firmly, "have never been very noble ones. It's probably because I've always thought I had to have life on my own terms—no one else's. I wasted twelve years looking for a better life—*out there.*" He gestured into the darkness. "I walked away from everything—family, friends, community—just to satisfy some selfish dream. And what did I find? Nothing, absolutely nothing. I didn't fit out there. But I refused to understand that until I'd wasted twelve whole years."

"Nothing in life is a waste," Ruth responded, suddenly feeling very disturbed by Jacob's words. "There's a reason for everything that happens to us."

They reached the house and stopped beside the porch steps.

"You may be right," he answered. "Those years of bumming around from job to job taught me one thing, Ruth. I learned that I belong right here, right where I started. I'm a farmer; I want to be a farmer. I love the life; I love watching the earth turn green each spring."

He put his hand to her chin, lifted her head, and looked deep into her eyes. "And now," he said slowly, "I've come to know my own people, and I've come to realize how much I gave up to follow that foolish dream when I was young."

Ruth touched his hand and closed her eyes. She suddenly knew what he was thinking. She knew it, and the thought of *hearing* it filled her with abject fear.

"Believe me when I say I'm sorry that I hurt you before. You aren't like anyone I've ever known. You're very special, Ruth. But I was afraid that night—afraid I'd betrayed my heritage again. Can you understand that?" She nodded. Hot tears formed in her closed eyes. "But now I appreciate my heritage as I never did before. Because of you . . ."

His throat tightened, forcing the words back down. He wanted to tell Ruth he loved her, but what good would that do now? "I know what I am, because of you. And I have a strong sense of what I should be. I want my life to have purpose—a reason for living. Not *out there,* but here, where I was meant to be." His kiss simply brushed against her mouth. "Thank you," he whispered.

Ruth's body went rigid. Her mind froze on the

meaning behind Jacob's words. *I was meant to be Amish,* he was telling her.

Numbed by the power of his resignation, Ruth could only follow Jacob up to the porch steps—silently surrendering to the reality of his decision.

In the wooden swing, his head resting on her shoulder, Jacob fell into exhausted sleep, leaving Ruth alone to contemplate another kind of grief.

They buried John Troyer two days later.

Ruth trudged down the lane and stood, secluded near the gate, watching the funeral procession of somber black buggies as it filed past the farm that clear, fall morning.

At Jacob's request, she and Mamie did not join the mourners.

When the sad caravan had passed, Ruth walked to the signpost and took down Mamie's greenhouse sign —just as her aunt had requested.

CHAPTER FOURTEEN

Belonging is a precious thing, Bishop Stoltzfus had told Ruth.

And belonging was that precious thing Jacob Yoder sought.

In her mind, Ruth could comprehend the meaning of his words, even as her heart denied it.

Often, as she lay in bed late at night, alone and

troubled, Ruth wanted to go to Jacob and confess her love.

Ruth imagined every detail of their dialogue. She would tell him that, together, they could make a life of their own free from the *past*.

In her dreams, Ruth promised Jacob her support, her love, and her understanding.

In her dreams, Jacob's answers were always the same: *Yes, Ruth, you are right. I can forget everything with you.*

But her heart's illusion of truth vanished with every dawn. For in the light of each new day, Ruth was forced to deal with cold reality.

Jacob Yoder was as much a product of his culture as she was of hers. His traditions were no less important than her own. And Ruth did not have the right to deny him a heritage—to dream that her world could be a viable substitute for what *he* wanted.

And how fair would it be to confess her love?

In many ways, Jacob had been more honest than she. He had never spoken of love, he had never asked for commitment. Did Jacob *deserve* more emotional conflict than he'd already been dealt? No. The answer was clear. Ruth refused to cause him more conflict. She would show her love by allowing Jacob the right to find his own happiness.

"Wait till you hear who came visitin' today," chirped Mamie as they sat down to dinner one mid-September night. "And you'll never guess what he wanted."

Jacob put his jacket across the back of his chair and sat down across from Ruth. "Monroe Sullivan," he answered with a smile, playing along with Mamie's good-natured guessing game. "And he wanted you to go in partners on a rattlesnake ranch."

Ruth laughed, pleased that Jacob's humor had resurfaced. Since John's death he'd been lost in thought and thoroughly withdrawn.

"Nope. But that's a *good* idea. Wonder why T. Monroe never considered it? Probably 'cause he's *lower* than a *snake's* belly." Mamie chuckled, thankful her little joke had Jacob laughing again. "Them rattlers might stampede right over him." She'd been so worried over Jacob's melancholy that Mamie was willing to do anything to make him feel better.

"Perfect occupation for Sullivan," added Ruth, winking at Jacob. "Then he could even branch out and go into rattlesnake rustlin'." She was working to sustain the light-hearted atmosphere between them all as long as possible.

"Enough *Rattlesnake Sullivan* jokes," Jacob protested, shaking his head. "You shouldn't discuss T. Monroe at the supper table. We'll all end up with indigestion." He reached for the bowl of mashed potatoes. "*Almost* as bad as trying to eat with a naked man at the table," he muttered, eyeing Mamie.

The old woman laughed. "Worse." She giggled and passed the meat platter to Ruth.

"So, who *did* come over today?" Jacob asked.

Ruth looked over at her aunt, expecting her to answer.

"*You* tell him," Mamie insisted. "It's *your* news."

"Okay," she replied. "Bishop Stoltzfus came over to see me today."

"He did? And *what* did the bishop want?" Jacob asked.

"He wants her to teach at the Amish school!" Mamie announced.

Ruth looked back at her aunt with narrowed eyes.

"I wanted to surprise Jacob," Mamie responded quietly.

"I *am* surprised," he countered. "Are you going to do it, Ruth?"

"Of course I am," she affirmed. "I was really flattered. It won't be easy to fit it in with all my own research but I'll manage somehow."

"That's somethin', isn't it, Jacob?" continued Mamie. "I mean, the bishop actually trusting an English to teach Amish children?"

"That really is a vote of confidence. But then, Ruth isn't very English," he responded. His vibrant blue eyes sparkled with sincerity, but his voice had suddenly lost its enthusiasm.

"There's an awful lot to do before school starts. How long do you think I have?" asked Ruth, feeling the warmth of his gaze. Since the night of the accident, Jacob rarely looked into her eyes when they spoke.

"Not long," he answered, shifting his eyes away from her face and breaking the glow of energy between them. "Harvest's going along well, so I imagine the kids will be free from field work in a week or two."

"That means early October," she mused. "Not much time to prepare."

"Amish school doesn't take much preparation," Jacob replied, returning to his dinner.

"I wouldn't worry about that," added Mamie. "Reading, writing, and 'rithmetic. They still believe in the basics."

"Didn't Bishop Stoltzfus explain how the school is run?" asked Jacob.

"Yes. And *that's* what I need time to prepare for. I haven't the slightest idea how to organize forty children, at eight different grade levels, into one classroom," Ruth answered honestly. "He gave me sample textbooks; they're basic texts. That's no problem." Ruth shrugged, disheartened by Jacob's growing withdrawal.

"You won't have any trouble," Mamie said confidently.

"I wouldn't be so sure of that," Ruth replied, picking at her own plate. "I've never taught small children before."

"Maybe you should have told the bishop that before you accepted the position," Jacob responded evenly. "I think he would have understood."

"I *did* tell him, Jacob. But he said, 'Do you know how to read? Can you do arithmetic and write your name?' I said yes, of course. Then he said, 'Didn't you tell me you were a teacher? Then teach the children the things you already know how to do yourself.'" Ruth sighed. "And I guess that's how they work it. Their last teacher was a local Amish woman who only went the standard eight grades."

"Jemima Keim," Mamie clarified. "She's moving to Missouri to be with her husband. I guess he just got settled on some land there."

Jacob nodded in response and stood up. "The bishop knows what he's doing, Ruth. He thinks you can handle the job, and he knew you wouldn't turn down a research opportunity like this." He put on his denim jacket and started to the door. "It's a very practical approach. Stoltzfus gets a certified teacher for the school and you get the chance of a lifetime."

"Old Stoltzfus is getting a real bargain," Aunt Mamie said. "They don't pay Amish teachers a penny."

"You're right. He is getting a bargain," Jacob replied softly, looking at Ruth a final time. "But it has nothing to do with finances."

Mamie watched the door close behind Jacob, and then she looked to Ruth, who was only toying with her own dinner.

"Don't worry about this teaching job," Mamie said, patting Ruth's arm. "You'll do just fine."

"I'm not worried about it, honest, Aunt Mamie."

"I didn't think so," Mamie replied. "It's Jacob, isn't it?" Ruth nodded. "Well, I'm worried about him too.

"Did you and Jacob ever clear up that little misunderstanding about your research?" Mamie asked her simply.

Ruth looked over at her aunt. "It's not that. We talked it out the day of the accident." She pushed her plate away. "We're not angry at each other anymore."

No, Mamie had surmised that much. It wasn't anger that she sensed between them. It wasn't grief, either, that was pulling Jacob away from them. Grief had a way of bringing people together, not tearing them apart.

"I know Jacob's still grievin' over John, but there's something else too. Do you know what's troubling him, Ruth? Has he talked to you about it?"

Ruth looked away, collecting her thoughts.

"I don't know how to tell you this," she began, "but Jacob wants to join the order. I think it's just a matter of time before he does."

"Why? Do you know? Why, after all these years?" *Why now,* she thought, *after knowing Ruth?*

"He started reevaluating his own life the night John died, and he thinks his life hasn't had any real meaning or purpose. Jacob has never felt comfortable in our world—he doesn't think he *belongs*. Now Jacob only sees what John had accomplished—a family and all—the things Jacob could have had if only he had stayed with the order and held to tradition. He thinks his life has been meaningless."

"But he's done so much, can't he see that?" Mamie fought for words that would explain it all away. "He has the best of both worlds."

"But he doesn't want both worlds," Ruth explained

261

patiently, holding on to her aunt's hand. "He wants *one* world where he feels like he belongs."

Mamie sighed deeply. "And so he's pulling back from us—you and me—because we don't fit in his life anymore." Tears misted in her eyes. "That's why he's been working away at Troyer's farm and staying away from the house in the evenings?"

Tears welled in Ruth's eyes too. "Yes. I think he's trying to make the transition. He does the farm work here but spends all his other time with his own people."

"Then it's only a matter of time before Jacob leaves us." Her aunt shuddered.

Ruth nodded silently.

"I don't care if he wants to live Amish. I don't care," she grumbled, hurt. "I love Jacob like a son, and I don't want him to leave us."

Ruth leaned back wearily in her chair. "I love him too, Aunt Mamie. I think I've loved him from the first moment we met right here in this kitchen."

Shocked once more by Ruth's admission, Mamie took hold of the table's edge. "And you haven't told him," she said, with sudden, vivid insight.

"I didn't know if he felt the same way," answered Ruth, a tear falling onto her cheek.

"Tell him. Find out how he feels."

"I can't, Aunt Mamie. Not now. If I talk to him now, he might stay just to keep from hurting me—or worse. Jacob might think I was trying to trick him into staying for you and the farm's sake. He's making this decision free of any pressure from me, and I want it to be that way."

She reached out and covered Mamie's hands with her own. "I love Jacob too much to add to his confusion. If you really love someone, Aunt Mamie, you want them to be happy. I won't risk Jacob's happiness for my own."

"How can you tell that will happen? I thought scientists didn't make any decisions until all the facts were in."

"I've thought this through, believe me. I don't want to live without Jacob. But even if he loved me, I'm not sure I could be the kind of woman he needs. I can't dedicate my every waking hour to home and hearth. I want to go on with my career."

"But you don't *know* what Jacob wants. You're assuming an awful lot, Ruth Marie. Jacob has always been interested in your work. He's even helped with your research. Land's sake, Ruth. Wasn't he happy when you told him you were staying and taking that job at Goshen College?"

Ruth looked down at her hands. "I didn't tell him."

"Why not?"

"Because I didn't want him to think I was staying because of him." She looked up at her aunt. "I've never been in love before, Aunt Mamie. Not like this. I didn't want to pressure him. Jacob's never said that he loves me. Oh, it must sound pretty old-fashioned, but I didn't want to back him into a corner. We've known each other such a short time, you know. I just felt I should give him time, and then, maybe . . ."

"You *must* have thought Jacob loved you, Ruth," her aunt replied quietly. "After all, you made some real important decisions with that in mind."

"I felt that in time our love would grow—but now there is no time. I couldn't pressure him," she pleaded. "I just couldn't."

"You don't pressure someone by telling them I love you," Mamie told her.

"I only did what I thought best," Ruth said. "And as it turned out, I think I've made the right decisions all along. I do want to stay here with you, manage the farm, and teach at Goshen. Jacob didn't really influence that. It would only have been *better* with him. But that's not how it's meant to be. If Jacob did love me, he wouldn't be planning to leave."

Mamie had no reply.

Every day, after working a full day in their own fields, Jacob and a group of Amishmen went to harvest the corn that John Troyer had planted.

The workers rotated their visits, so that no one would have to neglect his own farm more than one day a week. Everyone, that is, but Jacob.

He went each midafternoon and worked until dark in the fields. After that, there was always something else to be done. A windmill to repair, a harness to mend, wood to chop.

The grueling physical labor seemed to help hold his resolve intact. It reminded him daily of the decision he must soon make.

Hard work served yet another less noble, but effective, purpose. It kept his mind from wandering back to Ruth; it kept him from dwelling on their past. As long as he pushed his endurance to the maximum, Jacob could hold her memory at bay. And if he drained himself completely in the fields, he did not have the strength to dwell on her at night.

"Jacob?" Barbara stood in the kitchen doorway silhouetted against the dim kerosene light from within.

"I fixed that pump handle," he answered, walking up on the porch. "I'll take a look at the barn door tomorrow."

"Enough fixing and checking," she said to him. "Come in. Rest now. I have a strudel just out from the oven." She held the door open for him and Jacob obliged.

The night air was crisp with autumn chill, but the kitchen was invitingly warm.

"Sit down and rest." Barbara pulled out a caned chair near the stove. "It's warm here. Coffee? *Mit Milch oder Zucker?*"

"Zucker, danke."

She filled a deep china cup with boiling coffee and handed him the sugar bowl. "You count how many," she said, handing him a spoon. Barbara brought her strudel to the table and sat down to slice it.

"My husband liked strudel, but then you know that." She placed a large portion of pastry on a plate and handed it to Jacob.

"John liked everything sweet," Jacob replied, smiling over at her. "That's why he picked you, Barbara."

Though her face was flushed with the oven's heat, Jacob saw Barbara blush a deeper shade of rose at his compliment.

"And how are you doing?" Jacob asked, bridging the silence.

"Well." Her voice was calm and assured. "I am well. And the children. Dannie doesn't understand. He was very close to my husband. But I tell him that this was meant to be, and we must not question. He will accept it." A tear glistened in her eye, but Barbara remained composed.

"The children will have a second father, Barbara. Someone much like John, I'm sure of it." His words were meant well, yet Jacob truly doubted Barbara would ever find a man as wise and caring as his friend.

Barbara nodded. "And how does *your* harvest go, Jacob?"

"Nearly finished. It will be a good year, even with the storm."

"I have thought so often these weeks, *how can Jacob*

keep two farms going like this? I am concerned that your land might not be tended as well as mine."

Jacob smiled and sipped his coffee. "That's nothing for you to be concerned about. I'm not the only man who comes to help."

"But you are the only one who comes each day and stays late to do the day chores too. I have watched you, Jacob. You have much energy. But I think you work very hard for very little."

"I like helping."

"My husband had such energy. We worked well together. *Two* can do much more than one, Jacob. Why do you choose to work alone?"

Jacob hesitated, staring into his cup, as Barbara's implication hit him.

"Is it because you haven't found someone who is well matched to your energy?"

"Yes" was all he could answer. But the truth was that he *had* found his match. A mental image of Ruth flashed through his head.

"You and I are well matched," continued Barbara in a soft voice.

"Barbara . . ."

"You need a wife, Jacob, and a family of your own. Will you grow old with no one to care for you?" Quietly, she petitioned him with pragmatic efficiency. "We are well suited, I think. We have known one another all our lives. Together we can work very hard for our children's future."

Jacob reached out and touched her hand. "Barbara, I don't love you in that way," he said without thinking.

The slight hint of a frown shadowed her face. "Jacob, you think as the English. What has love to do with this? In time we'll come to care for each other. Just as with my husband. This love, it's a prideful

266

vanity. Come back to us. Live the good life, as it is meant to be."

If loving was vain, then it was the only vanity that Jacob had ever wanted. For, in all that he'd known in both worlds, this English love had no Amish equivalent.

"You are thinking of Ruth, aren't you?" Barbara's quiet words shattered the silence.

Jacob stared at her, surprised.

"I watched you at the barn-raising, Jacob. Eating with the other men at lunch. From the barn roof. You were always looking for her. But you must forget this woman. She will go away when her work is done, and you will be alone again."

Jacob rose, silent, from his chair. Barbara Troyer had offered him all he had ever wanted—everything she had to give. Everything, except *love*.

A pale harvest moon illuminated the cold, clear sky of late September. Falling leaves covered the gravel road; they snapped and crunched beneath the buggy wheels as Jacob drove back to the farm that Sunday evening.

At farm lanes and crossings, Amish girls waited in the moonlight, their long woolen cloaks wrapped tight against the autumn chill. As Jacob passed one girl, standing in the shadows of the roadside, she turned from him and concealed her face behind the curve of her black bonnet.

At the crossroad, Jacob hesitated, then turned the buggy toward the campground. His mind, still battling with the day's events, was too unsettled to return to Mamie's farm.

A large group of spirited young men lounged in their carriages near the campground's entrance. Much the same group, Jacob thought, as had been there the

267

first night he took Ruth for a buggy ride. How many, he wondered, will return in the spring to gossip and tease away another carefree season of *rumspringa?*

Marrying time was near; many a young Amishman would soon take a wife. The *rumspringa,* for them, would become but a memory, its freedom simply ascribed to tradition and quickly forgotten.

"The harvest is nearly done, Jacob," Emma Yoder had said to her son that very day. "Soon it will be the marrying time."

Her aging eyes looked past him to where Barbara Troyer sat playing with Lizzie beneath a tree. Barbara and her children visited the Yoder farm every Sunday now.

"But, of course, that makes no difference for you, Jacob," his mother went on. "Only first weddings need wait for the marrying time."

His head lowered, Jacob worked a blade of dry grass between his fingers. "I will know when *my* time comes, Mother," he said firmly.

"Will you?" she replied, now watching him closely. "How do you know that *this* is not your time?"

He let the dry grass sift to the ground beside his chair. "Because I do not choose for it to be."

"Ah," she answered, her rocking chair slowly pitching back and forth. *"Choosing.* Always *choosing.* If your mind was set in the right way, Jacob, you would not waste time with all this choosing. You would see that things are either right or they are not."

"And Barbara is right? I have no other choice?"

"Not that I can see." His mother continued to rock, again watching Barbara across the lawn. "You're not a young man anymore, Jacob. The time of choosing is over for you."

Jacob stood and kissed his mother's forehead. "You

268

are right, Mother. I am *not* a young man anymore. But I will still do my own choosing."

Jacob drove the buggy only once around the campground trail. The hushed voices of courting couples, parked in the deep shadows, reminded him of a time not so long ago when he too enjoyed the private pleasures of *rumspringa*.

It was here, with Ruth, that he first experienced its secret delight—long after the memory had dulled for the others of his youth.

Jacob was not a young man anymore, nor did he wish to be. A young man could never appreciate what he had known.

CHAPTER FIFTEEN

Pulling her collar up, Ruth hunched her shoulders against the frosty morning air and quickened her pace. She was running late this morning.

Usually she was out of the house and on her way long before now, but she and Aunt Mamie had lingered over their breakfast, waiting for Jacob.

"This is a bad sign," her aunt said when they finally realized that he was not coming in to eat. "Jacob's never stayed away at breakfast time before."

She tucked Ruth's lunch into a small paper bag and brought it over to the table. "There's your Thermos of coffee," she went on, pointing to the cabinet. "What do you think it means—him staying away at meals now?"

Buttoning her coat, Ruth slowly gathered her books and lunch things. "I'm afraid it means he's gone another step toward . . ." She couldn't finish her thought.

Mamie nodded. "Probably." She sighed.

"I'll be home by five," Ruth told her aunt, giving her a quick kiss. "Maybe he'll come for supper."

Mamie was in slow-motion that morning. Try as she may, she just couldn't get motivated. Thoughts of Ruth and Jacob weighed heavily on her mind, her legs felt like lead, and she hadn't the energy to fight it.

She'd looked at the problem from every angle. Now she was forced to admit that there just wasn't anything she could do.

The pain of losing Jacob and her niece's anguish were bad enough, but the frustration of not being able to do anything about it was maddening.

She dragged through the gloomy morning, managing to start a pot of fresh vegetable soup for dinner and complete a few loads of laundry. At noon, when it started to rain, she finally surrendered to her depression and sat down with a cup of hot tea.

Heavy rain drumming at the windows muffled the sound of approaching footsteps on the porch. She never even heard Jacob, until he came into the kitchen.

"Lunch ready? I'm starving," he said evenly as he hung up his rain poncho. "I hope the coffee's hot; that rain's mighty cold."

Mamie hadn't expected Jacob for lunch, not after this morning. Trying to appear unruffled, she got up and walked over to the stove. "I'll bet you're hungry," she murmured. "Workin' all morning on an empty stomach. I oughtta make you eat all those pancakes left over from this morning."

"Sorry. Didn't have time for breakfast," he responded, reaching around her for the coffeepot. "Wanted to get that last load of corn over to the co-op before it started raining." He walked over to the window and looked out.

Smiling now, Mamie stirred the vegetable soup. Why hadn't she thought of that? So, Jacob wasn't purposefully avoiding them this morning.

"Weatherman says the rain is going to last all week."

"How 'bout a sandwich and a bowl of vegetable soup?" Mamie offered, not the least bit interested in the weather forecast. "I was making the soup for dinner, but it's tendered up already. Do you mind eatin' soup for two meals in a row?"

"I could eat your vegetable soup *three* meals in a row, easy," he responded quietly.

Walking away from the window, Jacob stepped over a pile of clothes in the middle of the floor and pulled out a chair at the table.

"I got a little behind this morning," she murmured nervously. "Just push that stack of towels to the end of the table and make yourself some room."

"Maybe it's time you fixed the dryer," he said looking about at the color-coded piles of laundry.

"Maybe," she said as if that explained away the chaos.

"Well, I'll take a look at it after lunch. You'll need it working right, now that the weather's turned bad."

She hadn't expected that response at all. Wasn't he going to the Troyer farm today? Why wasn't he there already, since the weather was deteriorating so quickly? Surely they hadn't finished with the corn there yet.

271

Mamie ladled out a bowl of steaming soup and carried it over to the table.

"There's a leaky faucet in the upstairs bathroom too," she said, still testing.

"I'll check it out."

"I guess it's *that time of year* again," Mamie continued, watching him closely. "Just about everything needs fixin'."

"Uh huh." Jacob blew into the bowl of soup. "Have you been keeping a list of things you need done here in the house?"

Mamie's heart skipped a beat as she lowered herself into the chair next to Jacob. He wouldn't be talking about the annual repair list if he planned to leave soon.

"It's a pretty long list," she told him.

"Well, it's gonna be a long winter. We'll get it all done by spring," he assured her.

Mamie took a deep breath and cleared her throat. "Well," she began, gathering her thoughts. "I think we should get started as soon as possible, don't you?"

Jacob nodded and continued eating.

"I figure it's gonna take a good month or more just to get the upstairs remodeled."

Jacob looked up from his soup.

"Now that Ruth's got this permanent job at Goshen, we're gonna need to rearrange things a might," she plowed on with renewed confidence. "I was thinking of makin' that smallest bedroom into a kitchenette, and what with a study room, the big bedroom, and a private bath, Ruth could have her own little apartment up there. You know, Ruth and I are both used to living alone, so I want to make this as comfortable as possible for both of us. Don't you think that's a good idea?"

Jacob nodded, his eyes fixed on Mamie.

"That's what I thought. Ruth can have the run of

272

the upstairs, and I can putter around down here. It'll work out perfect, 'specially when other professors come visitin' and students show up for counselin'. You know, Jacob"—Mamie leaned across the table, her voice confidential—"it's not easy for two grown women to live in the same house."

"No," he answered quietly. "I don't suppose it would be."

Every weekday morning since Bishop Stoltzfus's visit, Ruth had gone out to the Amish schoolhouse. With only two weeks to go before the term started, she concentrated on the biggest single problem of her new job: orientating herself to a one-room school.

From the very first day, she'd decided to walk the one-mile course from the farm to the school. After all, her students would be walking, so why shouldn't she?

A half hour of exercise each morning would be good for her. She could prepare herself and pull her thoughts into focus on the way.

But, more important, Ruth chose to walk out of respect for her students and for the responsibility the Amish community had entrusted to her.

And secretly, she walked out of respect for Jacob, who would always live for her in memory.

Hurrying along the road, arms laced around her books and bags, Ruth looked out over the countryside, wondering if she would ever find a way to close her mind to Jacob's memory.

The flat farmlands had been in bloom when she came back to Elkhart County. The earth had been full of spring's promise; the whole world quickened in another season of hope.

And her love for Jacob had blossomed then, in the season of hope.

But now, the green furrowed fields were endless

273

dotted lines of brownish corn shocks that scrapped the morning air with eerie rustlings. Everything that had been was dead or dying. Their season had passed.

Ruth felt as barren as the earth that gray October morning.

Entering the schoolhouse, Ruth deposited her books and lunch on a bench next to the door, removed her coat and hung it on a wall peg. The building was cold, so she set to work building a fire in the potbelly stove that sat squarely in the center of the single, large room.

She must come early each morning, Ruth reminded herself, to start a fire so the place would be warm when the children arrived.

The kindling caught, and Ruth closed the stove door. Rubbing her hands, she paced around the stove, taking her mind from the cold and from Jacob by planning lessons.

The classroom was clean and bright, but sparsely furnished with surplus wooden desks and chairs. A well-used blackboard shone inky bright along one entire wall of the classroom, dwarfing the small oak library table that was Ruth's desk.

It was an hour before the fire really began to warm the place. But even so, the heat was uneven at best.

Near the stove, it was too hot; in the corners, it was still cold and uncomfortably damp. How would they ever manage when winter came and temperatures hovered below zero all day—when the wind would whip the heat away faster than she could feed the fire?

Absorbed in the problem, Ruth sat at her desk, running over alternative solutions. Thoroughly engrossed, she didn't hear the door open until the wind caught it. The heavy door slammed shut with such force that the windows rattled.

Startled, Ruth jumped and looked up.

Two tiny girls, no more than six or seven, stood frozen with embarrassment—their blue eyes wide as saucers in the aftermath of a grand, if rather undignified, entrance.

A hint of pale blond hair peeked from under both their wool bonnets, and one carried something wrapped in a shawl against her chest.

"Can I help you?" asked Ruth, trying not to laugh at their discomfort.

"Ve come to see the school," braved the one with the bundle in her arms.

"Ve come to school this year," the other offered.

"Would you like to come sit by the fire?" she asked approaching them.

Both girls shook their head no.

"Would you like to see the first-grade books we are going to learn from?"

"No, thank you," the one with the bundle replied. "Ve just learn the *vay* to the school today."

"Do you live far?" Ruth sat down at a desk near the door.

They shook their heads no again.

"What do you have there?" she asked, pointing to the shawl, trying to be friendly.

The little girl smiled. *"Meine Puppe,"* she said proudly.

"Can I see your doll?"

The girl looked warily at her friend, then shrugged and turned back a corner of the shawl.

Ruth tried to smile, because she couldn't speak.

"She's like me," said the girl before covering the doll again.

"Ve go now," announced the other, and they left.

Ruth stared after them, tears mounting in her eyes. The muslin doll had been dressed in Amish black—its body clothed in a cotton dress and white pinafore apron, a miniature bonnet was tied on its head.

But the doll had no face. No eyes or mouth. No expression. Nothing to give it an identity beyond its plainness. Nothing to hint of prideful vanity.

She's like me, Ruth heard the little girl's voice in her mind.

"And like Jacob," she whispered to herself as tears streamed down her face.

There wasn't any way Ruth could fight the awful heartache that overcame her. She sat, huddled by the stove, and let the tears form and flow in rhythm to her anguished memories.

Her loving Jacob was a man without a face—a man looking for identity. Why hadn't she understood that from the beginning? What was all her scientific training good for if it couldn't help her see such an obvious conflict as that?

Had she been more observant—had she been more objective—perhaps if only she had been able to look beyond her own need—all this would have never happened.

Ruth blamed herself for not being more rational. But, even so, she could not blame herself for falling in love with him. That much she wouldn't have changed.

It was love that had kept her from seeing Jacob's real need—his need for an identity. A man, Ruth thought to herself, does not change his identity by walking away from his past. For in the past, we all have *made* our fundamental identities, and without that foundation, we can add little more.

Yet, if Ruth could have asked for one wish that cold, rainy October morning, she would have asked for Jacob to find a lasting place for her, as part of himself, and that he would identify with her love.

The thought only made her cry harder. The time

had passed for wishes, and Ruth realized, even as she wished, that Jacob needed more than just her love. He needed to establish a place for himself in the world. A place where his Amish heritage and his personal needs could live in harmony. Her love alone could not displace all that had come before.

In desperation, Ruth turned to her work again, trying to escape the painful reality of the inevitable.

The kerosene lamp on the desk began to sputter again, and Ruth reached over to adjust the flame. The lamp was running low, but she didn't want to refill it now. The day was nearly over, and as soon as the kerosene ran out, she'd start for home.

Looking over the lesson plan for a final time, she penciled one last idea in the margin and closed the notebook. She hadn't really accomplished much that day; nothing seemed to block thoughts of Jacob.

Ruth stood and stretched her sore arms. A hard wooden chair, the smoke-laced air, and hours of futile soul searching had taken their toll. Both her body and her mind ached with equal force. Never had she felt so empty and so utterly defenseless.

The room was growing cold again, so she went to check the stove.

As she stood gazing at the dying embers, the door creaked open. Thinking that another child had wandered in, she turned, smiling.

There, across the room, stood Jacob.

Stunned by his sudden appearance, the breath caught her throat.

"I thought I'd give you a ride home," he told her simply, closing the door against the wind and rain. "Don't let me bother you. I'll wait till you're done."

"I was just waiting for the fire to go out," Ruth replied. Seeing him only made her pain worse. She

277

walked back to the desk and started gathering up her lesson plans.

Jacob went to the bookcase and thumbed through the books. "I don't suppose you have a copy of *Moby Dick* in here, do you?"

Ruth winced. "No, sorry. Just the basics." Tears welled in her eyes. How could he bring his favorite book and its telling memories to mind without any sign of emotion? He sounded so *Amish* just then—so stoic and accepting.

Jacob nodded. "I didn't think so." He took a child's reader from the shelf and slowly flipped through the pages. "Good old McGuffey," he mused. "Kids are still learning to read from *McGuffey's Reader.*"

Suddenly Ruth felt a flash of anger. Was she carrying the pain for them both? Had she been suffering through the heartache that Jacob had already reconciled?

She forced the tears away. No, she thought, it was less than that. Jacob did not feel the same love for her that she felt for him. He was simply holding his memories and her at a distance. Just as the Amish held the whole world at a distance.

Jacob closed the elementary reader and paced to the stove. "You really need two stoves in here to even up the heat a little." He rubbed his hands in the faint heat. "I could get another stove," he offered, not looking at her, "and install it before classes start. Maybe *three* would be better." He turned to look over the room. "This is an awful big area for just two . . ."

"Talk to Bishop Stoltzfus," she snapped back at him as her anger suddenly broke through. "You know he makes the decisions for the school." She piled her books together and knocked her notebook on the floor. Pages scattered all around the desk.

"Let me give you a hand," Jacob offered evenly, and walked to the desk.

"I *don't* need your help anymore," she replied, tears flowing from her eyes.

"Ruth?" Jacob's voice was soft as he knelt beside her next to the desk. "I—" He touched her wrist, but Ruth tugged away.

"How can you stand there"—she pointed with a trembling hand to the stove—"and just talk about heating stoves? And over there?" She motioned, shaking, to the bookcase. "About . . ." Her tone was not angry, not accusing. Not what she expected it to be. Her voice crackled with pain, and the tears belied her emotional agony. "Don't you ever *feel* anything? Why did you even come here? I *don't* want you here. Just leave me alone."

She gathered what papers she could reach and stood to walk over to the desk chair. But as she passed him, Jacob reached out to her and took both her wrists in his hands.

"Sit down," he said softly. "Here." Still kneeling, he gently pulled her down into the chair. "Let me take these."

She let Jacob take the papers from her hands. He laid them on the desk and turned back to her.

Trembling from the power of her own emotions, Ruth sat numbly before him, crying. Too upset to move, too lost to speak again, she was powerless to look away from his smiling blue eyes.

"Do you really think I'm so heartless and unfeeling?" he asked. Ruth closed her eyes against him. "Do you think I could forget you or that you said you loved me once?"

The kerosene lamp finally flickered out. The schoolroom was illuminated by the faint gray light of afternoon.

Ruth opened her eyes. "Why are you doing this to me, Jacob? Why now? Don't you know how deeply this hurts me?"

"Remember the first time we went out in the buggy?" Jacob asked her without responding to her question.

"Yes," she replied angrily, as if to defy the pain his words caused her. "We went to the campground and . . ." But her defiance failed her, and she couldn't complete the thought.

"I'll never forget that night at the campground, Ruth," Jacob continued, holding her hands tight in his. "I felt just like one of those teenage boys, courting my first girl."

A cool draft swept across the room and wrapped around her legs. Ruth shivered. But it wasn't that cold that made her numb. It was Jacob's words. They were spoken too late; Ruth's heart had frozen in the past because she had no future.

"You *are* my first girl, Ruth. Can you understand that?" She shook her head and wanted to look away, but couldn't force herself. "There never has been anyone but you. There never will be. I want . . ." He stopped abruptly and raised her hands to his lips and kissed them. "Why didn't you tell me about the job at Goshen?" he asked softly.

"I couldn't," she whispered as her anger was transformed once again to heartache. "Not after . . ." Tears fell from her eyes again. Her throat tightened. "I just couldn't."

"Why? Why couldn't you tell me?" he pleaded with her. "My God, Ruth, I never dreamed you'd want to stay here. Why didn't you tell me?"

All the hurt and longing within her swelled to the surface. Uncontrollably her body shook beneath a pounding wave of remorse. "What difference does it make?" She sobbed, turning to face him.

"What difference? It makes every difference."

Jacob kissed one palm and held it tightly to his chest.

Ruth could feel the heavy beat of his heart—the pulsing warmth of his body. "I love you, Ruth."

"But you never . . ."

"I know. I never told you. I thought you were happy with your life just as it was. I couldn't ask you to give up everything you'd worked for, not if that's what you really wanted."

"But couldn't you see how much I cared?" she asked him through the tears. "Couldn't you tell I loved you too?"

"Oh, yes, Ruth. I *did* see it," he admitted slowly. "Here, in my heart, believe me. But my head was so set on our differences, I wouldn't let myself believe it. But this changes things. You've chosen to stay—it's *your* decision."

Ruth ran her fingers along his cheek. "But the differences are still there, Jacob. My staying doesn't change that, even though I wish it could."

Her hand smoothed the damp curls at his temple. "I love you, Jacob. And now I know you love me. But that doesn't erase our differences, it only compounds them. I'm still English, and you are . . ." Her voice failed as the tears began again.

"I am *Jacob,*" he said firmly, still clasping her hand to his heart. "Jacob Yoder, the man who loves you."

Ruth shook her head. "You don't understand."

"Listen to me, please." Jacob put two fingers to her lips. "You once told me that everyone's life has its own special purpose. Do you remember?" Silently she nodded. "I didn't agree with you then, but I do now. And that's what I've been looking for all these years: my

281

purpose—my reason for living. It wasn't a question of being Amish or English. If it were that simple, I'd have never gone out there. I see that now, because of you."

Unable to speak, Ruth sat mesmerized in the light from his eyes. His fingers cupped her chin.

"You showed me things I'd never seen before in myself and my people. And you loved me as I never dreamed I could be loved." He kissed her hand again. "I don't know my life's whole purpose—maybe we never know it all—but I *do* know that you're the most important part of it. Without you, Ruth, my life will never be complete."

"Oh, Jacob. My Jacob," she cried, her chin trembling against his fingers.

Gently he kissed her quivering mouth and she wrapped her arms about his neck. His lips, warm and tender, trembled against hers as his own anguish was released.

"Oh, Ruth," he murmured against her cheek, before pressing his head to her breast. "I want to prove how much I love you."

Ruth rubbed the soft brown curls with her cheek. "You have, my Jacob," she whispered. "Believe me, I know."

Through the cold gray rain of autumn, the black buggy rumbled down the farm lane. From her kitchen window, Mamie watched as Jacob, his arms wound around Ruth, slapped the reins and urged the horse toward the house.

Wiping a tear from her eye with the corner of her apron, Mamie turned and, with open arms, welcomed them home again.